Praise fo

No

*_Publishers Weekly_ Best Book of the Year

*_Library Journal_ Best Book of the Year

*_RT Book Reviews_ Seal of Excellence

*_RT_ Reviewers' Choice Finalist,
Best Book of the Year

*_RT_ Reviewers' Choice Winner,
Best First Historical Novel

"A genre-bending, fast-paced whirl with fantastic characters, a deftly drawn plot, and sizzling attraction..."
—*RT Book Reviews* Top Pick of the Month, 4.5 Stars

"Sexy, edgy, and stunningly inventive...will have readers begging for more."

—*Library Journal* Starred Review

"A compelling debut that smartly mixes history, action, romance, and magic."

—*Publishers Weekly*

"High-stakes, world-saving magical adventure with wonderful characters and a sexy romance."

—Susanna Fraser, author of *An Infamous Marriage*

"A stunning mix of new age and old school makes this one sensational!"

—*Fresh Fiction*

"A strongly written, well-constructed magical world with complex characters."

—*Dear Author*

"Fresh and a little addictive."

—*Once Upon a Chapter*

"A great read with caring, worthy characters. The mix of cultures (past and present) makes for a wonderful story."

—*Long and Short Reviews*

"Fun, exciting, and different…too hot to touch and very enjoyable."

—*BookLoons.com*

"Written with details, depths, and has characters that will take your breath away."

—*My Book Addiction and More*

"A surprisingly engaging and action-packed read."

—*Bookaholics Romance Book Club*

"Very strong and solidly constructed characters in a vivid backdrop."

—*Night Owl Reviews*

"An intriguing story with part *My Fair Lady* and part Sarah Connor."

—*Leslie's Psyche*

"A nice twist on historical romance with a touch of magic."

—*Drey's Library*

"I was surprised to learn that this is a debut novel... Very entertaining."

—*Books and Quilts*

Praise for Isabel Cooper's *Lessons After Dark*

**RT* Reviewers' Choice Finalist,
Best Historical Fantasy/Paranormal

"Sizzling chemistry… Sexual tension propels the story forward, and Cooper's demon-haunted Victorian England is enticing and well-built. Fans will be eager for more."

—*Publishers Weekly*

"Seamlessly weaving the paranormal elements around the romance… Cooper's world-building is solid and believable."

—*RT Book Reviews* Top Pick of the Month, 4.5 Stars

"Funny, sensual, and occasionally dark, this charmer is laced with both humor and danger; another magical romp that fans are sure to enjoy."

—*Library Journal*

"A twist between X-Men and Harry Potter, with romance…and demons."

—*Literary Escapism*

"Intelligently written, in some places brilliantly written… The romance amused and delighted me."

—*One Good Book Deserves Another*

"FANTASTIC: magic, seduction, and overcoming obstacles...what more does it need?"

—*Fresh Fiction*

"An interesting concept that made me draw comparisons to X-Men."

—*Booked Up*

"The supernatural elements are perfectly intertwined and the excitement of the developing romance, combined with suspense, make this a real page-turner... Enticing and magical."

—*Romancing the Darkside*

"The excitement and danger in the story kept the pacing quick... This book is firmly on my keeper shelf."

—*The Romanceaholic*

"The drama and tension worked into the story as the war begins between human and demon is well expressed by the author."

—*Long and Short Reviews*

"Isabel Cooper is an author to watch!"

—*All About Romance*

Legend of the Highland Dragon

Isabel Cooper

sourcebooks casablanca

Cover design by Shane Rebenschied
Photography by Richard Izui
Model: Donovan Klein

Published by Sourcebooks Casablanca, an imprint of Sourcebooks, Inc.
P.O. Box 4410, Naperville, Illinois 60567-4410
(630) 961-3900
Fax: (630) 961-2168
www.sourcebooks.com

Printed and bound in the United States of America
VP 10 9 8 7 6 5 4 3 2

To Professor Robert Mathiesen, with many thanks for assistance, advice, and support.

One

"I NEED TO SEE CARTER."

The voice was deep, with a pronounced Scottish accent and a distinct sense of urgency. The owner was already speaking before the door to Professor Richard Carter's outer office had closed. The words were all too familiar to Mina by now.

"Professor Carter isn't in at the moment," Mina replied without lifting her gaze from the typewriter.

She spoke firmly, with emphasis on the *Professor*, careful to round off her vowels and clip her consonants and to leave time between each of the words. All of that had taken considerable effort when she'd first taken her position. Now, two years of constant practice—especially with that line—made her speech almost unconscious, like the motion of her fingers over the typewriter keys.

The next line was "If you'd care to leave your card, I can give it to him," but as she finally looked up, the visitor's appearance made Mina pause.

He stood in the doorway like a knight out of some storybook illustration, or perhaps an American outlaw from a penny dreadful: someone ready to do battle, at least, and not necessarily someone on the side of the angels. He was tall and dark, broad-shouldered and square-chinned. His clothes were well-tailored and the fabric looked like it was of good quality, but the respectable dark suit looked somehow incongruous on him, as if he were wearing a very expensive costume.

He also didn't wait to hear Mina's next line.

"Where is he?" the man asked.

That sort of response was not *precisely* new either, though it was rarer than the opening gambit. Most people had the sense to realize what *not in* meant, and the grace to respect it. This man was clearly going to be one of the other sort.

Mina put her papers to one side and fixed her eyes on the visitor. "He isn't in at the moment," she repeated, more sternly and with a greater if-you-catch-my-meaning inflection. "But I'd be happy to let him know you called."

The man crossed the room, moving like a panther—or at least like what Mina imagined a panther would move like, as she'd never seen one of the beasts herself. "I need to speak to Carter," he said, planting his hands on the edge of Mina's desk and leaning forward. "The matter is urgent. Now, if he truly is out, you can tell me where he's gone—"

"I'm afraid Professor Carter isn't in the habit of leaving me with a detailed itinerary of his movements. Sir."

"Then tell me the first place he went, and I'll proceed from there."

Up close, the stranger's hair wasn't just black. There were shades of red to it in the lamplight: not ginger, but true red, like wine. His brown eyes had more than a hint of gold in them, too.

Mina wasn't sure why she was noticing such things, except that danger was supposed to make one more aware of details, and this man could certainly be dangerous. She shifted one hand to cover the ivory-handled letter opener on her desk.

Then she lifted her chin. "Professor Carter doesn't employ me to give out his personal information to anyone who asks," she said. "And there are at least three bobbies on this block, sir. I can scream very loudly."

"What?" He seemed honestly surprised. Seemed, at least. He did back up a step. "Don't be ridiculous."

"*I* try never to be ridiculous, sir."

Unconsciously, Mina had risen to her feet. The new position still left her looking up some distance to meet the visitor's gaze, and she was by no means a short woman. Against the pale-papered walls and the chairs with their curving limbs and white upholstery, against the faint gray sky that she could see through the window, the man looked even bolder, more vital—as if he'd sucked all the color around him into himself.

She took a breath.

The man let his out. "My name," he said, as if conceding a point, "is Stephen MacAlasdair. Lord…" Only it came out *Laird* when he said it. His accent was stronger now. "MacAlasdair. I'm an old friend of the professor's, and the matter that brings me here is an extremely serious one."

Every matter that brought someone to the office was "extremely serious," in Mina's experience, or at least almost every visitor claimed as much. Most of them sounded sincere, too. Still, if MacAlasdair *was* an old friend of the professor's—

She looked around the office quickly. There was nothing particularly valuable or portable. A statuette of Anubis on one of the bookshelves and perhaps a number of the books themselves might have brought more than a few pounds, but the room held nothing whose absence would ruin Professor Carter.

"Have a seat," Mina said. "Please. I'll see if he's come back."

She waited until MacAlasdair had settled himself before turning and walking through the back door—and she made certain to lock it behind her.

Up a narrow staircase, where the smells of cabbage and bread mingled with that of old brick, she came to another door. This one opened onto a world of bookshelves and curio cabinets, with a desk and chair in the center of the room. The elderly man who sat there was short and stout, with white hair considerably longer than the current fashion. At the sound of the door opening, he looked up, his face lined and leathery and more worried than Mina had ever seen it.

Professor Carter tried to disguise that last aspect when he saw Mina, of course. He'd been trying for the last day and a half, and the strongest inquiries Mina could make had only been met with the staunch insistence that everything was fine, and he'd like a cup of tea when she could manage it, there's a good girl. Or that there was nothing to worry about, and had the Museum received that letter he'd sent the other day? Why didn't she go check, just to be sure?

She'd had more pointless errands over the last thirty hours than at any other time in her employment.

Now she knew better than to ask, and she hated to disturb Professor Carter yet again. Still, MacAlasdair probably wasn't going to leave without some response—and perhaps he'd be a distraction.

"Professor," she said, "there's a Stephen MacAlasdair to see you."

The professor stiffened. "MacAlasdair?"

"Yes, sir. I can send him away, if you'd like, but—"

"No. No, by no means. I'll see him." Professor Carter got to his feet, brushed at his coat, and pulled on his tie, the creases in his brow never fading. "Have Mrs. Evans send up tea and scones, Miss Seymour."

The brief diversion to the housekeeper's lair meant that Mina entered the office just a step ahead of the professor himself, who looked over MacAlasdair with, to Mina's eyes, considerable shock. "Good Lord, MacAlasdair, you haven't aged a day."

"Flattering," said MacAlasdair, "but untrue. It's good to see you looking well, Carter. Professor, I should say."

They each smiled, but Mina didn't think either expression genuine. Professor Carter kept playing with the top button on his coat, a sure sign that he was nervous, and MacAlasdair had lost none of the tension in his frame. There was more to this than two old friends meeting again.

When the door closed behind them, she broke her own rules and listened for as long as she was able.

"And when did you post Cerberus at your gates?" MacAlasdair asked.

Mina nurtured a brief but intense wish that he'd trip on the stairs and break his leg, or at least his nose.

Professor Carter made a reproving noise. "I've become an object of interest for more than a few people. Antiquities have caught the popular eye, you know. Miss Seymour does an admirable job of keeping the peace. And I daresay she'd have been more amenable if I'd known you were going to call."

"*I* didn't know I was going to call," said MacAlasdair, and now his voice was grim. "Not until I read the news. I take it you've seen the same piece."

"I—yes—" said the professor. They were climbing the stairs now, and their footsteps drowned out most of the conversation. Mina caught one name, though: Moore.

She stood very still for a second.

She'd read the paper too.

Colonel James Edward Moore, age sixty-three, had been found dead in his flat two days before. The *Times* said that "signs"—they wouldn't be more specific, and Mina was glad—pointed to assault with a heavy weapon. Scotland Yard was investigating but had named no subjects.

Apparently the professor had known Moore. Well, that might have explained his mood over the last day and a half. MacAlasdair had known him too. On the stairs, though, they hadn't sounded like they were discussing a brutal and mysterious crime. They'd sounded as if they might know what was behind Moore's death, and fear it.

Mina sat down again and resumed her typing. But she kept listening for noises from upstairs, and she kept one eye on the clock.

She knew, therefore, that half an hour had passed when MacAlasdair stormed down the staircase, slammed the back door open, and stalked through the office and out into the street. He didn't so much as look in Mina's direction on the way, and she found herself rather glad of that.

As soon as she'd closed the door behind MacAlasdair, Mina started toward the stairs, moving at a fairly rapid clip herself, and ran into her employer as a result. Her "Sorry, sir!" had a distinct note of relief to it.

Mina didn't think that Professor Carter noticed. He barely seemed to notice the collision. "Miss Seymour."

"Are you all right, Professor?"

"Yes, quite." Except that his face was at least a few shades paler than usual, and his eyes did not see her at all. He thrust a hand forward almost blindly, clutching a haphazardly assembled sheaf of papers. "Here are my notes from this morning. The section on Abyssinian relics might be a bit tricky. Let me know if you have difficulties. I'll be upstairs."

With the motion, the cuff of his jacket fell back a little, revealing a wide silver band around his wrist. Mina glimpsed strange, angular shapes running down the middle. Then, as Mina took the papers, the professor dropped his hand, somewhat hurriedly, and cloth fell over the bracelet again.

He'd never been a man for much adornment. Not as long as Mina had known him. And she thought she would have remembered the bracelet. "Sir," she asked, "what's troubling you?"

The urge to speak showed itself plainly on his face for a moment, as bright and wide as the bracelet—and as swiftly concealed. "An abundance of questions," he said gruffly, then cleared his throat and patted her shoulder. "You mustn't concern yourself about me, Miss Seymour. I've weathered more storms in my life than you've, er, typed notes on Abyssinia."

Mina smiled, as the professor clearly wanted her to, but shook her head. "If there's anything I can do—"

"Nothing anyone can do just now, much less a young lady." He was back to gruff. "Get on with your work, Miss Seymour. The day grows late."

Before she could reply, the professor turned away. The door closed behind him with a neat click, leaving Mina with unanswered questions and a pile of paper.

At least she could do something about the latter.

Sunday dinners were always a jolt these days. Scrubbed and starched, still with the better part of a week's pay in her purse, Mina squeezed into her old place at the parlor table on the Sunday after MacAlasdair had entered the office. With Florrie's gold curls to one side and Bert's tousled brown mop on her other, she ate beef and Yorkshire pudding under the gaze of her mother, her father, and, from the mantel, a much younger Queen.

It was a world away from either Professor Carter's book-lined office in Gordon Square or Mina's own whitewashed, bare-floored room on Bulstrode Street. It was also a world she entered back into easily after the first few moments, all the more rewarding now because she knew things could be different.

At least, her return was usually easy.

Mina ate with as good an appetite as ever. She

laughed at her father's jokes and Bert's stories, and listened as her mother read a letter from George, whose ship had docked in Shanghai a month ago. It was Sunday, Mina was with her family, and these both were excellent things. Still, the memory of Professor Carter's troubles weighed on her mind, and so did Lord MacAlasdair's contribution to those troubles, whatever it might have been.

When the conversation settled for a moment, Mina looked across the table at Alice, another of the Seymour daughters who only came home on Sundays. Alice was a housemaid up in Mayfair and frequently brought home stories that the other servants told, circulating the tales in a web of gossip that reached from one great house to another.

Someone like Lord MacAlasdair would certainly have servants.

"There was a gentleman throwing his weight around in the office the other day," Mina began, "and I was wondering if you'd heard anything about him. MacAlasdair?"

Alice put down her fork and considered the question. Only for a moment, though. Then she grinned, and her green eyes lit up with the joy of knowing Something Interesting. "The Scottish bloke? New?"

"I don't know how new. But Scottish, yes."

"Well, if he's the same one, he took a house in Mayfair a month ago. Came with just a valet and a housekeeper." Alice leaned forward. "And do you know what?"

Mina grinned back at her sister. "Yes," she said, as she'd been saying on these occasions for twenty-three years, ever since she'd started talking well enough to tease her sister, "which is why I asked you. I love hearing answers I already know."

Alice stuck out her tongue and went on. Around them, the family was listening. Gossip from the city was always interesting.

"Ethel"—another of Lady Wrentham's house-maids—"walks out with a policeman who knows the cook at MacAlasdair's."

"I thought he didn't have a cook," said Bert.

"He'd have hired one after he came, wouldn't he?" Florrie shot back, leaning across Mina to do so. "Stupid."

"I'm not—" Bert was beginning to raise his voice when a glance from Mr. Seymour stopped the incipient fight. Mina, whose best dress would have been much the worse for intercepting flung peas, sent her father a grateful smile.

"Go on, Alice," said Mrs. Seymour. "Does he still need servants? Your Aunt Rose knows a girl who's looking for a place in a kitchen."

Alice shook her head. "No. Well, maybe. He *has* already hired maids, though, and"—a significant pause—"Mrs. Hennings, the cook, she says he gives all of them *two hours off* every night!"

Few Drury Lane actresses could have given a statement more dramatic flair than Alice did with her announcement, and the Seymours, at least, were an appreciative audience. Even Bert, who knew little of domestic service but had heard stories from his sister, whistled—and got a glare from his mother for it.

"Any two hours?" Mrs. Seymour asked, her son's table manners safely corrected.

"No, just at dusk." Alice lowered her voice again. "He doesn't want any of them in the house then. Only he lets Mrs. Hennings stay in the kitchen, as she's got rheumatism, and any who want can stay there with her. But they're not to go into the house proper."

"I bet he's got a mad wife," said Florrie, who had been spending her pocket money on penny dreadfuls lately. "And he has to take her out sometimes to...to feed her, I guess, or let her walk around the place, and he can't let anyone else be around or she'll tear them to shreds."

"That's silly," said Bert. "Why wouldn't he just keep her in the attic? Or tie her up?"

"Because..." Florrie hesitated, buttered a roll, and then saw a way out of the problem. "Because he's still passionately in love with her. Even though she's mad. And he wants to be kind to her."

"He didn't seem the sort to be madly in love with anybody," said Mina, remembering being called *Cerberus* and MacAlasdair's demand that she stop being ridiculous. "And he certainly didn't seem very kind."

"His maids probably don't agree with you there, my girl," said Mr. Seymour, chuckling. "Still, he sounds like a strange sort."

"That's for certain," Mina said. "Alice, could you talk to Ethel for me? I think I'd like to have a cup of tea with Mrs. Hennings when she has a moment."

Two

Contrary to all general wisdom about cooks, Mrs. Hennings was neither short nor stout nor elderly, but rather a tall woman of handsome middle age, with the sort of black eyes that novels inevitably called "flashing" and glossy black hair that made Mina touch her own brown curls with envy. Her own figure was undoubtedly voluptuous, but that was as close as she came to the stereotype.

The kitchen of MacAlasdair's house was far more conventional than the cook. It included a black stove like a mountain of ironwork, shelves of stoppered jars, racks of pots and pans, and smoke-stained walls ascending toward rafters that Mina could barely see. Even though it was only dusk, the stars not yet out, the shadows were deep in the corners of the room. Sitting at the long oak table in the center of the room, she felt dwarfed and mouse-like.

Tea helped. She added three lumps of sugar to her cup, stirred, and sipped.

"You haven't been here long, Alice says," she began.

"Well, not here," said Mrs. Hennings, gesturing

around the room. The light caught a gold ring on her hand. *Mrs.* was more than a courtesy title, then, at least for her. "I've been in London for some years now. Worked at Bailey's before his lordship hired me."

"The hotel?" Mina grinned. "When I was small, we used to watch the people going in, some nights. My brother and sister and I. Saw all kinds of lords and ladies. George used to swear he spotted a sultan or a rajah or the like once, but Alice and I never credited it."

Mrs. Hennings joined Mina in laughing. The atmosphere in the room lightened a little, although when Mina glanced toward the corner of the room, the shadows seemed even deeper.

Well, it was getting on toward night.

"He might have been telling the truth, at that," said Mrs. Hennings. "We had a few." She set down her teacup. "But that isn't why you wanted to talk to me."

"No," Mina said. "Actually, I was hoping you could tell me something about his lordship. What kind of a man he is."

Mrs. Hennings's eyebrows lifted. "I see," she said. "Made you an offer, has he?"

"Lord, no!" Mina's face burned. The topic was embarrassing enough, but a sudden, treacherous memory of MacAlasdair's powerful body leaning over her desk suggested that such an offer might have its attractions.

She couldn't meet Mrs. Hennings's eyes for a moment. She looked off into the corner again, and this time she thought she saw something move.

Well, rats showed up in the best-kept kitchens, Mina had heard. She didn't want to call anything of the kind to the cook's attention, though.

"He's...he came to visit my employer the other day," she said, "and he seemed cross. I was hoping to find out—"

She hesitated, caught between several choices of phrase. "Whether he's actually a murderer" was almost certainly too blunt. "What exactly is wrong with the man" probably was too. And she didn't want to bring Moore into it unless she had to.

More movement caught her eye. That was a *large* rat, if it actually was a rat. A cat, maybe? If so, Mina was surprised it wasn't under the table begging. In her experience of cats, their reaction to food was almost universal.

"Hoping to find out if there's anything I can do to help things go more smoothly," she finished belatedly.

"That would depend on what 'things' are, wouldn't it?"

"I wish I knew," said Mina.

Mrs. Hennings smiled quickly, which might have been either sympathy or a rebuff. "His lordship's a private creature, I fear. Certainly doesn't confide in me, at least not about anything other than a fondness for lemon tart."

"But he's a pleasant enough man, generally? Not angry or demanding?"

"Pleasant enough from what I've seen. If he does cut up rough with anyone, it's not been me, nor any of the maids. I'd have known, believe me." Mrs. Hennings rolled her eyes.

Mina smiled, remembering some of Alice's stories of hysterics in the scullery. "Speaking of maids," she said, "I suppose they're all out at the moment? I've heard his lordship's generous that way."

"The night's too pretty to be inside, if you've a choice in the matter." Mrs. Hennings made a wry face and patted her left knee. "I broke this as a girl, and it's never been quite right since, so I'm as happy to sit down at the end of the evening. As long as—what the bleeding *hell*?"

Her gaze had suddenly focused on something over Mina's shoulder, something that had drained the blood from her face. Mina whipped her head around to look.

There was a man stepping out of the shadows.

No, not a man.

Not entirely.

It was nothing but shadow and silhouette, something that didn't quite look human. It stepped unerringly toward them, moving with a slowness that was more frightening than speed.

It had no need to hurry.

She should scream, Mina thought. Maybe it would bring help, though she couldn't imagine what sort of help would be effective against a…ghost? Spirit? It didn't look solid. Still, she should scream and run. But her throat was locked tight, her legs numb.

This wasn't happening. This couldn't be happening.

Movement, at the corner of her vision.

Mina turned her head, so slowly she thought she could feel each muscle working individually. There was another one of the shadows, stepping toward her from the other corner of the room.

Pain shot through Mina's arm, not intense but sudden and sharp enough to break through her paralysis. She looked down for a second and saw Mrs.

Hennings's hand just above her elbow, the other woman's nails digging in through layers of cloth.

Then they were both on their feet, Mina's chair clattering to the ground behind her. She grabbed the half-full teapot and hurled it at the closer of the two shadow-men. She was beyond surprise or dismay when she saw it go through the shadow and smash against the floor. Tea spread out, a dark pool against the polished stone.

"The Lord is my shepherd," Mrs. Hennings recited too high and too fast as both women backed away from the figures approaching them. "I shall not want. He—"

Unimpressed, a shadow flicked one whip-arm out toward her. She shrieked as it curled around her knee, or maybe Mina shrieked, or perhaps they both did. Mina lunged toward the cook, grabbing for one of her arms, even as the shadow-man tugged forward. Mrs. Hennings fell hard. Her head made a noise like a cracking egg when it hit the stone floor, and she stopped struggling.

Oh God.

The shadow-man paused for a second. Its head turned toward the cook's still form. Then it seemed to shrug, and the tentacle withdrew. As if Mrs. Hennings had never been there, the figure and its companion continued their advance—this time toward Mina alone.

Oh God.

The shadows were between her and the door to the outside. The windows were too small and too high to crawl through. Mina fumbled behind her, found the doorknob, and yanked open the door that led to the rest of MacAlasdair's house.

She ran, darting around tables and through doors and not really knowing where she was headed, holding on to enough self-possession not to flee upstairs but to try and find a way out of the house, hoping that the spirits wouldn't follow her even then.

This wasn't happening. This couldn't be happening.

One of the shadows had gotten close enough, a room or twelve back, that the tip of its "arm" had brushed Mina's ankle as she fled. Pain and numbness had run up from the spot almost instantly, as if she'd fallen hard on the leg. She tried to ignore it now.

She wondered if Mrs. Hennings was dead. If so, she suspected it was a better fate than Mina would have. Whatever the shadows intended, a broken skull would probably be kind in comparison. Moore had been beaten, the papers had said, with a large object. Maybe the shadows didn't need an object; maybe they just needed to touch a human body for long enough.

She had no strength left for either panic or sorrow at that thought. It just was, like one more table to veer around.

Another room. This one had light coming from under the door. Not normal light: a strange, wavering reddish glow, as if someone inside was messing about with Chinese lanterns. Was there someone inside?

She sprinted for the door anyhow. Maybe anything that strange would be able to take care of the shadows chasing her. If not, it was still a door, and it was still ahead of her. She reached out and grabbed the doorknob.

It didn't turn. Mina twisted frantically at it, with one hand and then two, and nothing happened.

Locked.

And there was nowhere else to go, no side passage to flee down, and the dark shapes were coming onward.

"Go *away*!" she screamed at them, knowing it wouldn't work, still not wanting to die doing nothing. "Begone! A—avaunt! In the name of God!"

No wavering. No change. Only oncoming, expressionless shadow.

A roar came from the room behind her.

It was a bit leonine; it was a bit like a train whistle; and it was loud enough to make Mina's ears ring. Hearing it, the shadows froze. If they'd had eyes, Mina thought they would have been looking at each other. She sensed some sort of uncertain communication between them anyhow.

Then a claw half the size of her body smashed through the door behind her, carving through the wood as if it were wet paper. Mina ducked away, flattening herself against the wall, just in time to see an immense dark shape charge out and into the first of the shadows.

A shrill scream went up from the monster. Mina thought that it was likely a dying wail—she hoped so, with a hot vengeance born of fright—but she couldn't see the shadows clearly any longer.

She could see their attacker.

She saw a scaled body as tall as the hallway ceiling and almost as wide as the hall itself. She saw great leathery wings folded against the beast's sides. She saw a long snaky neck that ended in a great wedge of a head, the same deep red as the rest of the creature. It had blazing gold eyes, that head, and a mouthful of teeth like railroad spikes.

Even her mind, which felt like so much jelly by that point, could grasp the meaning of those attributes.

Dragon.

The shadow lashed out at it with its arms. There was a hissing noise as it struck the dragon's flesh, but Mina didn't stay to see the rest of the battle. The shadow was distracted. The dragon was distracted. She took a deep breath and bolted forward, away from the locked door.

As she'd hoped she would, she passed under the dragon's neck as it flinched backward from the shadow. The beast snarled, terrifyingly close to Mina's ears. The sound gave new energy to her exhausted frame, and she scrambled onward past the folded wings and the scaled bulk of the dragon's body, past the lashing tail, and into the empty hallway beyond.

She didn't have time for relief. She ran again. Behind her, she heard movement, then footsteps, if something so loud could be called that.

Another door lay ahead. This one was unlocked. Mina felt the dragon's presence behind her as she ran through. Did they breathe fire? She was dead if they did—unless this one simply didn't want to burn the house down.

Why would it care?

Why would a dragon be in a house at all?

She wanted to wake up. She wanted to slap whoever was responsible for this final insult. Her week hadn't been enough. Running from shadow monsters and being pinned against a room with—something unnatural—in it hadn't been enough. No, there had to be dragons, too. If guardian angels existed, hers was due a kick in the shins.

The next door opened easily enough, at least, and deposited her in what must have been a drawing room. The curtains were mostly closed, but Mina could see a little bit of night sky through them. The stars would be out any moment. So would she, in all likelihood.

But there were windows and the street and—yes—a poker by the fireplace. She grabbed it just as the dragon burst through the door.

It shouldn't have fit through the door at all. Not the beast she'd seen at first.

It was smaller now.

There was a *blurriness* about it too. Mina couldn't make out its features, or even its form, particularly well. Terror might do that, but she'd been terrified before, and the dragon had seemed vivid enough then.

It didn't matter. She lunged for the window. The poker smashed through a pane of glass.

Then the dragon was in front of her, between her and her escape route. Mina shrieked again, this time in frustration as much as fear. It had to be *fast*, too?

She couldn't even look at it properly. It kept twisting, or being twisted. She could tell that it was rearing up now on two legs, which there shouldn't have been enough space to do. Otherwise it was as if she couldn't focus her eyes, or as if some prism hung between her and the dragon, splintering its image into many angles.

Well. *Fine*. She'd at least make it have a bad night.

Mina drew her arm back, tightened her grip on the poker—

A hand grasped her arm. A human hand, by the feel of it, since her bones were in one piece and there were no claws piercing her skin. But when Mina looked down, the skin on the hand was deep red and scaly.

That shape lasted for a moment, long enough to burn itself into Mina's mind. Then the scales vanished, the skin turned pale again, and she was looking at a hand that might have belonged to any gentleman.

Her own hand dropped to her side, the poker in her grasp suddenly very heavy. Mina looked up at golden-brown eyes, deep red-black hair, a square chin, and a thin mouth.

"Cerberus," said a familiar deep voice, heavy with irony and resignation. "Might I ask what you're doing in my house?"

Three

The best laid schemes of mice and men, as another Scotsman had observed, often went awry. Stephen had heard as much quite a few times in the century since Burns had written his poem, but the phrase had rarely seemed as true as at that moment. Granted that his plans hadn't been that well-laid; still, at no point had they featured either a battle with manes or further conversation with Miss Seymour.

Miss Seymour herself did not look like she found their current situation either an expected or a desired development. The muscles of her arm were rigid under his hand. Her whole slim body was tense—torn, Stephen thought, between the primitive urge to flee and the more intellectual knowledge that it would probably do no good. Even knowing the woman as little as he did, he would also have wagered that the impulse to belt him with the poker was in there as well, which was why he hadn't let go of her arm.

"I… You…" In the dim light, her eyes were very wide, very dark. Shock. She shook her head violently, though, and then turned from disbelief to defensive hostility, raising her voice and thrusting her chin forward. "I told people I was coming here tonight. Plenty of people. They'll know it if you do anything to me."

"Wise of you," said Stephen. "But not necessary. Contrary to rumor, I don't really eat virgins."

If Miss Seymour blushed, it was too dark for him to see it, at least in human form. The dragon wouldn't have found the dim light a problem, but the dragon would also have gotten a poker in the face some minutes back.

"And what," Stephen went on, "did you tell these people? I can't imagine you're advertising your services as a housebreaker."

Miss Seymour drew herself up. "I didn't break in anywhere. I came to 'ave a cup of tea with—oh. Oh, Lord." Indignation and suspicion both vanished, at least for the time being, and her mouth dropped open in horrified realization. "Your cook. Mrs. Hennings. She fell when they came in—hit 'er head. I don't know if—but we should go see to her, and quickly."

'Er and *'ave*, Stephen noticed, even as he turned and started down the hallway, pulling the girl along with him. Also, her vowels were broader than they'd been when she'd spoken to him in Carter's office. Hers wasn't a strong accent, and she'd clearly tried to get rid of it, but it was there.

He wasn't sure why her dialect, trained or native, mattered, but it was more information, and one never knew where or when that could prove valuable.

"Would you let me go?" Miss Seymour snapped as

they hurried down the hallway. "You're pulling the arm right off of me."

Stephen winced and stopped. "Sorry." It was easy to forget his strength; usually, he dealt with that by not making much contact with pure humans. He started to remove his hand, then stopped. Miss Seymour could manage a fair turn of speed when she ran. She was also still armed. "Perhaps—"

She glared up at him. "Do you really think I'll run *now*? You know who I am. You're a lord. You can go to Scotland Yard if you want, disgrace me and the professor both. What do you think I'll do if you leave hold of me?"

"Ah," said Stephen. She was right, but agreeing with her would have been gloating, and her voice was already spiky with frustration. "Well," he said, "then I must ask you to put down the poker."

Clang.

"I'm much obliged," he said, and released her arm.

Miss Seymour rubbed at her bicep. "Likewise, I'm sure," she said, formal and icy.

They went on.

The kitchen was still decently lit. Stephen could see the remains of a teapot and an overturned chair and Mrs. Hennings, lying on the floor with a pool of blood around her head.

Stephen rushed to her side and knelt down. The woman was still breathing, at least, and her pulse was steady when he felt the side of her neck. He lifted her head carefully, all the more aware of his strength since Miss Seymour's outburst, and began what examination he could manage. Near at hand, he heard Miss

Seymour moving around the kitchen: light footsteps, cabinet doors opening and closing, and the sound of water being pumped.

At last, he let himself sigh with relief. "It's a nasty cut," he said, "and she'll have a lump for a few days, but there's no dent in her skull. Head wounds always bleed considerably, even the mild ones."

"I know," said Miss Seymour, kneeling down herself. She had a basin of water with her and a small stack of clean napkins. "My brother's friend Harry copped 'im on the forehead with a bit of rock once when we were young. Bled *sheets*, he did, and Mum almost fainted when she saw him walk in, but he was right as rain by dinnertime. Here. You wash the cut. I'll see if some water on her face can't bring her round."

It did. After the first touch of the cloth, Mrs. Hennings made incoherent, pained noises and opened her eyes. "…Your lordship?" she asked, looking vaguely alarmed to see Stephen so near at hand.

"Lie still, please," he said. "Can you see clearly?"

She blinked a few times. "Yes, sir. What—oh, dear God. What *happened*? There were these dark…dark men, weren't there? They *were* men. They had to have been…but…no—"

"Ah," said Stephen. "Well—"

"Burglars," Miss Seymour said quickly. "They had masks over their faces. Probably ladies' stockings, though I didn't get much of a look. One of them hit you with a bullwhip, of all things. Seems he fancied himself Jesse James. Your knee gave out and you hit your head."

Mrs. Hennings frowned, but in disapproval now, rather than the confusion and incipient hysteria of before. "Well, what happened? Are they still around? Did they get anything?"

"No," said Miss Seymour. "Lord MacAlasdair," there was only a slight pause, "shot one of them. In the leg. That subdued them both fairly quickly. The police have taken them away."

Mrs. Hennings relaxed. Over her head, Stephen took a moment to stare at his involuntary companion.

After their first conversation, he'd mentally filed Miss Seymour away the way he did most people: Girl; Typist and Threshold Guardian; Professor Carter, For the Use of. Hair: Brown, Light. (Under the kitchen light, it was the color of caramels, somewhat curly, and more than somewhat escaped from its pins.) Eyes: Blue, Dark. Dress: Dark, Serviceable. Personality: Unfortunate, Deeply.

He hadn't considered, as facets of her character, the existence of brothers, the ability to lie swiftly and convincingly, or the willingness to hit a dragon with a fireplace poker. The subjects had not occurred to him.

Stephen cleared his throat. "Yes, well," he said, looking back down at his cook. "How are you feeling?"

"My head hurts a bit," said Mrs. Hennings, and raised a hand to touch the cut. "Ugh. But I'm right enough otherwise, I'd think."

"I'm glad to hear it," said Stephen, "but you should still get some rest. You'll have tomorrow off, and you'll tell me if you're feeling at all unwell afterward."

Mrs. Hennings seemed about as well as a person could be after a knock on the head, and there wasn't much that a doctor could do in any case, but such things could be tricky. Stephen remembered a boy, kicked by a horse, who'd been fine for days and then dropped down stone dead.

That had been more than fifty years ago. Back at home, Stephen wouldn't have thought anything of such time. Here, surrounded by mayfly people, the gulf of years seemed wider.

He began to help Mrs. Hennings to her feet, a process that went fairly well until she put her weight on her left leg. She cried out then, not loudly, and grabbed involuntarily at Stephen's arm as her knee buckled.

"A week off," he said, bracing her calmly. More memories came back to him: the aftermath of fire and flood, battle and plague. "At least. And we'll have a doctor in as soon as you're settled."

"Why don't you go and send for one?" Miss Seymour stepped forward. "I'll help Mrs. Hennings get comfortable. Unless—is there anyone else in the house?"

"Not yet," said Stephen. Even Baldwin and his wife had left: Baldwin had mentioned taking in a show. Neither of them had been to London before, and they were evidently determined to enjoy it.

Stephen met Miss Seymour's gaze again—You can disgrace me and the professor both, he heard her say in his memory—and then bowed to the inevitable.

A short walk later, he returned to find Miss Seymour sitting at the kitchen table, her hands folded in her lap. The broken teapot was gone; the tea and the blood had both been mopped up. Everything about the scene was calm. Outwardly, at least.

Miss Seymour looked up at the sound of footsteps,

eyes narrowed and body tense. When she saw Stephen, she relaxed, but only a little.

"I've sent an errand boy for Doctor Gregory," said Stephen. "He'll be here shortly, I'd imagine. How is Mrs. Hennings?"

"Lying down," said Miss Seymour. "One of your maids is with her. Jenny. She got here a bit after you left."

"And what does she know of the incident?"

"Only that Mrs. Hennings had a nasty fall. No need to mention burglars. Mrs. Hennings thinks it'd only scare the girls." Miss Seymour looked up at him and lifted an eyebrow. "You wouldn't want that."

"I certainly would not." Stephen pulled out the chair opposite Miss Seymour and sat down. "I try not to frighten women and children, as a rule. Particularly when they work for me."

The look on Miss Seymour's face was, for a moment, one of undisguised skepticism. She opened her mouth, seemed to think better of whatever she'd been going to say, and turned it into a sigh.

Stephen sighed too. Eight in the evening, and already the night felt very long.

"My lord," said Miss Seymour, and the title felt wrong coming from her. Stephen wasn't sure why. "I'd guess there's a reason you've kept me here, and I'd also guess it's not for my company. And you'd have called the police by now if you were going to. Unless you sent for them when you were out just now," she added, and her mouth went thin. "In which case, I'll point out to them that there's nothing illegal about having a cup of tea with your cook, and I only went farther into the house because I was running away from those things. What *were* those things?"

"Manes," said Stephen. "The Romans thought they were the spirits of the restless dead. I'm…less certain of that."

"They don't act like anything that was ever a person. Or look it," said Miss Seymour. She wrapped her arms around her chest, defensive. "Either way, you're talking about ghosts, or—or devils, or something like."

"I am."

"Why did they come here? Why'd they go after Mrs. Hennings and me? And what are you?" Miss Seymour fired the questions across the table, stopped, and reloaded for a final shot. "And what've you got to do with Professor Carter, anyhow?"

"That last question brought you here, I take it?"

"Yes."

Stephen rubbed his forehead with one hand. "Have you had supper?"

Miss Seymour blinked. "What? No."

"Then," Stephen said, getting to his feet, "we're going to eat. Even if it's only cold meat and bread. I'm not fond of making either explanations or plans on an empty stomach."

"I wouldn't say no to a bit of a meal," Miss Seymour admitted, "but—plans? What sort of plans?"

Stephen, who'd been on his way to the pantry, turned to look back at her. "You've seen a great deal tonight," he said, "and at a very dangerous time. We cannot pretend otherwise, I think, even if you were the sort of girl for that, which you are not."

"No," she said, sounding both pleased and annoyed at the same time.

"So—" Stephen spread his hands. "Here we are, you and I. What do we do now?"

Four

The pantry turned out to hold bread and cold chicken, as well as butter and plum preserves, though the previous difficulties with shadowy invaders meant that there was no more tea.

"You have to have another teapot somewhere," said Mina.

"Have I?"

"For company, at least." Ordinarily, she wouldn't have suggested that she was "company" for a peer—even now, she could feel her mother's hand on the back of her head—but this night had been anything but ordinary.

"It may surprise you to learn, Miss Seymour, that I don't often entertain here."

"Ah," she said, thinking of the dark rooms and the things that had chased her through them. No, she wasn't very surprised.

Mina drank water instead, tried not to let her hands shake while she held the glass, and eyed the food. Half-remembered fairy tales and a few of the myths she'd heard while working with Professor Carter made her hesitate, thinking of fairy food and drinks that made you sleep for years, but this was London, MacAlasdair employed a cook, and she'd never heard of anyone, in any story, enchanting cold chicken or plum preserves. Any decent spirit would probably snicker into its airy sleeves at the idea.

She took a slice of bread and buttered it, keeping her eyes on MacAlasdair as much as she could manage without buttering her cuffs by mistake.

"Well," she said, when the silence grew so that she could no longer bear it, "*I* can't tell *you* very much, I'm sure."

"No, I'd imagine not," said MacAlasdair, and the uncertainty in his voice made him seem slightly less remote and sinister. "I was going to wait until you'd had a chance to eat."

"Suspense doesn't make me very hungry," said Mina, but she took a bite of her bread anyhow. Eating was only sensible, considering the circumstances.

Chewing was an effort, swallowing a worse one, but after the first few bites, her body remembered itself and demanded more. The food did help. It was solid and normal and made her feel grounded again, not tossed about on uncanny events like a leaf in the wind.

"You'll have to stay here," said MacAlasdair. "For the time being, that is."

Atrocious timing. Atrocious man. Mina almost inhaled a morsel of bread, succumbed to a brief but undignified coughing fit, and got herself under control in time to wave MacAlasdair away. As a result, the first word she got out bore no resemblance, in either form or tone, to the icily proper "I beg your pardon?" that a lady would have used under similar circumstances.

"*What?*" Her voice practically shattered glass.

"I don't mean anything..." MacAlasdair coughed indicatively. "I've a cook and a housekeeper, Miss Seymour, and a number of maids."

"I'm happy for you," said Mina. "Are you in the habit of keeping women prisoner, then? Or just anyone who wanders in here?"

MacAlasdair sighed. "Hardly. But the circumstances make it necessary."

"What circumstances."

"The things you've seen tonight."

"And do you really think I'd *tell* anyone?" Mina rolled her eyes. "Oh, yes. I hear the weather's real pleasant at Colney 'atch this time of year, thank you so much." She heard her accent slip, stopped, and took a long breath, her hands tight fists at her sides. More carefully, she went on. "Even if I did tell, which I'm not going to, who on *Earth* would believe me?"

"Enough people," MacAlasdair said, "to cause me considerable trouble."

"One in specific?" she asked, picturing the shadow demons.

"That," MacAlasdair said, leaning forward with narrowed eyes, "is none of your concern."

Even human, he was a good bit larger than her. Mina suddenly couldn't take her mind from that fact, nor from the tightness of his square jaw and the way his hands had clenched on the table. There was no poker here. The table itself might be an obstacle, but not for long.

Catching the look on her face, MacAlasdair sat back and dropped his hands to his sides. He closed his eyes. "You have my apologies," he said roughly. "I didna' mean to frighten you."

"I'm fine," Mina lied.

Opening his eyes, MacAlasdair looked at her dubiously, but said nothing. Instead, he took a bite of his sandwich. He'd devoured half of it while she blinked, it seemed, which made him far less intimidating as a gentleman and far more when she thought of his other form. He chewed slowly and finally spread his hands. "One hundred pounds," he said. "I'll draw up the check for you myself, once this is over."

Almost from the moment of his ultimatum, Mina had expected a bribe of *some* sort. You couldn't lock a girl in a dungeon these days, after all, and she'd hoped MacAlasdair wasn't the blackmailing kind. All the same, the sum was a jolt. One hundred pounds was four times what she made in a year, and MacAlasdair tossed it off as casually as if he were buying a pint of beer.

She could almost be angry about that—how much it meant to her and how little to him—but, she reminded herself, it would serve no purpose. The world was as it was.

Still, her voice was a little sharper than she'd meant when she answered. "How long will that be, pray? And what will I be doing in the meantime? You'd have to give people *some* reason I was here, and I don't think you could pass me off as your ward, not to anyone with eyes or ears."

"I—" He frowned for a second, dark eyebrows

slanting together, before hitting on an idea. "You'd be my secretary, I suppose. I'm sure I can find something for you to type."

"Or a threshold to guard?" Mina asked. "And what about Professor Carter? He needs my services—come to think of it, what *about* Professor Carter? Is he in any danger?"

"I wouldn't be sitting here if I thought he was," MacAlasdair said stiffly. "I've given him what protections I can, and I assure you that they're effective. As for your services, Carter will understand. He and I are acquainted."

"Old friends, you said."

"So I did."

"How long is 'the time being'?"

"Until I settle a certain matter. I shouldn't think it'll be more than a few months," MacAlasdair said, and then his thin mouth twisted in dark amusement. "One way or another."

The room around her was huge. The man across from her was large and wealthy and, well, a dragon. *Scary* didn't half begin to cover it.

But a hundred pounds would set her up well; the dragon seemed to be at least something of a gentleman; and Mina Seymour had never let being scared stop her from doing anything before.

"All right," Mina said. "I'll take your offer. With three conditions."

"I should have known," said MacAlasdair. "What do you have in mind?"

"First of all, it's a hundred a year. And I get the first hundred however long your business ends up taking."

One corner of MacAlasdair's mouth twitched. "Agreed."

Briefly, Mina wondered if she should have asked for more. Oh well. "Second, I want to talk with Professor Carter. I want to be sure he'll have me back after this, *and* I want a good character from you. If I get a bad reputation from living with you, I'll have the devil's own time finding another place, and that might happen no matter how many maids and cooks you've got."

"Strictly speaking, Miss Seymour, that'd be two conditions. But I'll agree."

"Third, I want you to tell me exactly what's going on here." That banished MacAlasdair's incipient smile. Before he could say anything, Mina folded her arms across her chest and went on. "I've a right to know why I'm risking my good name and my career, and maybe my life. And with whom. I don't need to know Crown secrets, but I want to know who you are, and what you are, and why someone's sending shadow monsters after you."

"For my safety and your own," MacAlasdair said, "the less you know—"

"The less I know, the more I might accidentally let slip. Or walk into. You're paying to keep an eye on me so I don't tell what I *do* know. There's not much more you can do by keeping mum about the rest of it, I'd think. And I'm not staying here half-blind."

Mina lifted her chin and did her best to look calm and immovable. MacAlasdair couldn't know how fast her heart was going—unless dragons had spectacular hearing, which they might. She tried not to think about that.

Finally, MacAlasdair sighed again. "Very well," he

said, and Mina heard *Cerberus* as an unspoken echo to his words. "I should have guessed that you'd not make this easy."

Five

"Carter and I met on an archaeological expedition," Stephen began. "We went to Bavaria to investigate some recently uncovered ruins. There was some controversy about whether the builders had been the local tribes themselves or the Romans, and I had an interest in the latter at the time."

Regret pricked him for a moment: wistfulness for the days only a few decades ago when he'd been free to pursue his own interests.

Nostalgia didn't last long, though. It couldn't, because Miss Seymour was already holding up a hand to stop him.

"Yes?" Stephen asked with what he felt was considerable patience.

"Professor Carter's last expedition was fifteen years ago. And that was to Egypt."

"Well, Egypt seems a pleasant place for an excursion," Stephen said. He knew what Miss Seymour was trying to hint at, and he knew that a more gentlemanly man might have saved her the process. Neither the evening nor her intrusion left him inclined to be a gentleman. "I hope he found it pleasant."

Miss Seymour's long fingers twitched on the piece of bread she was holding, but she gave Stephen no other reaction. Slowly, deliberately, she let her gaze travel down his body, then up to the crown of his head, lingering particularly on his face and his hairline.

For all the skepticism in her look, it was a rather intimate appraisal, and Stephen felt the path of her eyes as if she'd trailed a finger along his skin. Before he was aware of what he was doing, he'd lifted his head and straightened his shoulders, aware both that it made his chest look broader and that it was absurd to care what impression he made on a woman who had so far only caused him trouble. His less rational impulses were always harder to control just after transformation.

Fortunately, Miss Seymour chose that moment to speak, and to speak with a level of asperity that quenched any remaining urge to pose for her. "I can only assume," she said, "that you weren't traipsing off to Bavaria when you were ten. And a skilled hairdresser and a bottle of dye can only do so much."

"I'm certain I wouldn't know."

"Are you immortal, then?"

"We're all immortal, if you believe the preachers," Stephen said. "I'm no more so than the next man, but I do age considerably slower." The real scions of the MacAlasdairs—his grandfather and back—were a different story, but he preferred not to bring his family into the discussion. He lifted his eyebrows. "And I'm not sure how my age has much bearing on our situation."

A hit: Miss Seymour's pale cheeks flushed, and she suddenly found her bread and preserves very interesting.

"Go on, then," she said, as if the interruption had been all of Stephen's doing.

He decided to be gracious in victory. "As I was saying, Carter and I went to Bavaria. The party also included Colonel Moore and a young businessman, Christopher Ward. Carter was the one with the real knowledge, even then. Moore and I were dabblers—and so was Ward, we thought. He owned a string of factories, and it seemed that archaeology was by way of a hobby for him."

"Seemed?"

"I suppose it would depend on who you asked," Stephen said. "He was as familiar as Moore and I with mythology and history and all of that. None of us had anywhere near Carter's expertise, although Ward forgot that fact a time or five." He shrugged. "His parents had died some time before. He'd inherited the factories from them. Otherwise, I didn't know very much about him. We weren't close."

"It doesn't sound as if you wanted to be," said Miss Seymour.

"No. He didn't endear himself to any of the three of us. Moore and I had each known Carter for a while, in our own ways. Ward was the newcomer and perhaps felt it more than we'd intended him to. Still, as I said, he was often arrogant—" Here Miss Seymour's dark eyes glinted a little, and her full lips twitched. Stephen thought that he could read her mind without any magic at all, and that it contained references to pots and kettles. He went on quickly, "—and he'd a manner with servants that I disliked."

"Ah," said Miss Seymour, "and what sort of manner might that be?"

"Temper, mostly. He wasn't a man to bear well with being thwarted or frustrated in his purposes. Especially not when there was someone he could blame for it, even if they weren't truly *to* blame. We'd have gone through five guides before we reached the site if he'd had his way. Still"—Stephen spread his hands—"he was putting up a considerable bit of the funding, and he wasn't a thief or an overly violent man. At least not that we saw. Now I wonder.

"We reached the site and spent a few days there." He remembered the smell of the south wind, sharp with snow while the sun warmed his shoulders. He remembered rough stone beneath his hands and the pleasant exhaustion after a long day at good work. He'd accompanied Carter half hoping to find something of his own ancestry, but the trip itself had been well worth his time.

At least, he'd thought so then.

"On the fourth day," he said, "we found a secret panel in the floor. Once we'd managed to open it, we found an old chest bound and inscribed with a great many holy symbols. Some were Christian. Not all. Moore and I were uncertain about opening it. We wanted to speak to a priest first, at least. Although, in fairness, I'm not sure how much good it might have done if we had. Whatever traditions bound that box had long been lost."

Miss Seymour frowned. "You and Colonel Moore wanted to wait," she said, "but Professor Carter?"

"Carter was quite the skeptic in those days," Stephen said. "He'd had some trouble before that with priests and churches and the like. Perhaps he was in the wrong then, too—but he wanted nobody interfering, and Ward was not a patient or a reverent man. Neither Moore nor I felt very strongly, either. There was a fair chance that the symbols were only superstition, to keep raiders from the village's treasure.

"So we opened it. We took care, of course, but no more than you would with anything so old. When we worked the binding free…I'm not entirely sure what happened. I felt different: not myself. I managed to keep this shape, but it was difficult," he said, skipping over the way his bones had ground together and the feeling that bits of broken glass were running through his veins. He skipped, too, the smell of his companions' blood and the sudden awareness of how fragile they were, how strong he could be.

The woman across from him, intruder that she was, didn't need to hear such things—and he didn't need to remember them in any more detail.

Miss Seymour tilted her head. "You were already"—she made a small circle in the air with one hand—"like you are, back then?"

"I've been a dragon my entire life," said Stephen. "Though it's only since Bavaria that I've *needed* to transform."

"Hmm," she said, as if making a note of it. "Every night, I take it. For two hours at dusk."

Miss Seymour spoke matter-of-factly enough, but she still left Stephen staring at her. "How did you know that?"

"Your servants haven't taken a vow of silence," she said, "or if they did, they haven't been faithful to it. Did you really think they wouldn't talk?"

"I hadn't given it much thought," said Stephen.

"Of course you hadn't," said Miss Seymour, and chuckled a little in the back of her throat. It was a pleasant sound—she had a good voice, rather rich—but not a good-humored one. "I beg your pardon, my lord. *Why* are you a dragon?"

"Why aren't you?" Stephen shot back. "You have one shape in your blood. I have two."

"Does your whole family?"

Since she had no idea how big his family was, or who was in it, that was a safe enough question to answer. Stephen nodded. "But this is hardly to the point."

"I suppose you're right. What was in the box?"

"A crown," said Stephen. "Gold, or so it looked, though it must have been impure. Pure gold could never hold the shape so long. There were rubies in it. A great deal of wealth. That was the problem."

"How do you mean?"

"Our guide was from the village, ye ken," Stephen said, half-conscious of the way memory broadened his accent. "He said that the crown was theirs by rights, and that we weren't to do anything until he'd spoken with their mayor. They werena' a wealthy people."

"And you disagreed?" Honey-colored eyebrows went up again, and Miss Seymour regarded him with undisguised skepticism.

"No," Stephen said, more quickly than he might have. Then, irritated by the need to justify himself to this woman—this mortal who had never been his servant or in his charge, who had no claim at all on him—he corrected himself. "I might have, perhaps. We'd done the work of finding it. Carter and Moore werena' certain. But Ward didna' take it well, even the suggestion. He began to shout at the guide, and the guide shouted back. I was distracted."

He had wanted to be distracted. Back then, disputes between mortal men had seemed both inevitable and irrelevant. Men shouted. They stopped in time. When these two stopped, he would step in. Until then, he had better things to think about. Stephen had turned back to the box and its inscriptions, trying to ignore the raised voices. Then he'd heard something else.

"Ward knocked the fellow down. Then he picked up one of the stones we'd pried up, and—well, the guide was dead before even I could reach them. Brutally dead by the time I could pull Ward away." Stephen had seen messier deaths over his lifetime, but the sheer rage in Ward's actions had given even him pause. Carter had been sick afterward.

"Ward grew angry with *me*, then. He hadn't thought I'd interfere, not for a man we'd hired for a shilling a day. I knocked him down. I thought he'd stay down for a while, so I turned away and told Carter to go get the local constable. That was when Ward grabbed the guide's knife."

Stephen touched his stomach, just below his last rib. "It was a fair wound, but we're harder to kill than most. It did take me by surprise, though, and Ward ran off before I could recover myself, or before the others could step in."

"What happened to him?" Miss Seymour asked.

"We'd thought he was dead. The police never found him, and his estate passed on—to a nephew, for the most part. There was no body, though."

Miss Seymour reached for her teacup and held it in both hands for a moment. "Right," she said. "So this man, Ward, blames you and the others for getting him in trouble—"

"For losing him everything he had. He'd been a wealthy man, as I said, and a man of some position in the world. He became a fugitive. He had the money he'd carried, which was no small amount, but he couldn't draw on any of the rest. If he did survive, and it seems he did, I can't imagine what he had to do."

Stephen sighed. "And to his mind, it could all have been avoided if I and the others had simply agreed to say nothing of the guide's death, or perhaps even if we'd been more firmly on Ward's side at the start of the matter. We did give the crown to the guide's village in the end. They sold it to a museum for a great deal of money, and that probably makes Ward all the angrier."

"Hmph," said Miss Seymour, which seemed to cover her entire opinion on the matter. "And now he summons shadow monsters?"

Stephen ran a hand wearily through his hair. "The wound I took, and how lively I was afterward, made it clear enough I wasna' a normal human."

How often in the last few decades had Stephen scourged himself mentally for opening that path to Ward? How much more often in the last few weeks? He'd lost count.

Half expecting Miss Seymour to reproach him on the subject, or to at least ask, he felt an immense relief when she merely nodded and went on, her eyes like honed steel. "He wants to kill you?"

"He wants to take everything I have from me, I'd imagine," said Stephen, "the way he thinks I took it from him. As he's not been terribly direct, I think he wants more to discover what he doesna' know about me and to use it against me. One man saying that Lord MacAlasdair is a beast... Well, as you said, the asylums are very pleasant these days." At Miss Seymour's dubious look, he shrugged. "Comparatively. But a man with proof, or with another witness, could do me far more damage. I'd prefer not to be a monster, and I very much prefer not to be a target."

And he would be damned before he saw his family made into either.

Across the table, Miss Seymour listened, her face pale gold in the amber lamplight. In it, her eyes were very large and dark. She took a long breath and looked up at Stephen. "You haven't heard from Ward at all between then and now? This is the first time he's tried anything?"

"Moore's death was, yes. To the best of my knowledge. Ward wouldn't have known where I was until I came to London. He'd hate Moore and Carter, as well, for throwing their lot in with the guide and for not lying for him, but I think he hates me most of all."

"Because you stopped him," said Mina.

"Because I was stronger than he was, and he couldna' kill me," said Stephen, "and because he didna' know what I was. Being powerless can give a man a powerful hunger for revenge."

"Ah," Miss Seymour said, and Stephen was relieved to hear neither judgment nor sympathy in her voice.

She let a moment pass in silence: perhaps a measure of respect, perhaps just buying herself time to think. "Why are you here now?"

That question was easy enough to answer, if still painful in its own way. "My father passed on six months ago. He conducted our business affairs. They require a presence in the city. I'm his heir."

"Speaking of heirs—Ward's family, or what there is of it?"

"Not very much. One nephew, who never met him. The police questioned him about Moore's death, once I'd given them the information. The nephew is over thirty, with a wife and three children, and a fair bit of history in his neighborhood. That doesn't mean he's not working with his uncle, but Scotland Yard hasn't found anything on him."

"Besides," said Miss Seymour, with a cynical little smile, "you made him a rich man. If anything, I think he'd send you flowers. You've talked a good bit to the Yard, then?"

Stephen nodded. "Carter, as well. We told them… as much as we could, with certain alterations. We said it was an older cousin of mine involved in the original dispute."

Before Miss Seymour could respond to that, Stephen heard the kitchen door open and a maid's exclamation of surprise cut hastily short. He didn't turn. "Is that satisfactory?" he asked.

"It will be, for the moment," Miss Seymour said.

"Good." Stephen did turn, then, and faced the maid. A moment's fumbling brought him a name. "Polly, this is Miss Seymour, my new secretary. Kindly find an appropriate room for her. Miss Seymour, make yourself at home as much as you can."

"And my things?"

"We'll retrieve them tomorrow," he said, and stood to leave.

Six

Polly, a short blonde girl who looked a little younger than Mina herself, stood silent for a moment after Lord MacAlasdair departed. From the way she chewed on her lower lip and the way her gaze shifted between Mina and the middle distance, she was trying to figure out whether the house even *had* an appropriate room. MacAlasdair had said he didn't entertain often. He also didn't keep that many servants, clearly, and "secretary" was an odd position, somewhere between the two.

Not to mention that Polly, unless she was a *very* trusting soul indeed, had to doubt that "secretary" was Mina's real role.

Mina bit back the urge to say anything—Polly wouldn't believe it, anyway—and tried not to blush.

Finally, the maid sucked in air through her teeth and nodded to herself. "Wait here, please, miss," she said, and took herself off, leaving Mina alone in the dimly lit kitchen.

As she'd done before when Lord MacAlasdair had left to seek a doctor, she folded her hands in her lap and made herself sit still, taking slow, deep breaths. Panic would help nothing, she reminded herself. Fretting would help nothing; anger would help nothing. She was where she was.

And the shadows in the corners weren't moving this time. She kept checking. *That* wasn't panic. That was just reasonable caution, although MacAlasdair wouldn't have left her alone with Polly if he thought the manes could come back. On the other hand, he hadn't exactly anticipated them the first time.

She jumped and squeaked when she heard footsteps in the hall. Luckily—God bless wooden floors and hard-soled boots—she had enough warning to collect herself before Polly opened the door again. "This way, miss. If you please."

Polly led Mina through some of the same halls she'd run down earlier but turned well before the passage that led to the locked room. Instead, she took Mina up two flights of stairs, casting curious glances at her all the time when she didn't think Mina was looking.

No wonder. One didn't hire secretaries in the middle of the night, particularly not female secretaries, who hardly anyone hired anyhow. Polly must have known by now that she was working for an eccentric; all the same, she must have had a dozen questions. Mina might have heard some of them if MacAlasdair had hired her as a maid, or even a housekeeper. However, secretaries, like governesses, were always a little apart from the servants.

It was too bad. If Mina had met the other girl under any other circumstance, they could have been friendly.

Perhaps they could even have been friends. She would have liked to have a friend in this house.

The room was a neat, sparse little place with dark wooden furniture and pale flowered wallpaper, clearly not a room for family or guests but also a few steps above Mina's regular lodgings. She guessed that it had been for one of the more senior servants, perhaps a lady's maid from a time when the house had had a mistress.

Polly waited in the doorway, and for a moment, Mina couldn't figure out why, or why the girl didn't say anything. Then she remembered more of Alice's stories: maids didn't speak until spoken to. That was true even with a secretary, she supposed.

She cleared her throat. "That'll be all, Polly," she said, keeping her voice as clipped and even as she ever had. "Thank you."

The maid nodded and departed, leaving Mina alone in the room.

She took a more careful look around, noticing a small window set high on the wall. The view out of it was gorgeous, though the night was cloudy. Mina could see the outlines of the London roofs, lit against the sky by the still-awake city below, and the dome of Saint Paul's rising above them.

Turning reluctantly back to the room itself, she had to admit that it wasn't at all bad. As far as she could see, there was no evidence of spiders or rats, nor any dust. The air was a little stale, but if she opened the window tomorrow, that would be all right soon enough. For a hundred pounds, she could imagine staying in far worse places.

There was gas lighting too, she found when she examined the lamp on the wall. MacAlasdair, or more likely his father, wasn't far behind the times when it came to modern comforts. She wouldn't have expected it from creatures who lived…however long they lived.

Mina shivered at the thought. It was an important thought, though, and an important thing to remember. However human MacAlasdair seemed—however handsome she thought he was, at odd moments when he stopped being aggravating—he wasn't human at all. He didn't live like one; he didn't die like one, or at least not at the same rate; and he might well not think like one.

And the man who opposed him had been human once but was clearly willing to deal with creatures who were anything but.

Mina wrapped her arms around herself and eyed the corners of the room, the shadows that fell from the bed and the writing desk. They didn't move. Anything hunting MacAlasdair would hardly start up here.

All the same, after she undressed, she got into bed with the light still on. She could sleep in almost any conditions, and MacAlasdair could damn well foot the extra bill.

Mina woke to clear light, a pair of starlings fighting somewhere near her window, and an immediate sense of unreality. Shadow men. *Dragon* men, for God's sake. If she hadn't been in an attic room in a strange mansion, she would have dismissed the whole affair as a dream and cautioned herself against whatever she'd had for supper.

The thought of supper brought on an immediate and most worldly hunger. She washed and dressed in a hurry, though she was careful to look respectable, coiling her hair tightly back and pinning her collar very straight. Word got around quickly; Polly wouldn't be the only one with questions.

Mina soon found that she was right about that. She'd risen early enough to find the servants still at breakfast, and all of them—four maids, a butler, a groom, and a gray-haired couple who were probably the valet and housekeeper Alice had mentioned—turned to look when she entered the room.

The older woman got to her feet. "You'd be his lordship's new secretary, then," she said in a much broader Scottish accent than MacAlasdair's. "I'm Mrs. Baldwin, the housekeeper here. You've met Polly. That's Lizzie next to her and Sarah, and the wee one next to her is Emily, and James and Owens and Mr. Baldwin on the other side. And Mrs. Hennings upstairs, poor woman, and that's all of us under this roof." She smiled and spoke readily. It could have been friendliness; it could have been duty.

Mina gave the most polished smile she could manage in return. "Miss Seymour," she said. "Good morning."

"Good morning," said Emily, who was "wee" indeed—no more than fifteen, by the look of her—and thus probably from the scullery. The others produced a variety of nods and smiles, pleasant and careful and distant.

"Have yourself a seat and a bit of a breakfast," said

Mrs. Baldwin, "and then his lordship will see you in the drawing room. Polly will show you how to get there."

Breakfast was porridge, bacon, eggs, and scones, as well as very strong hot tea. It was also largely silent. Mrs. Baldwin observed that the weather was likely to be fine, James mentioned needing to have the blacksmith in one of these days, and Mina asked if the Baldwins had come up from Scotland with Lord MacAlasdair. Yes, they had; no, the trip hadn't been very difficult. That was nice.

Mina wanted to ask about Scotland, about how long the train journey had taken and what it had been like, about Lord MacAlasdair's horses and how the maids were finding the house. Miss Seymour, who had to keep the distance becoming to his lordship's secretary, sipped her tea, made polite inquiries about Mrs. Hennings's health—she was recovering nicely, it was really a bit of bad luck for her to have slipped on the staircase as she'd done, and clearly the story about the robbers hadn't gotten out—and excused herself as soon as she'd eaten sufficient food to see her through the next few hours.

MacAlasdair's house was rather handsome, now that she saw it in the daytime and without supernatural pursuit. However, it was still a rather intimidating place. The walls were mostly dark, with plenty of mirrors and gilded picture frames, and the furniture tended to be dark as well, not to mention rather massive.

Portraits were abundant. Mina saw an icily blonde woman with a ruff and a lapdog, a pair of bright-eyed children posed in front of a bay window, and a succession of men who looked more or less like MacAlasdair in clothing of various decades and centuries. She didn't *think* they were all MacAlasdair himself—he hadn't owned the house for very long, and scattering such pictures around the place would have been arrogant even for him—but, combined with the knowledge of his longevity, they still gave her a chill.

She lagged a little behind Polly as she walked, looking around, and so she gave a little start when the other woman said her name.

"Yes?" she asked.

"Come in," said MacAlasdair, from the room beyond an open door, and embarrassment swept over Mina. The maid had been announcing her. She should have known, and now she looked like a complete fool.

She drew a deep breath and stepped into the drawing room. MacAlasdair was lounging in one of the chairs by the fire, folding the day's paper in a leisurely manner, his long legs stretched out before him. He stood up and looked her over slowly, as if confirming her reality and the fact that he'd have to deal with her.

"Good morning, sir," she said, with as much cool politeness as she'd ever used for three short words.

There was equal caution in the golden eyes that met hers, but Lord MacAlasdair spoke more smoothly. "And a good morning to you as well, Miss Seymour. You may go, Polly." As the maid left, he indicated one of the chairs. "Have a seat. You seem to be well enough."

"One adjusts," said Mina, which she supposed was the truth. Her lack of hysterics had surprised *her* a little. She was glad that he probably didn't know anything about the light in her room. "Besides, if those things come back, I'd guess I wouldn't be the first they'd go after. Not from what you said."

"You wouldn't," said MacAlasdair, "and they'll not. Not for a few weeks yet. You canna' summon manes save in the dark of the moon, and that's past. Now that I've sent them back where they come from, Ward will have to wait a fair bit to play *that* trick again—though I'm sure he can lay his hands on other tools."

"Nothing like starting your day with a bit of good cheer, I suppose," said Mina.

"I'll take what cheer I can," said MacAlasdair. "Especially if it means not having manes tearing through my house. You can have your breakfast with me from now on," he added. "It would be sensible for me to give a secretary the day's instructions then."

It wasn't a gracious offer, and the first response that rose to Mina's lips was a stiff *I know my place, sir, thank you all the same*. But she checked it, remembering the stares and the stilted conversation over breakfast. She *didn't* know her place, not in this house. Or rather, her place was betwixt and between in a way it had never been with Professor Carter, who had only the one housekeeper and ate in his study without looking up from his latest book more often than not. Here, MacAlasdair at least knew her real situation better than the servants.

He was trying, too. And it wasn't as if their circumstances were entirely his fault.

"I'd be glad to," said Mina. "Will you actually have instructions for me?"

"Perhaps," said MacAlasdair, startled. "Nothing

immediate comes to mind. I'm in the habit of handling my affairs personally."

That was possibly the least surprising thing Mina had seen or heard since she'd crossed MacAlasdair's threshold. She bit the inside of her cheek to keep from saying as much.

"Today," MacAlasdair continued, "we'll go and retrieve whatever belongings you need. Whenever you're ready: my own plans are far from set."

It took a moment for Mina to realize what he was saying. When she did, she couldn't help laughing. "*We* won't do any such thing, thank you."

MacAlasdair raised dark eyebrows. "Pardon?"

"I live in a lodging house, my lord. A *female* lodging house."

"Ah. And they won't—"

"Not hardly," Mina said. "No men. Not even wealthy men with titles. Maybe *especially not* wealthy men with titles," she added, and saw MacAlasdair look away. Ha.

"I'll wait for you outside, then," he said after a moment.

"You'll wait for me in the tea shop," said Mina. "There's one on the corner. If I suddenly can't walk safely from there to my flat and back in the middle of the day, neither of us has any business staying in this city."

"You'll not talk to anyone on the way."

It wasn't a question, and Mina narrowed her eyes. "I won't be rude to anyone I know, but I'll be quick—and I've been looking after myself for a few years now. I gave you my word on your secrets, if that's what you're getting at, so you'll just have to trust a little bit that I meant it. You *can't* watch me every minute. For one thing, I won't let you."

"We have a bargain—" MacAlasdair began, glowering at her.

If Mina let him continue, his look and the authority in his voice might start working on her. She glared back instead and raised her voice. "Which says I'll stay here. So I'm staying. And I'll put up with more supervision than most people have outside of Newgate, because it's an awful situation all around and because you're paying me, but I have my limits. Anyone would."

Part of Mina was surprised that the table between them didn't start smoking in the seconds to follow. Apparently he didn't breathe fire, or he had it under good control if he did. All that happened, after a very long moment, was that he sighed like a man beset on all sides. "Verra well."

His accent was stronger again. From her own experience, she knew that wasn't a sign of composure. Mina wasn't sure whether she was pleased about that or not.

Either way, she had to take one more step. Walking about with MacAlasdair might cause enough talk to be trouble, even as careful as they were being. She wanted to be sure of her future before rumors started. "And before we do anything of the sort," Mina said, "I want to talk to Professor Carter. Alone."

Seven

So, for the second time in less than a week, Stephen cooled his heels in Carter's outer sanctum while Miss Seymour and the professor held their own council beyond the door and up the stairs. This time he was waiting longer—long enough to sit down, grow tired of sitting down, and begin pacing the room again.

He hadn't tried to argue this time. Carter was his friend, even if the two of them hadn't seen each other in a long time, and Carter had less than no love for Ward. Even if Miss Seymour did decide to betray Stephen, Carter would be no accomplice to her treachery. She had to know that. Granting them privacy carried very little risk. It certainly hadn't seemed worth *another* wrangle with the woman. Stephen had encountered actual bulls who were less stubborn.

Besides, he did want to put her at ease, as much as he could manage. Much as Stephen hadn't wanted Miss Seymour—or anyone else—entangled in his affairs, he had to admit that her entanglement had come from noble motives, and that she'd showed more courage over the last day and night than he would have expected from most mortal women. And, even had those things not been true, she would still be living with him for some unknown length of time.

Still unknown, dammit. Stephen glared ineffectually at a figurine of Anubis.

The manes provided some clue: the summoner had to be in the same city as his target, more or less, and the rite to summon them was far from common, even where magic was concerned. Stephen, who was no scholar, had only heard about it from a demon hunter he'd met some decades ago and who'd been dead for the last twenty years.

That was a pity. He could have used Abraham's insights into this particular matter. He would also have welcomed the German's company again. As it was, he was stuck with letters to the occultists he knew, ineffectual requests to talk with Ward's remaining family, and whatever information Scotland Yard wanted to pass his way. It wasn't much.

Now he could add one sharp-tongued, mistrustful mortal female to—well, not to his list of resources. Typing and correspondence wasn't likely to be Ward's bane. Miss Seymour went on the list of encumbrances, then, which was quite long enough already.

A sound from outside stopped Stephen's pacing and spun him toward the door.

Someone was coming up the steps outside, someone moving quickly and more furtively than most people on legitimate business ever did. Stephen crossed the room in three steps and seized the doorknob, just as the letter slot banged open and something spherical dropped through onto his foot.

Instinct sent him backwards, kicking the thing toward the wall before it could bite or sting or explode. The footsteps outside scurried off.

The sphere was about the size of a man's fist, wrapped in brown paper and tied with string. It wasn't hissing or ticking. It didn't smell like smoke. Still, nobody with an ordinary package to deliver dropped it through the letter slot and ran, and Stephen doubted that Carter had any secret admirers.

Miss Seymour might have, of course. She was a pretty lass with an undoubtedly nice figure, that mass of honey-gold hair, and a set of very red lips in her sharp little face. A man could take quite a fancy to her until she spoke, and perhaps one who *had* spoken to her wouldn't have the nerve to give his gifts properly.

The thought made Stephen curl his lip. They bred a spineless lot of young men these days, if that were the case.

There was nothing for it. Stephen faced the east and said a few quick Latin words, invoking the Wind That Parts the Veil, and saw the world before him turn misty and gray. The desk shone faintly golden through that fog, and the bookshelves were a bluish violet, but the package stood out like a full moon, glowing an eerie, shifting silver-green.

Stephen took a few steps toward it but made no move to touch it yet. At this distance, with the Wind at his back, he could see through both the physical wrappings and the object itself, and knew that it was no coward's courting gift—though it would look like a harmless bauble of some sort, probably a polished crystal or a metal bowl. It would be something to keep on the mantel or to put flowers in, so that the mist inside it would have as much time as possible to disperse.

That mist would be somebody's eyes and ears, and a truly skilled enough magician could whisper suggestions through it. It would take a great deal of power to change a human mind that way, but one could certainly change moods, twisting a target toward despair or madness. Even if Carter or Miss Seymour had gotten rid of the thing, the mist that came out on opening the package would probably have been enough to suit Ward's purposes.

Even with the package wrapped, there was only a little time before the mist would begin to seep through the paper.

Fortunately, April in London was still a chilly month.

Stephen took off his coat and wrapped it around the sphere, careful not to let his hands touch even the outer layer of the paper. With the bundle in his hands, he stood, walked over to the fireplace, and uttered another invocation, this one to the Flame at the Center of the World.

Then he dropped the ball, coat and all, into the flames.

In retrospect, he thought when his head stopped ringing, he probably should have expected it to explode.

"...and so here I am," Mina said. She'd told Professor Carter everything that had happened the previous night, though she'd excluded Stephen's real form. In her version of the story, he'd sent the manes packing with pistol and holy water and wanted to keep her there because she'd seen them.

"Well," said Professor Carter. He drew a breath and then repeated: "Well."

"I know it must all sound rather improbable—" Mina began.

"How could it, my girl, when I was there for half of the proceedings?" Professor Carter chuckled, though there was as much ruefulness as mirth in it. "I may have been a skeptic at first, but the Bavarian expedition went a long way toward curing me of that, and it wasn't the last such experience I had, either! There was a time in Jamaica—but that's neither here nor there, is it?"

Mina had to admit that it wasn't. She smiled, though, as she hadn't been able to do since she'd entered Professor Carter's office with MacAlasdair at her side. Despite everything MacAlasdair had told her, she'd still worried that the professor would think she'd gone mad. Seeing his face animated by curiosity and without a trace of disbelief did more good for her spirits than any tonic she could think of.

"And if I hadn't been convinced already," said Professor Carter, "Stephen would have done it the other day. Bless the man, I'd hate him if I was a vainer fellow. Doesn't look a day over thirty, does he?"

"No," said Mina, another admission. "Then—he *is* a friend of yours?"

"Oh, yes. Not that I know a great deal about him, mind you, but we went on a number of journeys together when I was a younger man. Quite a dependable sort of a chap. If you *had* to go poking into this affair of ours"—Professor Carter tried for a reproving look—"I'm glad you've ended up under his protection while it lasts. He'll see to it that you're all right, if anyone can."

Mina decided to ignore the uncertain postscript and kept herself from bristling at the mention of *protection*. After all, an evil magician with shadow demons at his command was hardly a figure that even the most independent of New Women could be expected to handle on her own.

"You won't mind if I work for him, then? Or even if I stay in his house? He does have maids and a housekeeper. It's not as though we'd be alone—"

"Not at all, not at all." Professor Carter waved a hand. "The situation's rather an unusual one, after all, and besides, Stephen's quite honorable. Never known him to…well, ah…" He coughed. "I mean to say, you'll be quite safe with him."

Men didn't always know these things, Mina reflected, and fifteen years could change a man, or a not-quite-man, considerably. Still, MacAlasdair had so far seemed honorable in *that* regard at least, though Mina was relieved to hear the professor confirm her impression. She was more relieved to see that the situation didn't scandalize him.

"Then I'll still have a place with you, afterward?"

"Well, certainly," said Professor Carter. "Wouldn't dream of having things otherwise. If we're both still alive, of course."

Downstairs, something went *BANG*.

Luckily for everyone concerned, Mrs. Evans had been visiting her daughter in Kensington for the last two days. Otherwise, events after the explosion would have included a great deal more panic and secrecy.

As it was, Mina made it down the stairs, Professor Carter's letter opener in one hand, to find the study empty save for MacAlasdair, who was picking himself up off the floor.

The man who'd accompanied Mina to the professor's office had been polished and distinguished looking, if also distant and intimidating. His clothing had still seemed like a costume—all the more so, now that Mina knew something of his true nature—but it had been a good costume, and he'd worn it well.

Now his coat was missing, and his shirt and waistcoat were torn in several places. More than that, Mina saw blood matting at least one of the still-whole sections of shirt at MacAlasdair's side. A few more cuts, though these were not much more than scratches, littered his arms and face.

"I—" she began. Unsure where to go after that, she seized on the injury. "Sit down, will you? And don't move. Are you bleeding anywhere else? We'll need some water. Is it safe for me to go to the kitchen? Is it safe for us to be down here?"

"Your inquisition, Cerberus, lacks a wee bit in the way of priorities," said MacAlasdair.

"My name's Mina. Miss Seymour," she corrected herself, irritated. "And you haven't answered my questions. Or sat down."

"I'm a man of many failings, I see." He did sit down, though, and shook his head as if coming back to himself. "It's quite safe now. You may go anywhere you please—in this house, of course."

"Trust you to remember *that*," said Mina, and took herself off to the kitchen.

She fetched a pitcher of water and several towels quickly, and returned by the time Professor Carter had made his way downstairs. "Are we under attack?" he was asking MacAlasdair.

"Nae more than we were a day ago," said MacAlasdair. "Someone was tryin' his hand at spy work. Dropped a cursed little bundle through your letter slot. That's all."

"How reassuring," said Mina. "Does 'spy work' generally blow up like that?"

"No," said MacAlasdair. "That was me. I saw no other way to rid us of the thing."

He glanced toward the fireplace. Following his look, Mina saw that the flames had turned a dancing blue-silver. It was really quite pretty, though she wouldn't have said so in front of the two men.

Professor Carter had no such reservations. "For a curse, Stephen, that's a remarkably pleasant little aftereffect."

"It wasn't evil magic in itself," said MacAlasdair, "only used for evil. And rather showy in its destruction."

"Yes," said Professor Carter, and clicked his tongue as he looked at Stephen. "Should we call a doctor? I don't know of any *really* discreet ones, but I'm sure we could think of a story—"

"No. It'll heal quickly enough, once it's clean. If I may beg your pardon," he said to Mina, and then began to remove the remains of his shirt.

Mina decided to examine the desk. One never knew, after all, what might have broken in an explosion, or where the bits of whatever had exploded had gotten to. She tried to focus on finding them and not on seeing how graceful MacAlasdair was despite his size, or the slow exposure of his body. If her heart was going faster than it should and her cheeks felt warm—well, that was only natural in the wake of spies and mysterious explosions.

She dipped a napkin in water, went over to where MacAlasdair was sitting, and then could no longer avoid looking at him. His arms were muscular; his pale chest was broad and solid, lightly covered with red-black hair that narrowed to a thin line trailing down his flat stomach. So near at hand, Mina seemed to feel an unusual warmth rising off his skin—or perhaps that was just her.

The cut was thin and shallow, not bad at all. She concentrated on that, which only helped a very little bit. "I do hope this won't be a daily occurrence," she said, keeping her voice steady and not at all breathless. "I'm not any sort of trained nurse, you know."

"For your sake, Miss Seymour"—MacAlasdair's voice was very close to her ear, a deep rumble that went through her body and almost made her drop the cloth she was using—"I'll do my utmost to avoid it."

"How generous of you," said Mina, and looked up into a pair of gold-brown eyes fixed intently on hers.

She stepped back quickly. "I think that's as much as I can do," she said, and cleared her throat. "I can't sew it up and I can't get you any other clothes. And what—what about you?"

As she spoke, she turned back to Professor Carter. That was a relief on one level—although also a disappointment in a way Mina resolved not to think about—but the thought of leaving the professor alone was more alarming, and in a wholly unmixed way. "If people are trying to kill you or spy on you," Mina said, "shouldn't you come back with us? Or leave London for a bit?"

"No, I think not," said Professor Carter. "If Ward had wanted me dead, he would have made some overt move in that direction. I think I'm more valuable to him as a living source of information—and this bracelet should prevent him trying to get anything out of me the way he did Moore, poor fellow." He raised his arm again to show the silver bracelet and looked toward MacAlasdair for confirmation.

MacAlasdair nodded, but reluctantly. "As far as I know," he said. "Even so—"

"Even so, we've had this discussion," said the professor. "I've no reason to believe Ward's reach is limited to London, and your house is far from impregnable. In fact, if he makes another try at it, I might be in more danger there than here. And I would far prefer to remain where I am for the present time. I'll discuss it with you again if anything changes materially, MacAlasdair, but nothing has."

He was still tense, but far less so than he had been after MacAlasdair's previous visit or during the week just before it. Watching him, Mina wondered suddenly if the difference might have had to do with secrecy, or even with worry over *her* welfare. Perhaps they'd each been trying to protect the other all along.

Eight

Although Mina hated to admit as much even to herself, and although the proverbial wild horses couldn't have dragged the confession out of her anywhere near MacAlasdair, the first few days of her captivity were actually a jolly good time. She slept until nine, as she'd not done since she was sixteen and laid up with influenza; she managed to finish all of the mending that she'd been putting off, and even added a new collar to her second-best blouse; and she finished reading *King Solomon's Mines*, which she'd been working on since the new year.

She became almost used to breakfast with MacAlasdair. It was generally a silent affair, but as Mina had suspected, a less uncomfortable one than the similarly quiet meal she'd had below stairs. She didn't get the same sense of suppressed conversation or of scrutiny, only of a man who wasn't often up to speech before noon. Mostly, the two of them read the paper.

The first time Mina picked up a section, MacAlasdair hadn't been able to completely suppress his surprised look, and Mina had bristled inwardly. "I'm very fond of the *Times*," she had said in her most polished, clipped voice. "I'm glad to see you get it."

"Always happy to oblige a lady," he'd said, recovering quickly.

To his credit, MacAlasdair didn't put even the slightest irony on *lady*, nor did he ask whether she'd started reading the *Times* after she'd come to work for Professor Carter. Mina was slightly disappointed about the latter. She'd prepared an indignant response, and MacAlasdair never had to know that she *had* started reading that particular paper about the same time as she'd begun looking for secretarial posts, with an eye toward impressing her employers.

After all, she'd quickly started being interested for other reasons—and perhaps the other reasons had been there all along, just looking for an excuse.

Mina took her other meals with Mrs. Hastings, volunteering to take the cook a tray while her knee mended. It was a good excuse to get out of dinner and supper without making much more work for the servants, and MacAlasdair hadn't invited her to join him for those meals. He ate them out at his club, more often than not, and ate supper very late indeed. So, while the rest of the servants sought their own amusements for the hours between sunset and starlight, Mina sat upstairs, talked with the cook, and tried not to think about the creature penned in some room downstairs.

She wasn't entirely sure what MacAlasdair did when he wasn't eating breakfast or being a dragon. Neither was Mrs. Hennings when Mina very casually brought the conversation around to that subject. He went out a lot these days. He hadn't back when he'd first arrived. He didn't really tell anyone where or why.

Mina hoped that at least some of his trips had to do with hunting down Ward. She wasn't completely comfortable sharing a house with a sometimes-dragon. She was even less easy knowing that somewhere in the city was a man who hated both her host and Professor Carter, and who could summon shadow demons and conjure mists. If she'd been the kind of woman who lost sleep over anything, she would have spent a few restless nights on that account.

As it was, she took shameless advantage of both free time and food, and managed to enjoy herself tolerably well—for the first three days or so. (It helped that the first two were rainy.) Then came an evening when she'd finished both her book and her mending, when Mrs. Hennings was down in the kitchen again and not inclined toward conversation, and when Mina was certain she couldn't have slept any longer if she'd polished off a bottle of laudanum. Professor Carter was all right, MacAlasdair had told her that morning, but he had nothing for her yet.

She couldn't go out.

She didn't need to. MacAlasdair's house was large enough for any amount of exploring.

Mina began with the servants' hall, although that didn't take very long. The bare walls and wooden floors weren't particularly interesting, and she was hardly going to enter anyone's bedroom. Even if she'd been willing to pry, which she wasn't, it would only have been another room like hers, except perhaps smaller. There was no attic room at the top of this house, no imprisoned wife like the ones from Florrie's imagination.

The thought made Mina smile. Then, descending the stairs, she wondered if MacAlasdair might not have a wife after all. Not a mad one, of course, but it was common enough for even normal men to take a house in the city and leave their wives and children in the country, if they were rich enough. MacAlasdair was.

Perhaps his kind kept their women locked up, as a rule.

That line of thought brought up several other questions: just what kind of women *were* these hypothetical wives, anyhow? It didn't seem likely that dragon-men just grew on trees, though Mina supposed it was possible. Who did they marry, then? Mortal women? Did that…work?

Mina was glad nobody was around, since she could feel her cheeks burning. The memory of MacAlasdair with his shirt off came to her unbidden, and a small unwelcome voice in the back of her head said: *He certainly looked like a man then.*

"Well, it's nothing to do with me," she said aloud, and hurried into the next hallway.

Mostly, this one held more bedrooms, all of which had clearly been vacant for a while. The doors were unlocked, the blinds drawn, and the furniture covered with white cloths. In the dim light, the draped sofas and chairs made Mina think of ghosts. In truth, the whole place had a spooky feel to it, of places meant for people and action and life that now held only stillness.

Maybe all big houses felt like that when the family

wasn't about. She'd have to ask Alice after all of this was over.

Hunting scenes and landscapes hung on the walls. Mina saw one of a castle somewhere green, at sunset. Shadows flew across the background. To a casual observer, they might have been birds.

The picture looked like something out of a book of fairy tales, like it should have had a knight in armor at the bottom of the castle and a princess leaning out a window at the top. Or maybe those were sensitive subjects to dragons. Mina giggled, then heard herself and stopped. In the empty room, she felt conspicuous, as if she'd laughed in church.

The ground floor should have been more familiar after four days, but Mina paused at the bottom of the stairs and looked around with the same uncertainty that she'd felt upstairs. She knew the drawing room where she and MacAlasdair ate breakfast; she knew the kitchen; she was passingly familiar with the rooms between them; and otherwise she'd kept to her room or Mrs. Hennings's like…

Well, there was that image of a mad wife again.

She turned right and started off boldly, though she made sure that she was heading away from the room where MacAlasdair kept himself. Curiosity was one thing, foolhardiness quite another.

She opened a door and found a library, shelves covering three of the four walls. The books on them ranged from red-leather-bound volumes that looked almost new to haphazard bundles of peeling binding and crumbling papers. She lingered there for a while, testing the inviting armchairs in front of the fireplace and flipping through a few of the hardier-looking books.

When she opened the next door, she found the room where she'd broken the window.

Mina paused in the doorway for a few seconds that felt much longer, then stepped inside and pulled the drapes apart. The window was whole again—that could have been magic, but was more likely an expensive and hasty bit of work on the part of a glazier—and the lights of the London evening came shining in through it.

By those lights, dim as they were, she could see a long sword hanging over the fireplace. It was in a scabbard with lots of brass, and the twisted handle looked like silver. Although Mina didn't know much about swords, this one wasn't shaped like any kind of officer's saber she'd seen, even from a distance. She thought it was older than most Army swords, maybe even older than the Army as she knew it.

Below the sword, little ornaments marched across the top of the mantel: a giraffe, carved out of what was probably ivory; a portrait of a gray-haired woman; and a small bronze box set with red and blue gems—most likely real rubies and sapphires, Mina thought, though small ones. On top of the box was a bronze bird, its mouth opened to sing.

Very carefully, Mina picked the box up. As she'd thought, there was a key on the bottom. When she wound it, a slow, graceful melody began to play, one that sounded as old as the sword looked. She'd certainly never heard the tune before.

Then she heard something else: footsteps in the hall outside.

After the transformation had passed, Stephen's human form felt new and foreign. Before Bavaria, it had never done so—one shape had been as natural as the other. Now every night was an adjustment, and when he didn't have the pressure of manes and strange women in his house, relearning his human body went, or seemed to go, much more slowly.

At home, he'd walked in the woods, secure that he could handle any threat there. The London streets weren't nearly as safe, and Stephen didn't wish to accidentally break a pickpocket's arm, so he wandered through the halls of his house—trying, he'd thought sometimes, to make *it* feel his as he made his body do the same.

Music was one more new element in a world full of them. Pleasant as it was, the tune brought his head up and his senses to full alert. Someone was nearby. Stephen hurried down the hall toward the sound, opened the drawing room door—

—and saw Miss Seymour.

She stood in front of the windows, the city lights casting a pattern of light and shadow over her coiled hair, with her hands cupped around something that gleamed bronze.

As Stephen entered, she lifted her head and turned, full lips parting in surprise before she spoke. "Good evening, Lord MacAlasdair."

Over the past few days, he'd come to know that careful, polite tone as the sound of drawn steel: not striking out, but very prepared for an opponent's blow and letting him know it. Even if that opponent hadn't thought of himself as an opponent. Even if he was in his own house.

"Miss Seymour," said Stephen, "I wasn't expecting to find you here."

"Oh? It looked like a public room," she said. Very carefully and very visibly, she put the music box back on the mantel. "I thought I'd look around a bit. I hope you don't mind."

"Not at all," he said, as he more or less had to at that point. "Any room I care much about is locked."

"And you won't give me a ring of keys to test me?" Miss Seymour smiled thinly. "Probably just as well."

"Yes," said Stephen. "I wouldn't be sure of you passing."

"I'll have you know I respect privacy quite well, once I know something *is* private."

"I'm glad to hear it." Stephen leaned against the mantel. He could turn the lamps on, of course, sit down in one of the chairs, and wait for the staff to come back, but somehow he was disinclined toward any of those actions. In the dim light, with him and Miss Seymour both standing, talking to her felt more natural, as if they were in some scheme together—which, in a way, he supposed they were.

It had been a long time since he'd had a partner in anything he did. His siblings and his cousins had their own interests; few other people knew exactly what he was, and those were either servants or had different loyalties as well. Miss Seymour wasn't a real *partner*, of course, he reminded himself, but he'd take what moments he could.

"Any news?" she asked.

"A little. The Americans had a gentleman resembling

Ward in custody a few years ago. In Boston, it was. There was a young man bringing accusations. Breaking and entering, he said, but it never came to anything, and they released the man. It might not have been Ward. Though it did take place in…esoteric circles. Spiritualism and that. Rather a troublesome sect, too, from what little I could find."

"What happened to him then?"

"We'll be trying to find that out. Among other things. If he's in London now and still interested in magic, I've a few places I can go with that."

Miss Seymour nodded slowly. At her side, her long, graceful fingers played with the plain material of her dress. "This might take a while, then," she said.

"That it might," said Stephen. Was the girl that impatient to be gone? Not that he wanted her as a visitor, but God knew he'd treated her well enough. "I told you as much."

"You did," she said almost absently, and then went on in a much firmer voice. "When do you go see Professor Carter?"

"Tomorrow, most likely." The professor had probably been right about his danger, or lack thereof, now that he had the bracelet. All the same, Stephen wanted to keep checking since Carter wouldn't be able to sense something like the mist.

"All right," said Miss Seymour. "I'll go with you."

"You'll be doing no such thing," Stephen said immediately.

"And why not? I'll be with you. Then I'll be with the professor *and* you. Then I'll be with you again." Miss Seymour snapped her hands outward, illustrating a void between them. "There's no time when I can say anything to anyone, is there? Besides, I'll have to give him letters to send to my family, won't I? Unless you want me receiving my mail here."

"You want to send *letters*," said Stephen. He remembered and cursed the existence of the penny post.

"Of course I do. I can't go home on Sundays now, can I? And I'm not likely to let my family think I've died or—been kidnapped." Miss Seymour gave an ironic little chuckle. "Truth aside."

"I didn't kidnap you." Stephen almost growled the words, though he hadn't intended to. He could feel his control slipping: not of his shape, not precisely, but of *this* shape's reactions and of the situation as a whole. "If you hadn't noticed, we're in a bit of danger—"

"And writing to my family, or seeing the professor, isn't going to make Ward any more of a threat to you than he already is. People already know I'm here. What are you worried will happen?"

"I don't know. I can't know. And if you keep springing your own plans on me—"

"Oh, yes." Miss Seymour tossed her head back, and Stephen followed the slim, proud arch of her neck with his eyes even as he heard her sneering at him. "God forbid your captive have plans. Or ties to other people. Or anything that doesn't go your exact way."

A few steps forward let Stephen glare down at her, a look that had gotten him through many a conversation in the past. "I've been very generous wi' you so far, Miss Seymour. I'm prepared to continue that course of action, up to a point, but I'm a man of limited patience. Must you always be arguing with me?"

Her eyes flashed cobalt fire. "When you're being unreasonable, yes!"

"Unreasonable, is it?" The words came from deep within his chest, as deep as the impulses he stopped trying to resist. Reaching out, he wrapped an arm around Miss Seymour's waist, then pulled her forward. Now her slender form was a hair's breadth away from him, and the anger on her face was rapidly changing to surprise. "Lass, you don't know what unreasonable is."

Miss Seymour's mouth opened again. One hand grabbed at Stephen's arm, while the other came up to his shoulder. Before she could push him away or make whatever snide comment had occurred to her, before she could say anything at all, Stephen bent and kissed her.

She froze against him for a second. Stephen almost let her go then, as the human part of him asserted itself. The feeling of Miss Seymour in his arms had his blood pounding almost at once, but he wasn't in the habit of tormenting women. He began to relax his grip on her—

—and then her lips parted beneath his and the stiffness in her body became tension of another sort entirely. Her fingers curled into the fabric of his coat. Pressed against his chest, her breasts rose and fell rapidly; and she kissed him back with inexpert—and perhaps unconscious—hunger.

That was the end of thinking for Stephen just then.

With one arm, he drew Mina—he couldn't keep thinking of her as Miss Seymour, not now—even closer, pinning her to his body, feeling the outline of her through far too many layers of cloth. She could feel him, Stephen was sure. He was hard and aching, hungry as he'd almost never been for a woman, even in his youth. She didn't draw back from his arousal, though she did catch her breath. Stephen wound his free hand in her hair and kissed her more deeply, stroking his tongue against hers and sliding his other hand down from her waist.

His palm was gliding over Mina's hip when she pulled away. She shoved at him when she did it, the hands that had been clenched on his coat now flat and forceful. The gesture wasn't quite as good as a bucket of cold water, but it sufficed. Stephen dropped his hands and took a step backwards.

Panting, Mina stared up at him. Her hair was disheveled now, light-brown strands tumbling down around her face. Her eyes were dark and her lips slightly swollen, but the face she turned on Stephen was full of cold anger.

"That didn't prove a bloody thing," she said, the East End as thick in her voice as Stephen had ever heard it. "Not one thing, *my lord*. An' if you try winning an argument that way again, I'll leave straight away, an' you and your money can both go to Hell."

She spun on her heel, her loosened hair almost hitting Stephen in the face, and stormed out.

Nine

Mina almost didn't come down to breakfast the next morning.

It hadn't been a good night. She'd left MacAlasdair's company without any clear idea of where she was going and had finally sought refuge in her room. There she'd tried unsuccessfully to start reading her book again, tried even less successfully to lie down and calm her mind, and ended up alternately pacing the room and hitting the pillow.

She should have slapped MacAlasdair, she thought, lord or not. *Dragon* or not. After all, he obviously wasn't willing to kill her, and if the kiss had actually proved anything, it was that in some respects, he was just a man like any other.

She wished she had something to throw at the wall, but she didn't own anything breakable in her room. Not that MacAlasdair would notice if she broke the lamp or the mirror; he probably didn't even know they existed.

But no. It didn't do to get into that habit. It didn't do to lose control. She'd done quite enough of *that* for one evening already.

That, of course, was the other problem: she'd liked kissing MacAlasdair.

Actually, she'd liked it quite a lot.

He hadn't been the first man to kiss Mina—though the others had been boys, really, and she'd been much younger as well. She'd gone further than that with one of them, though never as far as he'd wanted. Even at seventeen, Mina had known what risks she didn't want to take. She'd liked the experience then too, and had, in truth, wanted more herself. Sometimes her breasts would ache, after their…encounters…or the place between her legs, and she'd had some idea of what satisfaction her body craved.

The feelings had seemed almost overwhelming. Mina had understood how girls could get carried away. In comparison to the longing she felt now, even through her rage, those earlier sensations were pale and cold and abstract.

Perhaps it was that she was older, or that Stephen was older—well, *much* older—than those lads from her past. Perhaps it was that she was better rested now and better fed. But Mina didn't think either of those reasons explained all the difference. Even remembering MacAlasdair's mouth over hers, or the strength in his arms as he held her against him, had her body longing to repeat the experience. And *not* remembering was hard work.

She didn't even like MacAlasdair, not really. She certainly hadn't *wanted* to kiss him—not really—not then, at least. It had been horrible and arrogant and forceful.

And Mina kept wondering what it would be like to do it again.

Eventually, the remnants of lust subsided, the pacing wore her body out, and she could make herself sleep, though her dreams were restless and she was glad not to remember them in the morning. When she woke, for the first time since she'd come to MacAlasdair's house, she looked at the door as a safeguard. If she stayed in her room, she wouldn't have to face him yet.

But, if she stayed in her room, he'd know she didn't want to face him. She wouldn't see Professor Carter, either, and she wouldn't get out of the house. MacAlasdair would have won—and Mina would still be trapped and probably start climbing the walls any day.

She dressed and thought of girding her loins, then tried not to think about loins again.

When Mina strode into the dining room, it was with every particle of self-possession, every ounce of formality and propriety that she'd learned since she'd decided to become secretary to a scholar. Every muscle in her back felt rigid. She blessed her foundation garments.

MacAlasdair was at the head of the table as usual, with her place set nearby. As usual, he lowered the paper as Mina entered the room.

When he met her eyes, there suddenly seemed to be much less space around them. He filled the room as he filled the chair: big, powerful, commanding.

Mina quickly took her seat. Only then did she notice a difference in the table. At her right hand, a little ways away from her breakfast dishes, was a silver tray. Someone had laid out several sheets of stationery on its surface, as well as two envelopes, three black fountain pens, and a sheet of stamps.

Mina blinked.

Right, then.

Slowly, with careful, controlled movements, she poured tea. Added sugar and cream. Buttered a scone. Pretended that she wasn't watching MacAlasdair out of the corner of her eye.

Then, when she could trust herself, she spoke. "That's quite...comprehensive. Everything a correspondent could ask for."

"I'm glad to hear it," said MacAlasdair. "I'll be meeting with Carter this noontime, if you'll be ready by then." He sounded very casual, but his gaze never left Mina's face.

She smiled. There was certainly no harm in that. He'd keep his distance now, and so would she. It was a virtue to be gracious in victory, Mina had heard. "I'll write after breakfast," she said. "If you'd like to read the letter before I seal it, I'll be in the study."

The door opened as Mina was on the last page of her letter, finishing a paragraph about the view from her bedroom window. It could have been a servant coming in to clean or to tell her something, but she knew it was MacAlasdair even before she lifted her head.

"The first two pages are on the table," she said. "Have a look if you'd like. I'll be done in a moment."

"Thank you," he said and smiled—diffidently, for the first time since Mina had met him. He ran a hand through his dark hair and seemed about to say something, but ended up crossing the room in silence.

Mina bent to her letter, trying to ignore the way

her skin prickled at MacAlasdair's approach. She saw his hand, large and firm, out of the corner of her eye as he picked up the sheets of stationery she'd already covered with writing. She heard the steady rhythm of his breath and the sound of paper crinkling as he read.

I hope that you're all doing well, she wrote, concentrating—or trying to concentrate—on making the letters neatly. She'd mastered that particular art some ten years ago, but it never hurt to pay more attention, did it?

> *I'm not sure when I'll get to see you again, but I'll keep sending these letters. You can write to me in care of Professor Carter.*

"That's not a bad story you've told them." MacAlasdair spoke from behind her. "Very close to the truth."

Mina had said that MacAlasdair wanted her to help put his father's affairs in order, that some of them were the sort he didn't want anyone talking about, and that she'd be well paid and get a week's holiday after she was finished. She intended to take one, too. A hundred pounds should more than cover the time, and Professor Carter would understand. She didn't mention the hundred pounds in the letter—that much money *would* make people talk—just that she'd be well paid.

"Lying's a sin," she said demurely and then couldn't resist a smile of her own. "And more importantly, too many lies are confusing."

MacAlasdair chuckled, deep and rich. "Verra sound

philosophy you have there. You don't think they'll talk about whatever secrets I want you to be keeping?"

"Not much. It's business, and business isn't really that interesting. They might think that your father had some opinions he didn't want getting around—"

"He probably did, at that," said MacAlasdair. "He was still bitter about the Rising, when I was young, and all that came after. Talked a great deal about it."

"The Rising?" It sounded familiar, but it wasn't new enough to be current or old enough to be antique, and so Mina sought for the reference amid memories of schoolbooks and the smell of chalk dust. "You mean the Scottish rebellion?"

"Aye." MacAlasdair's mouth was tight. "I wasna' born yet, nor for a few years after, but I heard stories enough, and I understand the bitterness."

MacAlasdair's hair was rich red-black, without a thread of silver in it; his strong-boned face held a few sun lines near the eyes, but nothing more; and his body was straight and strong and vigorous. Looking at him, you didn't think *two centuries old*, and then—

—and then she was in a room with someone who wasn't entirely human, someone who remembered the world before her grandmother had been born. She wanted to put out a hand and touch his sleeve, just to make sure he was real.

Instead, she said, "But he couldn't have fought in it. I mean—I don't think we'd have won if we'd been fighting *dragons*."

"And do you think that I and mine are the only such creatures in Creation?" MacAlasdair shook his head and laughed again, this time with a much darker humor. "Ye had your own creatures to send against us, you English, and your sorcerers and artifacts as well, the things that none of the history books mention. And we die from steel and lead if you put enough of it into us. My father fought, and one of his brothers died at Fort William and the oldest of my sisters at Littleferry."

"I'm sorry," said Mina.

MacAlasdair shrugged, and the darkness passed from his face. "It's a family wound, and not my own, nor of your making. As I said, I never knew either of them. I did my fighting elsewhere."

Still, there was nothing really to say to that, or at least nothing Mina could think of. She started to turn back to her paper, and then something MacAlasdair had said drew her attention.

"Your *sister*?"

"Our women are more…active than most," MacAlasdair said. "There's little difference between a female dragon and a male, at least where size and strength are concerned. It makes a bit of a difference in the way we view things."

"If only the Pankhursts knew," said Mina, thinking of the articles she'd read about the suffragists.

"There's a bit more of a difference for mortal women, I'll admit, but—no' as much as people have been in the way of thinking lately. And at that," said MacAlasdair, smiling again, "I'm surprised that you're not out there attending meetings yourself."

Despite the teasing tone of his voice, there was warmth in his smile and approval that Mina felt in her chest. Still, she tossed her head and fired back, "Well,

I would be, if I had a bit more time for it. Speaking of which, are you going to let me finish?"

"Forgive me," he said, still teasing. "I should have known your schedule would be crowded."

"Oh, if only it were," said Mina, and went back to writing.

Ten

Not too far from the British Museum and the office where Stephen had first encountered Mina, down several little side streets, one came to an ordinary-looking house. Like its neighbors, it was three stories of neat red brick, secure behind an iron fence and a tidy yard. Nothing was remarkable; everything was respectable.

At night, light and noise stole from behind the drapes, out the windows, and off into the spring air. That, too, was little different from other houses nearby. Some of the neighbors did say that the lights were odd colors at times and that the sounds were almost inhuman. Other, more skeptical sorts said that the first group of people were drunk or dreaming or seeing what they'd thought they'd see.

After all, London had heard rumors about Mrs. O'Keefe for years, and the Society of the Emerald Star was no real secret. Too many of its members were too fond of notoriety for that.

Secret or not, the Society did employ a butler who never spoke and who looked as if he could have given

Stephen some serious trouble, even in his draconic form. The man looked over Stephen, his card, and the letter of introduction he offered, all without moving a single muscle in his face. Then he retired to the inner sanctum, consulted with someone inside, and returned to gesture Stephen through the door.

Not only a door, as it turned out, but a set of red, gauzy curtains that clung to Stephen's evening wear and knocked his top hat briefly askew. He straightened it, took a breath of air that was redolent with both incense and opium, and turned to face the woman approaching him.

Selina O'Keefe was tall, pale, and willowy, with large gray eyes and a heavy mass of raven-black hair, which she was currently letting tumble down her back to match the gown she was wearing: flowing gold silk and lace, as unstructured as it was impractical. Gems gleamed on every finger and dangled from her ears, catching the light from many shaded lamps. Her walk was airy and she gave Stephen her hand as if she was Cleopatra bestowing a favor, yet there was something in her eyes and in the set of her chin that suggested more practicality than the dozen or so similarly dressed women, or their smoking-jacketed companions, who currently disported themselves around the room.

"Welcome, Lord MacAlasdair," she said quietly but in a voice that made the simple statement a theatrical pronouncement. "In what way might our Society aid you?"

If she mentioned anything about him being king hereafter, Stephen thought, he would leap out a window posthaste.

"I'm looking for a man," he said. "Can we talk somewhere a bit more private?"

"There's a couch near the window," said Mrs. O'Keefe, and put a hand lightly on his arm. The butler had disappeared somewhere. "I'm afraid I can't leave my guests alone just now."

As they walked toward the couch, Stephen understood why. He'd expected the lolling figures on other couches even before he'd smelled the opium. He hadn't expected the woman with snakes winding around her wrists, like living ribbons of bright green and gold, or the man who stood near her casting bone runes onto a velvet cloth. Near them, a tall, lithe man with coppery hair was staring into the fire. As Stephen passed, the man looked up with eyes that seemed to hold the flame themselves for a moment, and the angles of his face were inhuman.

Charlatans made up most of the Society. Hedonists. Harmless, if scandalous, degenerates. But a few were different—and Ward, if he was still interested in occult power, would have wanted to contact those few.

They reached a red plush sofa with a high back in a corner that afforded a good view of the room while still a fair distance away from most of Mrs. O'Keefe's guests. She took a seat, arranging her miles of skirts around her, and Stephen sat down at the other end of the sofa. Mrs. O'Keefe eyed the space between them, glanced up at Stephen's face, and then gave him a humorous, rueful smile—*Can't blame a girl for hoping*, it said—that looked much better on her than her former dramatic pose.

Then she said a few words in Latin to the group, and

the noise from the rest of the room died away. "What sort of man are you looking for, Lord MacAlasdair?"

"His real name is Ward, though he might have been using an alias. He's a tall fellow and skinny, with blue eyes sort of wide-set and blond hair, though it's probably gray by now." Stephen sighed. This wouldn't help, not really. There were thousands of tall, skinny men in London, and Ward could have dyed his hair as easily as not. "Has anyone been coming in asking a lot of questions? Anyone other than me, that is—asking about spells, perhaps, or magical trinkets or books?"

"Many people seek such wisdom as we possess," said Mrs. O'Keefe with a graceful gesture of one hand. "But," she added in a much more worldly voice, "there was one particularly insistent gentleman. He came in…oh, a month ago? My memory for these things drifts sometimes. One moment."

She rang a tiny silver bell, and the enormous butler drifted over, moving with astonishing silence.

"Saunders—"

Saunders, thought Stephen. For that hulk. He managed to keep control of his face. Mina, he thought suddenly, would be biting the inside of her cheek about now, her blue eyes dancing in that way they had when she was trying to stay solemn and proper and having the devil's own time of it. Just as well she wasn't here; he'd have never kept his countenance.

"Saunders," Mrs. O'Keefe continued, "how long ago did you have to, er, *escort* that gentleman out?"

"Six weeks past, madam," said the butler in a melodious tenor voice. "The incident, if you'll recall, was just after the occasion of Sir Cartland's epic recitation."

Stephen cleared his throat. "You had to throw him out, then?"

Mrs. O'Keefe sighed. "He impressed me as an unfortunate character from the first. He was quite incredulous that I was the head of the Society—well, one does get men like that." She shrugged, languid and indifferent. "But he was rather insistent on being admitted to the inner circles very quickly and on obtaining certain information that we were unwilling or unable to give."

"Were you now?"

"Lord MacAlasdair," said Mrs. O'Keefe, "contrary to the world's opinion—and I know full well what *that* is—we do have ethics here. There are lines we will not cross, and summoning certain creatures is one of them. Even if the risks were not surpassingly great, the price is far greater than I would allow."

Certain pages of certain books had burned themselves deeply into Stephen's memory. He grimaced and nodded agreement—and relief.

Ward, after all, was no footpad and no brawler. Getting inside locked houses or past watchmen would have been difficult for him, and he'd already known that Stephen had an inhuman resistance to injury. If he'd hoped to ruin Stephen, either through physical damage or by exposure, without risking his own person, he probably would have had to deal with some very nasty forces.

For that matter, he would probably have called on those forces to kill Moore. That would also have been safer for him.

"I'm guessing he wasn't pleased about your refusal," said Stephen.

"Anything but. He made a number of threats against me, but..." She spread her hands, gems catching the light, as Stephen was sure she'd intended. "I have protections enough."

And you're not his main target.

Stephen didn't know the full strength of Ward's arsenal, whether magical or financial. But from what he'd experienced and from Moore's death, he doubted the Society would survive very long if Ward made its members the sole focus of his wrath.

"Is there anyone else he could have gone to?" Stephen asked. Mrs. O'Keefe started to lift her shoulders and spread her hands again, and Stephen was certain that the next words out of her mouth would be something about how the city was crawling with dubious occultists. "Anyone in particular that you know of?"

"A few," said Mrs. O'Keefe, and reached for a sheet of paper and a pen. Many such objects were lying about on tables, Stephen noticed, presumably in case one of the Society members was struck with poetic inspiration. She wrote quickly in a graceful, flowing hand. "Of these, I think Reynolds is most likely to give your man Ward what he wants. He was a member of this society once, but his...tastes"—she almost hissed the word—"were profoundly unacceptable. Unfortunately, he has powerful allies now. Another thing your quarry would seek, from the sound of it."

"You're thinking your visitor was Ward, then?" Stephen asked. He'd have followed the trail anyhow since it was the only one he had, but he wanted to be sure before he got hopeful. "Another might have asked for the same information."

"He looked like you describe. The hair was darker—not blond or gray—but such things are easy enough to manage. I wouldn't have said he was particularly thin, either. But the eyes were the same, and he was tall."

Age could add a few inches to any man's waistline. The description was close enough.

"I'm very much obliged to you," said Stephen, getting to his feet. "Good day, Mrs. O'Keefe."

"Good luck, Lord MacAlasdair," she said.

Earlier that evening, Mina had set aside the last of Professor Carter's correspondence and made a decision. If she was going to stay in MacAlasdair's house for some unknown length of time, she was by God going to *stay* in the house and not skulk around in the attics. MacAlasdair and his servants could like it or not as it pleased them.

So, after a glance in the mirror to replace a hairpin or two and make sure she didn't have ink spots on her nose, Mina had descended all three flights of stairs with her head high and made her way toward the library.

The servants were back by then—the stars had been out for quite a while—and Baldwin had intercepted her on the way. His expression managed to be both polite and forbidding. "Laird MacAlasdair's out for the evening," he said. "If it's him you were looking for, Miss Seymour."

"Actually," Mina had said, even as she briefly

wondered where MacAlasdair had gone and why, "I was just going to find a book." She didn't explain that MacAlasdair had given her permission to look around the house. That would have been admitting that she *needed* permission. "There's quite a library here."

"It's verra large, yes," said Baldwin. "A bit disorganized, though. Will you be wanting anything in particular?"

"I thought I'd see what I could find," said Mina. She'd risked a smile. In return, she'd gotten a slight softening of Baldwin's heavily whiskered face. It was something, at least. "Could someone make a fire in the drawing room and bring me a cup of tea?"

Training had kept Baldwin from looking surprised at her request. He'd hesitated only an instant before saying, "Of course. I'll see it done."

Flush with minor triumph, Mina had proceeded into the library, managed to find a small subset of Dickens in the shelves' jumbled contents, and was curled up on the couch with *The Pickwick Papers* when the door opened again and MacAlasdair, dressed in spotless evening clothes, walked into the room.

"Owens said you'd come in here for the evening," he said, looking from Mina to the fire and back. "I hope I'm not intruding."

It's your house was the first response that came to Mina's mind. What she said, as she hastily straightened up, was "No, not at all."

It was true. The extent to which it was true was no more surprising than the thrill that had run up her spine when MacAlasdair walked in. Both were unnerving.

He did look good in evening clothes. That might

have had something to do with it. The close-fitting coat and trousers showed off both his broad shoulders and the firm lines of his waist and thighs, while the white shirt made his hair look almost garnet-colored and his eyes even brighter. Somehow, unlike most men Mina had seen, he looked more powerful in evening dress.

She resisted the urge to shift in her seat or to moisten her lips, although they'd suddenly gone dry. Thank goodness for tea.

"You've been out," she said, in a truly amazing feat of stating the obvious. "Er, Baldwin said you were. But not where." She kicked herself mentally for sounding like a prying wife, and then kicked herself twice for caring. "Somewhere fancy, I'd guess."

"You could say as much," said MacAlasdair, his mouth curling sardonically around the words. "There are a number of…clubs…around London that take an interest in mysticism. I thought some of them might be able to put me onto Ward's track."

"Ah," said Mina. "And did they?"

"Perhaps. There are a few hints I might pursue. The Emerald Star, for instance—" MacAlasdair stopped. "But telling you all of it could take some time."

"Time I've got," said Mina. "And I want to know."

"Very well, then," said MacAlasdair. He settled into a seat near the fire, leaned back, and began.

Eleven

THE NEXT EVENING, AS SHE STOOD BY THE DRAWING room window and watched night fall over London, Mina was still thinking over what she'd heard from MacAlasdair.

She'd heard about clubs like the Emerald Star, of course. Florrie brought home stories every so often, and other girls in Mina's boardinghouse gossiped about spiritualists and fortune-tellers. A few gauze-draped mystics had even called on Professor Carter from time to time, after which he'd usually had to have a lie-down and a glass of whiskey. Mina had just thought they were all frauds.

Hearing otherwise had brought on very mixed emotions. On the one hand, the presence of other magicians in London meant other people who could maybe deal with Ward if MacAlasdair really fumbled the matter. On the other hand, in Mina's experience, you could count on other people to foul things up more than you could count on them to be helpful, and now there was a whole other world of potential accidents—or *not* accidents.

The sound of shattering glass broke through her reflections.

Mina darted back away from the window and was halfway across the floor before she realized that it hadn't broken. The noise hadn't come from the drawing room. It had come from the fireplace, but nothing around that was broken, either.

The noise had come down the chimney.

Closing her eyes, Mina pictured the floor above her. The stairs led up from the hall, and the drawing room was on the right side of the lower floor. Retracing her previous exploration, she thought that the noise had come from one of the bedrooms she hadn't entered.

A bird or a bat had probably flown into the window. Granted, the second floor was a bit low for that and too high for children throwing stones, but stranger things happened.

In London, burglary wasn't really strange. In the house of a wealthy man who lived alone—who was known to keep few servants and to send those away at regular hours—it wouldn't be at all unusual.

And while Stephen had said the manes weren't coming back for a while, Ward could have conjured up other things.

Mina swore under her breath and found that her mouth had gone completely dry.

MacAlasdair was locked away being a dragon for a little while longer. Running to get the police would give the burglars or demons or whatever time to do their work and get away. If they were working for Ward and managed to see Stephen in dragon form, that would be awful. If they weren't human and caught either Stephen or the rest of the servants by surprise, that would be even worse.

She took the poker from the fireplace. It hadn't helped much last time, but she wouldn't be facing a dragon now—at least, not with any luck.

Mina went up the stairs slowly, keeping close to one of the walls and moving as quietly as she could. She wasn't bad at that. She was no burglar, but she *was* a slim woman with a light step, and one who'd spent her life in crowded houses.

Nobody was waiting for her at the top of the stairs. No hand lunged out of the dark hallway to catch her wrist; no chloroform-soaked cloth descended over her nose and mouth.

Not yet, at least.

She snuck down the hallway, passing one closed door after another. No noise came from within any of them so Mina kept going, the poker heavy in her hand.

Then there was a thump at the end of the hall, from a room whose door had been left open just a crack. From what Mina knew about the house and what she'd seen from the servants' routine, she thought that it was MacAlasdair's bedroom.

She stepped closer, pressing herself against the wall.

"...anything in there?"

It was a male voice, and the accent was familiar. The speaker might have been any of the men she'd grown up with.

"Lot of fancy clothes," said another similar voice. "You?"

"Nothing big enough. Couple sets of cuff links,

though," the first man added, clearly pleased by this unexpected development. "Look like gold, they do."

"Well, don't 'old out once we get clear of this place. *'E* only cares for one thing, after all."

Mina had heard enough.

Slowly, she put the poker down, then moved away and into the bedroom next door. Shuttered windows and dust cloths announced that nobody had slept there for some time, but the furniture still remained: a bed with a brass frame, a washstand, and most importantly for Mina's purposes, a dark wooden desk and a chair to match.

Good thing she was a strong girl.

Even so, when she lifted the chair, she knew she'd pay for it later—and that she wouldn't have managed it normally. Fear did wonders for the human body.

As she approached MacAlasdair's room again, one of the men inside spoke.

"Nothing 'ere but papers. Bloody desk was the devil to open, and it's just a lot of scrap."

"Anything look valuable?"

"Damned if I know, Bill. Do you take me for a barrister?"

Mina set the chair down very slowly, wiped her sweating hands on her skirt, and then grasped the doorknob. The door closed very quietly so she wasn't sure either man had noticed the click.

Then came the chair. Terror still fueling her muscles, she shoved it against the door and wedged the top under the doorknob.

"'Old up a tick, Fred," said Bill. "Was that door closed before?"

Mina didn't wait to hear the rest. She picked up her skirts in one hand, the poker in the other, and ran. Behind her, the doorknob rattled. Then the door itself thumped.

The chair was sturdy, but it wouldn't hold forever, nor against all force. Mina didn't know how strong the men in MacAlasdair's room were. She went faster, taking the stairs down two at a time. She didn't let herself look behind her because that wouldn't help anything.

It had been getting dark before she went upstairs. Surely the first stars would be out by now!

At the bottom of the staircase she turned left, trying to remember her first mad flight through this house—and she did seem to be running for her life every time she came this way. She'd have to have a word with someone about that.

Another left, and then a right, and oh, there was *that* room again, down the hall ahead of her. She couldn't see red light under the door this time. Maybe that was a good sign?

"Knocking" was an inadequate description for what Mina did next. She banged on the door with all her strength, rattled the doorknob as the men upstairs had done, and finally lifted her voice to shout. "MacAlasdair!"

Nothing.

"*MacAlasdair!*"

Had there been movement from within? She couldn't tell. Were there footsteps in the hall behind her?

"*Stephen!*"

The door banged open. Stephen stood in the

doorway, human, alert—and bare-chested. "Good God, Cerberus, what—"

"Burglars. In your bedroom." Mina spoke as quickly as she could, gasping for breath between the words. "I think Ward sent them."

A short Gaelic oath sprang from Stephen's lips, and he turned his blazing eyes on her. "Are you all right?"

"Fine. They never even saw me."

"Keep behind me, then," he said and strode out into the hall.

Mina followed, though not too closely. Two people were better than one only as long as she didn't end up a hostage. She'd be close enough to help but not to be in danger. She was also close enough to see the play of muscles in Stephen's back as he walked. She hadn't intended that, but it helped her morale.

Halfway up the stairs, they could hear loud, rhythmic thumping. When they reached the hall, Mina could see the door to Stephen's bedroom shuddering under blows from the other side. The chair was still roughly where she'd left it, but the edge under the doorknob was beginning to slip.

Stephen turned his head and flashed her a smile: wide and white, and probably terrifying to anyone who'd come up against him on a battlefield. Then, in one quick and noisy motion, he hurled the chair away from the doorknob, yanked the door open, and burst through.

Caught in the process of striking the door, Fred and Bill stumbled back away. They recovered more quickly than Mina would have liked, finding their feet and realizing that they outnumbered the new arrival.

After a quick glance, they rushed Stephen, one with a knife and one with a short club.

Stephen moved like a dancing flame, ducking away from the knife and letting the club glance harmlessly off his hip. With an elbow to the face, he sent the man with the club down to the floor. Then he spun around, and his fist smashed into the knife-wielder's jaw just as his booted foot took out the thug's legs.

It took maybe a minute. Mina wasn't exactly a stranger to fights, having taken George home from the pub often enough before he'd left for the sea. Still, she was now left standing, opening and closing her mouth like a carp.

Stephen straightened himself up and rubbed absently at his side. "There's one that could bruise a bit, I'm thinking," he said. "Not too shocked, are you?"

"No!" Mina answered, pride putting force into the half-truth.

"Good. We'll be needing to tie these up," said Stephen, "and ask them a few questions before we bring in the police. Best make it quick—and it'll go quicker with the two of us."

Twelve

Once Stephen had a moment to look at the burglars without trying to hit one or the other, they proved to be unremarkable-looking enough. One was young enough to still be spotty; one was old enough to have lost most of his hair.

Bound with several of Stephen's cravats—Baldwin was going to have a few things to say about this entire evening—the younger burglar shifted nervously, to the extent that he could, and looked between Stephen and Mina. "What're you gonna do now?"

"That depends on you, I should think," Mina said. Ice clinked in her voice. In her dark dress, with her hair loosened by her run through the house, she looked like the more attractive sort of avenging angel. "You got yourselves into this situation. I'd imagine you can get yourselves out, if you can be clever."

The man looked from her to his still-unconscious companion, chewed on his lower lip, and then sighed. "What do you want," he asked, "and what'll you give me for it?"

"Who hired you and why and when and where."

Stephen crouched down beside the thief. "You tell us, and perhaps you won't be seeing the inside of Newgate any time soon."

The threat of the law had lost some of its power. Fifty years ago, he'd have mentioned hanging or transportation. Perhaps mortals' fears adapted as easily to a changing world as everything else about them did, though, for the name of the prison made the thief's face go pale beneath its spots.

"We never got a name, m'lord."

"You must know what he looked like, though," said Mina. "Hooded cloaks stand out a bit these days."

"Tall and kind of fat. Dark 'air. 'Is collar was turned up, though, and it *were* dark where we met."

"And where was that?" Stephen asked.

"Dog an' Moon, m'lord. Cable Street."

Mina's eyes flickered for a second, but she didn't volunteer anything. "When did you first enter into your arrangement?" Stephen went on.

"'Bout three weeks ago, or the like."

"Then this wasn't the first job you did for him," said Mina. "What was that?"

The thief looked down. "Deliverin' a package, ma'am. Through a letter slot, it was."

"Ah," said Stephen, not at all surprised. "How did you meet?"

"The barman there sometimes passes word on to us, word of jobs and that. 'E's the one set up the meeting."

Stephen nodded. "What was your job this time?"

"'E wanted us to look around. Tell him about anything odd we saw, take anything we thought was important, that sort of thing. Said nobody'd be about at this 'our. Never should've trusted 'im for that. Bloody toff."

"Watch your language," said Stephen, though Mina's face hadn't changed a bit at the words. Indeed, he'd heard her use similar terms, though rarely. Still, he felt a need to make the gesture. "Anything else?"

"Not for 'im, no."

"When did he hire you for this job?" Mina asked.

"Two days back. Said we'd get money when we brought 'im the crown." The young man sighed. "That's all I know of it, m'lord, I promise."

He was, as far as Stephen could tell, speaking the truth. Stephen sighed and got to his feet. "For what it's worth," he said absently, "I very much doubt that he would have followed through with the payment he promised you. And I suggest that you avoid his company in the future."

"Yeah, o'course," said the young man. Perhaps he meant it; perhaps he didn't.

It probably didn't matter either way. He and his companion hadn't seen enough of the house—or of Stephen—to be a threat. The police couldn't get any more useful information from them than Stephen already had and wouldn't know how to follow up on it anyway. At least, Stephen's prior experience with Scotland Yard had led him to expect no great feats there.

Stephen bent and picked up the knife from where it had fallen. It was cheap work. Even if its wielder had landed a blow, the blade might have broken before doing Stephen any real harm. The club had been more effective—he had a sore place just under his ribs now—but there was something visceral and intimidating about a knife, and he didn't keep them lying about his bedroom these days.

"Would you be kind enough to untie our visitor?" he asked Mina.

She set to work, her slim fingers flying over the knots. The cravat fell away, leaving the young man rubbing his wrists.

"Get up," said Stephen. He adjusted his grip on the knife—casual, but not too casual, just enough to make the thief aware of its presence. "Pick up your friend."

That process involved some grunting. "'E's *heavy*," the young man said.

"That's very unfortunate for you," said Stephen. "Now walk."

At knifepoint, the two thieves went out the door, through the hall, and down the dark staircase. Stephen followed closely behind, as did Mina, who had stopped briefly to re-arm herself.

At some point, Stephen thought, he'd just have to *give* her a poker, perhaps one with her initials on it. Certainly she looked as natural holding the thing as anyone could under the circumstances.

At last, after a dim and silent journey that was mercifully free of further incident, they reached the back door. Stephen stepped forward and jerked it open, then gestured to the small street beyond, where a gas lamp barely cut through the growing night. "You'd best be getting on your way, hadn't you?"

The young burglar started forward, moving slowly under the weight of his older companion. As they crossed the threshold, Mina spoke again.

"I'm going to send for the police now. I'll tell them I saw someone lurking around the house. It'll take them"—she looked off down the street and did a few mental calculations—"oh, about ten minutes to get here, I should think. If you move fast, I might just be a silly girl spooked by the fog."

Then she shut the door.

"I don't suppose," she said, looking up at Stephen, "that this sort of thing happens often?"

"It's the first time of it to my knowledge," he said and then cleared his throat. "I've you to thank for making sure they didn't do worse or see more. You had no reason to risk yourself the way you did."

The flush on Mina's cheeks deepened, and she shrugged. "A hundred pounds seems a fair reason to me. I don't go back on a bargain."

Being tactful, she didn't add *whatever you may have thought*.

She was looking down again, Stephen noticed, and her hair fell across her face. Tired? Worried? He stopped at the foot of the stairs and put a hand gently on her shoulder. "Is anything wrong? Other than the obvious, I mean?"

"I—no. Not really. Um..." She took a breath and then gave a what-the-hell sort of shrug.

Oh, this was going to be good.

Thirteen

"What happened to your shirt?" Mina couldn't believe she was even asking. "What I mean to say is, well, you were fully dressed last time I saw you. And you'd just transformed then. So I was wondering if everything was all right, or you'd had to turn back quicker than normal—"

But why would Stephen have speeded up his transformation now, if he hadn't the first time they'd met? Mina's mind caught up with her mouth and left her momentarily silent.

Of course, he'd already fought off the shadows when she'd first seen him transform. He must have known then that Mina wasn't a threat. He hadn't known anything earlier that night except that she was alarmed.

Not that Stephen would have rushed things for her sake. The thought made her feel slightly dizzy. No, there was no reason for him to take Mina into consideration, and if he had, it had only been out of obligation or chivalry.

Why was she even *thinking* about it?

Why wasn't she finishing her sentence? Stephen was starting to look amused.

Mina grabbed for the dangling ends of her thoughts. "—or if there was something wrong. Besides housebreakers."

She said a brief and silent prayer that it was too dark for Stephen to notice her blushing. Then she realized that it didn't matter. Her voice had gone up substantially over the course of her question, and a broad grin was spreading itself over Stephen's face.

He hadn't taken his hand off her shoulder, either. It was resting there very lightly, probably the gentlest contact Stephen could manage, and yet a good half of Mina's awareness was focused on its weight and its warmth, even through her clothes.

The other half was conscious of Stephen's smile, the way his eyes turned up at the corners—and the bare expanse of his chest rising pale and firm from his dark trousers.

"A new shirt, I should think," he said, looking down at himself for a second, as if only now considering the situation. "The problem with being a gentleman in this day and age, truly, is that you've got a fair bit of clothing, and most of it looks the same."

The girl from Bethnal Green said *we should all have those problems* inside Mina's head, but it was the professor's secretary—and the woman looking for distraction—who spoke aloud. "What do new clothes have to do with it?"

"The law of contagion. No' germs or anything—" he added, as Mina's eyes widened. "The magical meaning's older than that. It says if two things—or people—have much to do with each other, they start being part of each other. So if I wear something often enough, the magic thinks it's a part of me, and it transforms back and forth. If I don't, the transformation destroys it."

"Oh."

The explanation made sense. It was even interesting. But it didn't do what Mina had intended. It didn't take her mind off the facts at hand, namely the fact that Stephen *wasn't* wearing a shirt and was standing rather close to her.

She took a long breath. The house was dim; they were alone; and every inch of her skin had suddenly become twice as sensitive as normal. This wasn't the time to give in to any kind of impulse.

But she only had so much self-control, and surely intellectual impulses were better than the other sort, and information could always be useful, so she asked. "Two people?"

"Aye," he said, and his accent was getting thicker again. He *still* hadn't removed his hand. "'Tis harder to use the connection there. A man changes a great deal with the years, you see, and an object is often changeless, or nearly so. But we're part of each other. People, that is. Someone threatened Carter and it brought you here, after all."

"That's not magic."

Stephen shrugged, and the muscles in his shoulders flexed a little with the motion. "As above, so below. The rules arena' that different, in the end."

"So—" Mina caught her breath.

No, she wasn't going to ask. Questions that began with "So you and I" would not lead anywhere remotely productive or good or wise. The phrase "you and I" was a very bad one, particularly when Stephen was looking down at her, only a few inches away, and he smelled rather like wood smoke, which she didn't want to notice, either. It *should* have reminded her that he was a dragon and she should be afraid.

Instead, she wanted to step closer and rest her face against his neck.

Bad idea. *Bad* idea. The whole thing called for a lighter topic.

Unfortunately, she'd started speaking before she realized the only thing that came to mind: "Why were you wearing a new shirt, then? If you knew that."

"The maids don't know it," Stephen said, "and Baldwin doesna', exactly. It was never truly a problem. Not—"

"Not until I came along," Mina said, quirking a smile.

"Something of the sort, aye. In this particular case, though, I've no objections to your presence. My awareness isn't quite the same when I'm transformed, and they could easily have seen too much if you hadn't been there."

Now Stephen did move his hand, but he didn't drop it. Rather, he slid it up her arm and along the line of her shoulder, then her neck. Finally he traced his fingertips down the side of her jaw before cupping her cheek in his hand.

She should move now, Mina thought, or push his hand away, or at least say something. There wasn't an etiquette guide in the world that would say this situation was proper, especially not with what had come before. She felt frozen in place, though. The world seemed to have stopped; she definitely didn't think she was breathing.

She didn't particularly want to start again.

"Cerberus," said Stephen, and this time Mina didn't mind the name as much. Stephen's voice mocked himself this time, and praised her. "Guarding my doorstep this time. I should ha' known."

"Oh," she said, light and breathless and a long way away from her actual mind, "this is all a bit pleasant for the underworld, you know."

"I'm no' much judge of that," he said, "but I'm glad to hear you say it." His fingers moved slightly against her face, stroking the skin behind her ear. "You're certainly a much less terrifying defender. And a much more appealing one."

Stephen's voice fell on the last sentence, and for a moment, the quiet, husky tone of it overcame the last of Mina's restraint. She took one small step forward, put her own hands on his shoulders, and lifted her lips to his.

Even caught up in the moment, she was a little uncertain at first. It had been a long time since she'd kissed a man, and she usually hadn't initiated the process back then. Besides that, Stephen was tall enough to make Mina worry that she'd judge the angle wrong and end up kissing his chin or his nose. The first brush of her lips against his mouth was light, tentative.

The fire it ignited was enough to drive her past any uncertainty.

All the same, the kiss was gentle this time too. Mina heard Stephen catch his breath as she leaned against him. The hand that had cupped her face was at the back of her neck now, fingers stroking down her spine, but he let her take the lead, responding to the pressure of her lips and the light touch of her tongue.

Beneath her hands, the muscles in his arms were bunched and tense. There was as much power in him as there had been when he'd pulled her to him in the study. He was simply containing it now. Leashing it.

The realization was as heady as the feeling of his skin beneath her fingers.

She took a step forward. That brought her breasts against Stephen's bare chest, sending a delightful sort of ache through them and turning her nipples instantly hard—and her knees weak. Stephen slipped his other arm around her waist then, so it was a very simple matter just to lean into him, to trust him to take her weight while she melted against his body.

Kissing a man, apparently, was one of those things that came back quickly. If the sensations were far stronger, the skills at least had stayed.

Realizing as much gave Mina more mental satisfaction. She wouldn't come off as a complete novice in this area. A nice girl probably wouldn't have been glad about that. A nice girl wouldn't be standing in a deserted house and kissing a man she barely knew.

Nice girls missed a great deal.

She broke the kiss, but not to pull away. Rather, she indulged her impulse of a few moments before and turned her face to rest against Stephen's neck. The wood-smoke smell was stronger there, mixed with a very human masculine aroma, and when she ran her tongue experimentally up to Stephen's ear, he made a rough and inarticulate noise.

Also, the hand at her waist was now cupping her backside. Very nicely, too. Then there was pressure, so she followed it, letting Stephen draw her right up against him.

Now her breasts were crushed against his chest so that she could feel its warmth right through the layers of her clothing. Lower down, a long, thick shaft pressed against her, even hotter and harder than the rest of Stephen's body.

Mina's practical knowledge of male organs was a little hazy. It was still good enough to produce several unclear but extremely tempting images and to make her squirm in Stephen's arms, rubbing herself against him.

That didn't quite work. Rather, it felt wonderful but was not quite what she wanted.

Stephen was too damn tall. Or she was too short. It would all be much better if they were lying down. The thought crossed her mind just as Stephen trailed his other hand down, his fingers maddeningly light as they grazed over her bodice, and gently cupped one of her breasts.

"Ohh."

The sound rushed out of Mina on a breath that seemed to empty her lungs. She felt Stephen tense, felt the flex of his muscles beneath her palms, and drew her own hands downward, feeling crisp hair and smooth skin beneath her fingertips. Touching his chest meant putting a little more space between it and her breasts, but that was all right—especially when Stephen started stroking his thumb over her nipple.

Then it was more than all right: it was enthralling.

The place between her legs was hot and wet and aching. It ached more with every motion of Stephen's hands, with every inch of his skin Mina touched, but she desperately wanted to keep going.

And then, from the window nearby: *thump*.

Mina didn't even see Stephen move. She barely felt it. One second she was in his arms, her whole being centered on desire; the next, she was facing the window from behind him. Her shoulders were a little sore, and when she had a second to breathe, she processed the whirl of movement. He'd grabbed her and spun her out of the way.

Contrary to all reason, the thought did nothing to diminish her lust.

A pair of green eyes, staring out of the darkness, did. Mina glimpsed them when she peered around Stephen, gasped—and then relaxed when the shape around them moved and she saw more of it.

"Just the cat," she said.

"*The* cat?" he grumbled. "I wasna' aware we had one."

"Well—a cat, then." Although it was more like *the*. Emily had started putting food out for the creature, and Mina had caught Owens with a saucer of milk at least once. Mina couldn't read Stephen's tone, though, and she wasn't inclined to tattle on the scullery maid who sometimes smiled and asked how her day had gone. "I've seen it round the back a few times. Strays, you know. You get them in the city."

"Probably harmless enough, then," Stephen said, and turned away from the window. His gaze fastened on Mina's face, and his eyes darkened, but he made no move to approach her.

Mina understood. Harmless as the cat was, its sudden presence outside had been an effective slap in the face for her. Now she was all too aware that she'd been standing in a deserted and dimly lit house, ready to do all sorts of unwise things with a man she'd known for all of three weeks—a gentleman, at that, and one who wasn't even human. She couldn't blame him this time, either.

Whatever he was going to say—scandalized lecture or gentlemanly apology—Mina didn't want to hear it. "People will be getting back soon," she said. "You should probably go and see to your room before one of the maids gets there."

"Oh. Aye." Stephen cleared his throat. "No, it wouldn't do to have them upset," he agreed and started up the stairs. Halfway up, as Mina was beginning to walk away, he stopped and turned. "Are—will you be all right?"

"Oh, well enough," said Mina, turning back with a smile she didn't really feel. "I'll just…I'll make myself a cup of tea."

"Because that," she added to the dark hall, once she was alone there, "is sure to solve everything."

Fourteen

In the morning, the wind spat rain against the window glass. Stephen looked up from his tea and made a sound that sounded unusually dragonish even to him. He should have known. He'd come to London in the spring—if one could call it that.

Oh, the sky was as gray at home and the weather as bad, or worse. He had to admit that. But he'd never minded there. In the city, the rain felt greasy, and the low, bleak sky was an imprisoning wall. There were walls everywhere here. Some of them granted at least a little safety—though last night had shown their limits—but all of them kept him trapped, even the ones that were only words.

Duty: there was a set of iron bars. *Honor* was another good one. He'd shut himself behind both quite willingly. He knew it was for the best, and yet—

He buttered a scone absently and ate it without tasting it at all.

It was going to be that sort of day. It had not been a particularly restful night. Stephen had seen to his most immediate needs in a matter of minutes with a few rough and almost punishing strokes of his hand. His sleep had still been restless, haunted alternately by red-lit shadows and a woman's flushed face, her blue eyes hazy with desire.

He wished to hell that his dreaming mind would at least settle on horror or lust.

The knock at the door took him from his thoughts for a moment. "Yes?"

"Miss Seymour, my lord," said Polly's voice.

"Good. Come in."

She always came to breakfast. Her presence today was no surprise and a bit of a relief, considering the previous evening. All the same, Stephen leaned forward to watch the door open, tense and alert for—God knew what.

It was some comfort, and troubling at the same time, to see that Mina didn't precisely look at ease. Pretty, yes, even on a day like this one and even in yet another combination of plain dark dress and tightly knotted hair. She held her body rigidly, though, and she looked only briefly into his eyes. "Good morning."

"And to you," he said. Out of the corner of his eye, he watched Polly disappear through the door and wondered if perhaps he shouldn't have asked her to stay. But what cause would he give? It was too late for him to start acting like a maiden aunt.

He poured Mina a cup of tea and pretended that it took his full concentration, that another sort of tension entirely wasn't threatening to make itself known. Her skin was creamy and pale against the dark dress, and her eyes were huge, but he wasn't going to take much notice of that.

He told himself that very firmly, addressing the thought particularly toward his groin, which seemed disinclined to listen.

"I hope your bedroom was all right," said Mina, fortunately *after* Stephen had put the teapot back down. It wasn't so much the words themselves as the way she caught her breath after *all right*, realizing what she'd implied. She bit her lip, small white teeth against crimson skin.

With that, Stephen's cock came to full attention.

Damn, he said again, silently this time and directed toward his unruly senses. He had to work with this woman, a purpose he wouldn't serve by acting like a schoolboy—or a satyr.

He managed to keep his voice from betraying his arousal. "I saw nothing damaged," he said. "'Tis good of you to ask."

"Oh. Good." Mina turned her attention toward her breakfast.

As far as Stephen knew, the walls and furnishings of his drawing room were completely mundane: stone, plaster, and wood, quite natural and certainly not given to changing. All the same, the room seemed about half its normal size. The air was warmer too; the clammy day outside had slipped from his mind entirely.

Business. Business would help—and making progress on that business would get Mina out of his house all the sooner. She'd been very clear about wanting that a few days ago, and it would certainly be better for both of them.

Stephen wished he hadn't felt the need to tell himself that.

"Speaking of last night—" Bad start. Mina jerked her head upward, eyes wide, and Stephen was very sure which part of last night she was recalling. He shifted in his seat. "Our visitors were mentioning a pub, and you looked like you knew the name."

"Not very well," Mina said. The mingled shock and desire left her face—it was probably just as well—and she tried to replace them with a severe, governess-like look. One side of her mouth kept turning up, though. "Not personally, anyhow. But I've passed by it a time or two, and I've heard a few stories."

"You'll need to tell me about the place today." Stephen glanced over at the window. "We're having good weather for stories, at least."

Mina laughed then. "I'll pull up a chair, shall I, and you can sit at my feet and listen? I only wish I had some knitting, and maybe a lace cap—" Then she stopped laughing, and her golden-brown eyebrows slanted downward. "*You're* not going there. And you're *not* asking about Ward."

She was almost asking a question, except that the sheer disbelief in her voice was too strong.

"And why not?" Stephen asked.

"Because you'll die." Mina put down her fork, half a slice of bacon still on the tines. "Definitely if you start asking questions and maybe even if you don't."

She spoke as if she was explaining some basic and obvious physical law—gravity or the need to breathe air.

"I've gotten the impression the last few years," Stephen said, emphasizing *years* enough to let her know what other words he might have chosen, "that I'm a fair hand at taking care of myself."

"Against a whole pub full of men? Without revealing more about yourself than you want?" Mina shook her head. "I wouldn't put money on it. Anyhow, even if you did come out on top, the story'd be all over the street two hours later. Do you really want that?"

No, he didn't. Last night's burglary and its results would doubtless get back to Ward anyhow, sooner or later, and the other man had to know that Stephen would be asking questions. Still, the less Stephen gave away, the better—including how good he was in a fight, how much he'd been able to find out, and where he'd gotten that information.

"But," he said, "if the man's been offering work, surely plenty of people must have been asking about it."

"Nobody like you," said Mina.

That might have been flattering, but Stephen didn't count on it. "I wouldn't just be walking in there like this," he said, a gesture taking in coat and waistcoat, pocket watch and cuff links. Although, in truth, he hadn't thought of that until Mina mentioned it, nor was he sure where he'd get other clothes. Perhaps he could borrow Owens's, though the groom's shirt would be tight across the shoulders.

It didn't matter because Mina, far from being convinced, laughed again. "You could go in wearing a convict's uniform and it wouldn't matter," she said. "You look like a gentleman, and if you didn't, you'd still look dangerous—and wealthy. And that's the sort of man gets talked about in a place like the Dog and Moon. Especially if he's asking about jobs. A gentleman might slum a bit, but he wouldn't go and ask for work."

"Thank you very much," said Stephen, trying to sound sarcastic and not gratified. "Could you teach me?"

"Well, thank *you* very much," said Mina, and the sarcasm was real for her. "But no. Teach you how to act like you've—like you've never had more than one pair of trousers without a patch on 'em? Like you've worried every winter about getting behind on the rent if the coal was too dear, or thought breaking a leg might break *you*? Maybe if I had a year." She looked from the china on the table to the portraits on the walls, and then back to Stephen. This time her gaze had no desire in it. This time, she looked as if she was calculating the value of his clothes down to the shilling. "*Maybe.*"

The hell of it was that she didn't even seem very angry. Her eyes shone like indigo glass, but the spark in them was at least half rueful humor. If the laughter in her voice had far more of a brittle edge than it had before, at least the laughter was still there.

Stephen flinched from it as he would never have winced at a blow.

"I hadn't known that," he said.

"Well, no. You wouldn't. That's my point." Mina reached for her tea and bent her head to blow across its surface. Her face became hidden: a pale blank between china and hair. "Some have it worse than others, of course."

"And which of those were you?" Stephen asked. He spoke before he thought; he wanted to reach out and cup her face again, to lift her chin and look into her eyes.

When Mina replied, he was glad he hadn't. All the

laughter had gone from her voice, leaving the crackle of ice in February. "We managed," she said. "And I don't see how my family's got any bearing on our situation."

"Look here, I was only—" Stephen began, and then he had nothing to say and no grounds for indignation.

Mina had never made any secret of where she came from. Stephen had always known; he just hadn't *known*. The plain dresses and the occasional accent took on a new weight now. So did her determination to keep working for Carter, her concern over her reputation, and the look of mingled wonder and frustration that had crossed her face when Stephen had so casually offered his payment.

Everything meant more, and so there was nothing he could say.

Gradually, the anger went out of Mina's face. That stung more, in its own way, because what replaced it was resignation borne of the knowledge that she couldn't really have expected any better. Then it too was gone, covered by a blank and businesslike expression that might have been worst of all.

"In any case," she said, "I can't teach you how to blend in. Odds are you'd just stand out more if you did try."

"Well, then," Stephen asked, glad and sorry at the same time to return to the immediate problem, "what is it you'd have me do?"

"Nothing at all," said Mina. "I'll go."

Fifteen

In the end, Stephen didn't argue as much as Mina had thought he would. That wasn't to say he didn't protest—he did, almost as soon as she'd spoken—but the skirmish hadn't lasted very long. After all, Mina had already pointed out all the reasons why Stephen couldn't go and ask. He'd said that it wasn't safe. She'd said that she'd already been in the neighborhood and that she'd probably be spending more time there than he would, once the matter of Ward had come to its end. He'd made several surly noises and eventually given up the fight.

Just as well. Mina still had one card left to play, but she hadn't wanted to lay it down. It went, roughly: there are plenty of women there, and plenty of them are more delicate than I am, and you don't worry about any of *them*, because you don't want to take them to bed.

That wasn't exactly fair—Stephen was enough of a gentleman that he'd probably be concerned about anyone he actually knew, even if lust hadn't come into the picture—but it would do for an argument. With her pride still smarting from his earlier questions, Mina had almost been disappointed that she hadn't had to go down that path.

She went down Cable Street instead. She wore her oldest dress and bundled her hair into an untidy knot at the back of her head. After a winter of smoke, rain, and crowded streetcars, her coat wouldn't give anything away, and she was glad to have it. The night was warm enough to be foggy, but the wind off the water didn't know it was May, whatever the calendar said.

Vague shadows moved through the yellow fog, stopping to join other silhouettes for a chat or a fight, then moving on. As she passed, Mina heard bits of conversation as disconnected as the shadows:

"...an' I told 'im that there weren't no more money, and 'e said..."

"C'mon, Ruthie, 'twas only the one time an' it didn't mean nothing. I swear it—"

"...don't think much of it, whatever she says. No great judge, my sister. The first flat she an' her husband took..."

It was all familiar enough; two years of Bulstrode Street and Professor Carter's office hadn't changed much, and neither had a few weeks with Stephen. The East End closed around her, and she slipped back into it, another almost formless shape in the mist.

Stephen was somewhere in it too—far enough away from her that people wouldn't think they'd come together, but near enough that he could see her. When Mina had scoffed at the idea that he could see *anything* in this fog, he'd said his vision was better than most people's, and she supposed that could be true, even though his time as a dragon had come and gone.

Still, Mina didn't like it. It would probably lead to trouble, for one thing. For another, she didn't like him seeing Cable Street, knowing that she was familiar with the place. That could only lead to more questions—and more pity.

Some vestige of girlish idiocy, which apparently still lingered well beyond its appropriate age, did take a warm pleasure in knowing that Stephen was nearby and that he worried about her. No good reminding herself that he would probably have done the same for any woman he thought was in his charge. Part of her mind refused to listen.

Luckily for the rest of her, Cable Street offered plenty of diversion, particularly as Mina drew near to the Dog and Moon. There she found no shortage of puddles and people to step around, hands to dodge, or requests—and offers—to ignore. She'd been doing such things most of her life, but now it felt more tiring, as if she had to keep a screen up around her mind as she walked.

Perhaps it was no wonder most of the women she'd grown up with were so weary.

She glanced up briefly at the pub's sign, making sure that it was the moon and baying hound she remembered. Then she pushed open the door and stepped into a world full of light, sound—and smell.

Not all the smells were bad, at that. The odors of vinegar and fish made Mina's mouth water, although she'd had an excellent dinner, and the dark, nutty smell of ale was relaxing and familiar. Above those, though, rose less pleasant scents: old drink, too many bodies in too little space, and things it was best not to name.

The pub was having a good night. Fog always helped. The bar was crowded, the tables were full, and the tired-looking barmaids were almost constantly weaving their way back and forth through the crowds. Mina pushed her way forward, using an elbow or two where she had to, and settled herself at the bar.

"What'll you have?" the bartender asked, somehow sensing a new presence without looking up. She'd seen him a few times growing up. Save for more gray in his hair, he looked the same: tall and square, broken-nosed, pale-skinned. Had his name been Smith? Smitty? She didn't remember.

"Pint of beer," she said, letting her voice slip back home, and slid a few pence over the bar. "An' a bit of talk." She added a few more. The bartender grunted but took them. Then he turned away.

Mina leaned on the bar—there wasn't a seat to be had, though fortunately her neighbors all seemed to be immersed in loud discussion—and waited. In a few minutes, a glass arrived in front of her, complete with a *thunk* and an inch of liquid sloshing over the side. She picked it up and sipped.

The bartender looked at her without recognition. Mina had hoped for as much. Her time in pubs like this one had mostly involved dragging George out of them so he could clean up for dinner, and talking with a few friends who served the drinks. It was enough that she knew the ways of the place, and hopefully not enough that anyone would spot her.

"What sort o' talk did you 'ave in mind?"

She shrugged. "Fred says as how you know ways a body can get work sometimes. 'Igh-toned men as are likely to want things done." She rolled her eyes as the bartender—Williams? William?—began to leer. "Not *that* sort of thing, thanks. A girl don't need directions to that kind of work. But Fred—"

"Fred runs his mouth considerable, don't he?"

"Just to me," said Mina and simpered, or tried to. She hadn't had much practice at it.

"Then why didn't you ask him?"

"Maybe I want work as doesn't go through him," Mina said. "A bit for myself. He said you know a bloke—"

The bartender's eyes narrowed, but his mouth worked thoughtfully. He took himself off briefly to pass on more beer and then returned. "Could be," he said.

"Well, 'as he got anything needs doing now?"

"Now? Nah."

Mina took another, larger drink. "Is there a name about 'im?"

"John Smith," said the bartender, and smirked. "Why do you want to know, anyhow?"

"Let's say I do," said Mina, with an inward sigh. "'E just comes in and asks for people?"

"Something like that."

"And how do you tell 'im when you've found 'em? You must have some way of getting the word out quick."

"You seem like you've got somethin' in mind."

She shrugged one shoulder, trying to look casual. "I might 'ave an offer a man might pay for," she said.

"If 'e was the sort of man who'd got ambition. But I want to put it to 'im myself. Saves misunderstanding."

"Saves money, too."

Mina dug a few more coins out of her purse and held them meaningfully in front of the bartender. "A couple shillings ain't my concern, is it? I'll mention your name to 'im if you like, and you can take your commission up with the gentleman."

She put the coins on the table but kept her hand over them. The bartender stared at her for a long moment. She glared back.

"Fine," he said eventually. "Like I said, the name's John Smith. Thirty-nine 'Unter Street. I send a note when someone useful turns up. 'E comes in after an' pays me. And is overdue, I don't mind telling you."

"Thirty-nine 'Unter," Mina repeated. "And if 'e comes back looking, can you let me know?"

Another shrug. "If you come back afore someone else asks. If you're done with the questions, I got customers." When Mina didn't answer, the man moved off.

It was good enough. Mina finished her beer, left the glass on the bar, and pushed her way out of the pub.

A short ways down Cable Street, she heard footsteps behind her. She knew it was probably Stephen, but she took a step away anyhow as she turned to face the new arrival, and she kept a tight hold on her purse. You never knew.

"It's only me," said Stephen, appearing out of the fog and once again confirming what Mina had told him. Wet-haired and dressed in his plainest, oldest clothes, he still didn't fit in. He carried himself wrong: shoulders too straight and frame too easy at the same time.

Then again, Mina didn't think she'd ever seen Stephen in a place where he *did* blend, just as she'd never seen him in clothing that didn't look like a costume.

Perhaps he looked most natural in his…natural state.

Perhaps she had no call to start wondering about that.

Still, she took the arm that he offered and let herself be glad of the closeness and warmth of his large body.

"You've got no gloves," said Stephen, looking down.

"Too new," Mina said. "We're looking for Hunter Street. Thirty-nine." She shut her eyes for a second, calling geography to mind. "It's not too near, but a hansom should be able to get us there quick enough."

"Ah—" Stephen began.

It had been a long evening already, and was going to be a longer one from the look of it. Mina had no patience for chivalry. "I suppose you can drop me back at your house first," she said, being even more careful than usual with her *h*'s as she spoke, "but I'd have thought you'd want to go as quick as you can. Before people start asking any questions. And I think two are probably better than one unless he's got a job lot of men there, honestly, but you're in charge."

"Oh, am I now?"

"You've got the money, anyway."

"Ah, well," Stephen said and passed a gloved hand over his mouth. "That's actually what I'd been coming around to telling you. The situation changed a bit while you were in the pub."

Mina looked from his hair—damper than the fog would explain, now that she was close to him—to the embarrassed look on his face. She tried not to grin. "Lose your wallet?"

"Aye."

"About twelve, was she? Big eyes, a bit tearful? Lost her mum in the dark?"

"Her grandmother," Stephen said and cast a baleful glance behind him. "Fast wee thing she was, too. Her and her friends."

"It helps to know the streets," said Mina. She patted Stephen's arm, the fabric of his coat soft and thick beneath her gloveless hand. "Don't feel bad. You're hardly the first, and I can probably get us a cab."

Sixteen

Thirty-nine Hunter Street was a squat and unwelcoming place: sturdy, square brick walls, white shutters, and the general impression of dour respectability. The woman who answered the door was as dour as the house itself, and gave Stephen and Mina a squinting, suspicious look.

"We only rent *single* rooms here," she began, a prune-like cast to her mouth, and added, "*sir*," as if it was more of an insult.

"I'm not here to rent," said Stephen. He tried to ignore the implication, but it did make him more aware of Mina's presence at his side. She'd turned toward him slightly, probably to put him between her and the wind. He wanted to put an arm around her and hold her against his chest—his people's abnormal warmth should serve *some* purpose—but this wasn't the time or the place. He wasn't sure either one existed. "I'm inquiring after one of your lodgers. A Mister Smith."

"What's your business with him?"

"It's a private matter. He does stay here?"

"He might," said the landlady, "and then he might not. It's a bit late to be paying a call."

"I'm not here for social reasons," Stephen began.

Then Mina put her hand on his arm. "It's all right," she said, when Stephen peered down at her. "I'll tell her."

"Tell me what?" asked the landlady, thrusting her chin forward.

As Stephen tried not to *look* as if he'd no idea what was going on, Mina looked down at her feet, gulped, and then looked back up into the landlady's eyes. "He's my brother. He's…he's in trouble"—her voice fell, implying all sorts of elements to the *trouble* that no decent girl would say aloud—"and…well, I don't want to go up there myself. He'd never forgive me if I saw—"

The landlady's face softened, a transformation almost as incredible as any Stephen had been through. "Well, well—" she began and cleared her throat. "Who's your friend, then?"

"Mister Smith served with me in the army," Stephen said, "some years ago. In happier days," he added, with a moment of pride for thinking of the phrase. "He spoke to me often of his sister, and any service I can do her—"

The landlady deflated the rest of the way. "All right, then," she said. "You can go on up. It's the second door on the right. And you'll come inside, miss. It's no weather to be out in."

Victorious, if dishonest, Stephen followed Mina into the boardinghouse's front hall, then climbed a narrow, white-painted staircase, dimly lit and smelling faintly of cabbage. The stairs creaked beneath him on every step; so did half of the boards in the upstairs hall, despite its runners of fabric.

Light came from underneath the second door on the right. All the others were dark. The other boarders either slept early, stayed out late, or didn't exist.

Stephen walked as lightly as he could to the lit door, grasped the doorknob, then broke the lock with one swift, brutal motion. He shoved the door open, removing his revolver from his coat pocket before he stepped inside.

The lamp inside illuminated a sparse, scrubbed room with a narrow bed, no belongings that Stephen could see, and a man in gray cotton sitting on the edge of the bed. He looked up when the door opened, saw the revolver, and froze. There was no panic about him, neither in motion nor in expression. Something had happened. That was all.

"This is my room," he said without passion. "What are you doing here?"

"You're John Smith?"

Stephen held the revolver steady and considered the picture before him. The man wasn't Ward. He was too short, his hair was almost colorless, and the structure of his face was too even, too round. Also, he looked up at Stephen with neither alarm nor hate.

"I am John Smith," he said. "What do you want?"

"Have you been hiring men down at the Dog and Moon?"

Smith blinked once. "No."

It was the wrong question, Stephen realized. The men he'd spoken to had described Ward, or someone like him. In truth, he wouldn't trust Smith to hire anyone himself.

"Do you receive the messages the barman sends?" he asked. That was the right question, if there *was* a right question.

Indeed, Smith nodded. Something about him shifted, too. Stephen wasn't sure what. He couldn't have placed it in the man's stance, or even in his eyes. The difference was like the faint smell of smoke on the wind or a sudden chill in the air. It roused the hunting instinct in his blood, the primitive awareness that the moment for action was fast approaching.

"What happens to the letters?" he asked, concentrating on his aim.

"I inform my master of their arrival," said Smith, as if stating the answer to a mathematical problem. "I take them to our meeting place."

Master, he'd said. Not *employer*, not *commander*. *Master*. On the back of Stephen's neck, every hair stood on end.

"How long have you been at this?"

"Forty-eight days."

Now there *was* a smell. Faint but sharp, it stung the inside of Stephen's nose. "What's that?"

Smith gave him a truly blank look.

Then, a sound. Sizzling. It came from somewhere near Smith's boots. Stephen took a hasty step backwards. "What in the world is wrong with you, man?"

"Nothing," said Smith. The sizzling sound was louder now, and the smell was stronger. "I am functioning exactly as designed. Good-bye."

Stephen lunged toward Smith just before he shattered.

There was no explosion, no grotesque rain of flesh. Instead, cracks ran up and down Smith's body, covering his hands and face within seconds. Another second widened them. Then there was no more Smith, only a small pile of bits that looked like a thicker eggshell—and a burning cloud of orange gas.

Stephen's free hand closed around one of the bits of shell. He stuffed it into his coat pocket without thinking, then bolted for the window. The butt of his revolver broke through the glass easily, and cold air rushed inside.

The window was small, though. The wall it faced was high, and the wind coming in blew the gas toward the open door. With every inhalation, the orange cloud poured into Stephen's lungs, scorching them like no fire ever had. As he ran forward, hand over his face, he felt blood begin pouring from his nose.

Even he wouldn't survive very long in the building. A mortal man would have been dead already.

Mina was downstairs.

"*Fire!*" Stephen yelled, and his throat screamed raw agony with the word. He drew a painful breath and shouted again. "Get out of the house!"

None of the doors along the hallway opened; no light came on underneath them. Stephen ran down the hall anyhow, trying one knob after another and getting no answer.

Then, from the bottom of the stairs, he heard Mina calling his name.

He turned from the final door and ran for the stairs. The mist was hazier now, diluted with the extra space. Still reeling from the initial cloud, he wasn't sure how deadly it remained. Halfway down the stairs, he had to stop and hold on to the banister while he coughed.

"Stephen!" He looked up through the mist to see Mina, holding a handkerchief over her face and ascending the stairs toward him.

"*No!*" The word came out bloody. Stephen reached forward, half-blind, and grabbed Mina by the shoulder. "You'll die. Get out."

"You too," she said, and now she'd grabbed *him*, her hand tight on his wrist. Without so much as a by-your-leave, she turned and began pulling him down the stairs. "Mrs. Grant's next door. She's called the police."

"Anyone else?" he managed.

"No. Move."

Mina dragged him, with considerably more strength than he'd have thought she had, and Stephen aided her as much as his pain-wracked body would allow. Keeping his eyes on her made it easier to stumble onward. He watched the strands of hair that hung down her back and the determined set of her shoulders, and he almost forgot how much effort it took just to put one foot in front of the other.

Then the doorway was in front of them; then Mina was through it, and Stephen staggered through after her, just sensible enough to slam the door shut behind him. He closed his eyes and leaned against the wall.

"My God," someone said, "what's happened to him?"

"Was it a fight?" another voice asked.

And then Mina, blessedly calm and steady and close at hand. "Can't I take you anywhere?"

They got back home. Stephen wasn't entirely sure how. Most of his attention was focused on drawing breath into lungs that felt lined with broken glass.

The voices swirled around his head, exclaiming and questioning. Mina's rose above them. They faded. Mina spoke again, sharply but unsteadily, with tears in her voice. Stephen tightened his arm around her, squeezing her shoulder with one hand. She was shaking. No wonder. He should do something, he thought. He should at least say something, but the coughing took over again.

"...get a doctor," said Mina.

Stephen shook his head. "Won't help. I'll be all right. Home."

He saw the carriage as a large, almost formless black shape. He thought briefly and uneasily of legends—the black coach on the Royal Mile, foretelling death or taking souls to Hell—but the elderly dapple-gray horse and the talkative cab driver dispelled that impression quickly enough. Inside, the seats were cracked and badly sprung. Stephen let himself fall back into his as if it had been a featherbed.

Slowly, he stopped coughing and his vision cleared. He saw Mina sitting opposite him. Her lips were a thin line, her eyes fixed on his face. Stephen lifted a hand and felt dried blood on his mouth.

"Sorry, lass," he said.

"Don't be stupid," said Mina. She passed him her handkerchief, cold and wet and smelling of tea. "And don't talk."

"I can talk," said Stephen, doing the best he could for his face. Now he could feel the scalded tissues of his throat repairing themselves—a gift from his heritage. "Quietly. Shouldn't move too much, either. Hope we have no more visitors."

"Right. Or I'll have to learn how to use a sword."

"I'd have to teach you," said Stephen. The idea had some appeal—guiding her hands on the hilt of a blade, seeing her figure in athletic costume—but his body was not in any state to follow through on it. Absently, he reached into his pocket and pulled out the bit of shell.

Up close, it looked like any bit of pottery. It was about the size of his palm, and one side was mostly flesh-colored. The other glimmered with a shifting green-and-red pattern.

"What's that?"

"John Smith," said Stephen, "or part of him."

Mina grimaced. "He wasn't human, then."

"No. I'm not sure what. I've heard a rumor or two. Constructed beings. Never anything concrete. As it were." He laughed, which made him cough. When he'd finished, and Mina was glaring at him, he went on. "This one had a trap inside."

"I'd say it did. Who could do that?" Mina wrapped her arms around her body. "Make a fake person with a cloud of poison inside? How do you figure that out?"

"Most people don't," said Stephen. "We can use that."

Seventeen

Stephen claimed he was recovering without help. He claimed he could talk. He might have been right. Mina didn't know much about either poison gas or dragons.

She did know that he was pale, even by the dim light through the cab window, and that he talked at half his normal speed, with frequent pauses to cough. She wanted to sit by him, or at least to keep a hand on his arm and give him what reassurance human touch could provide, but she hung back. Too much attention could just irritate an ill person, and she didn't want to be one of the fluttering women her brothers had both complained about.

Besides, that was a dangerous path to go down.

Mina kept silent for the rest of the cab ride, and Stephen seemed glad enough to follow her lead. At his house, she passed him into the hands of Baldwin, by way of an aghast-looking James. Baldwin himself kept his emotions well hidden, only a quick exhalation showing that he wasn't completely used to finding his master in such a state.

As Baldwin and James helped Stephen up the stairs, the older man also cast a sideways glance at Mina. She felt his gaze take in everything about her, from her disarranged hair to her lack of gloves. She said nothing.

Instead, she went upstairs by the back way, conscious of Emily's startled look as their paths crossed. When the door to her room closed, she leaned against it heavily for a minute, resting her head on the thick wood, then crossed a short distance to sit down on the bed, absently undoing her coat buttons.

She was supposed to be pinning up her hair again. That had been Mina's plan: make herself look respectable, then go see what she could find in the kitchen. When she undid her coat, though, she sat and stared at her hands. They looked the same as they'd always done: short nails, faint ink stains. The night had left no mark on them—even if she felt that it should have.

Poison gas. Fake people. And Stephen, coughing blood.

She shuddered. Her tears in front of the lodging house hadn't all been fake. Three near-death experiences in as many weeks were overdoing it even for her nerves.

Someone knocked at the door. Mina sucked in her breath and shrank backwards on the bed. Then her mind reasserted itself, but in no particularly reassuring manner. The other servants almost never sought her out.

"Come in?" she asked, her voice much higher than normal.

The door opened. Of all the people she hadn't been expecting, Mrs. Baldwin stood in the doorway, her hands clasped behind her back. "I hate to be intruding,

Miss Seymour," she said, "but I'm afraid I've a great need to talk with you."

"Do you?" Mina said faintly. "Oh, good."

"Aye." Mrs. Baldwin looked at the room over Mina's shoulder. "You see, his lairdship told my husband that you're the one with answers about this evening."

Mina's eyes hurt. Her head hurt. Her *mind* hurt, like her legs after a three-hour walk. She cleared her throat. "And why," she began, in the most clipped tones she'd learned for Carter's, "do you think you're entitled to answers?"

"We're living here," said Mrs. Baldwin simply. "And we're none of us blind or deaf or stupid. We may not know what's been happening the last few weeks, but we all know it's something odd." She took a breath. "Clyde and I have been with his lairdship some time now. We know there are often odd things happening around him, around all of his blood, and we haven't been in the habit of asking many questions. But he hasn't been in the habit of coming home injured, either."

"It's his own neck to risk, isn't it?"

"Is it, now?" Mrs. Baldwin asked. "Have you ever known a man's enemies to care much about making sure his servants were safe?"

"Well—" Mina remembered the shadows. And the thieves—had they caught her alone, she wouldn't have ended the night happily. "No," she admitted.

Mrs. Baldwin nodded. "Well, then."

"Maybe you should come in," said Mina.

With another nod—more polite, this one, and less satisfied—the housekeeper entered and settled herself on the small chair by the window. Mina perched on the edge of the bed and tried to think, to balance fairness with discretion.

"There are some things I can't tell you or anyone. Lord MacAlasdair might, but they're his to tell. He does have an enemy. Someone from his past."

At that, Mrs. Baldwin's eyes flickered just a little. "Ah. Not someone he can tell the Yard about, then?"

"He says he's worked with the police a little. But—"

"You can't be relying on…outsiders…entirely," said Mrs. Baldwin. "Saving your presence, Miss Seymour."

"No offense taken," said Mina, who didn't have the energy for it in any case. Besides, she wasn't quite an outsider now. She wasn't quite an insider either, of course, and that was part of the problem. Someone familiar with Stephen's world might not have felt so lost in it.

Mrs. Baldwin didn't allow her much time to think about that. "He'll have been taking his own measures, then. Is there anything—anything the others might need to be worried about? Anything that might do them harm, if they came across it?"

There had been a moon last night; the manes couldn't return yet. Ward probably would have sent other things after them by now, if he could manage it. "Thieves," she said slowly, "but I guess any house is a risk for those."

"Some considerably more so than others. What about a general threat? Fire, aye, or flood?"

"No," said Mina.

"You're sure of that?"

Mina closed her eyes and reached up to rub the

bridge of her nose. "If you want someone who's sure of things, ask his lordship. You've known him for a while, and you don't know me at all."

"Aye, well," said the housekeeper. Her shadow moved as she reached up to push hair back from her face. It was a movement as weary as Mina felt. "I'll put about the bit about thieves, at least. They'll take their chances here just the same, or we'll fill in a bit for them. Either way, I expect they'll survive."

"I can boil an egg or two," said Mina and looked back at Mrs. Baldwin, "and I know my way around a needle and a dust cloth, if it comes to that. Can't promise anything about horses, though."

For the first time since Mina had met her, the housekeeper really smiled. "Great ungainly beasts, aren't they? I was never so glad as when we came here, though 'twas a sad occasion for it." She got to her feet. "Don't fret over much about them. Clyde's always been fond of the creatures, God knows why. We'll manage even if Owens takes himself off."

"I'm glad to hear it." Mina managed an answering smile.

"I'll have a wee word with the rest of them, and we'll see what's to come." Mrs. Baldwin headed toward the door, then turned. "And should you be free of an evening, I'd be glad of a cup of tea. 'Tis a big house for so few of us, aye?"

"You're right about that," said Mina.

Eighteen

"You canna' be getting out of bed yet," said Baldwin, late in the morning after Stephen had discovered the homunculus.

"I can," said Stephen, slipping his arms into his coat. Baldwin knew his duties. Even as he protested, he offered clothes without missing a moment. "And I must."

"But only the last evening—"

"I'll not dash into any burning buildings. I'll not dash anywhere, I'm thinking." Even now that the coughing had stopped, his lungs still felt tender and almost bruised, and breathing too deeply or too quickly had a painful edge to it. "I've always healed quickly, Baldwin. You know as much."

His valet's face was full of thought, of old stories about half-seen shapes and places in the woods where nobody went. As Stephen watched, the tales passed like a river through Baldwin's eyes, relaxing him and yet rousing the old mortal tension that came with mystery, even an inherited one like the MacAlasdairs.

"Well," said Baldwin and turned his attention to Stephen's necktie. After arranging the linen to his satisfaction, he spoke again. "Mrs. Baldwin's had a word with your…secretary, my lord, as you advised."

"I'd advised *you* to have a word," Stephen said, "if you wanted to know."

"Miss Seymour had gone to her room already, my lord. It wouldn't have been proper."

"Of course not." Leaving aside the urge to be sarcastic about such modern developments in etiquette, Stephen found Baldwin's consideration a relief. At least the rest of the household was treating Mina with propriety, however much its master might slip on occasion. "What did she have to say?"

"That you've an enemy, my lord, and one you canna' be telling the Yard about. That he's been thinking to strike at you more than once, but that we're in no more danger than what we might be if you'd angered some sort of criminal syndicate. Which we've told the new lot you have, or your father has."

"'Criminal syndicate'? You've been reading the *Strand* a bit, haven't you?"

"I like to take advantage of such opportunities as the city affords, my lord."

"But you don't believe it yourself?" Stephen asked, watching Baldwin as he folded clothing over his arm. "What you've told the rest of the staff, I mean?"

"I believe you've an enemy, and that he's been acting in an unlawful manner, my lord. And I believe you've decided to place a great deal of trust in your Miss Seymour, and that we'll then be abiding by your decision."

Quite a number of protests and questions occurred to Stephen just then. They started with *she's not* my *Miss Seymour*, though the term did sound uncommonly pleasant, and continued to wondering whether Baldwin would have trusted Mina otherwise, or was simply resigned to the situation.

He cleared his throat. "How did the others take that news?"

"Lizzie and Sarah have given their notice, I'm afraid, and so have Owens and James. I'm afraid it was a bit of a shock to them, and they found the prospect rather intimidating."

"Yes, I'd imagine."

When, hoarse and in pain, Stephen had suggested that Baldwin apply to Mina for an explanation, he hadn't expected anything so close to the truth or with such consequences to the household. Anger stirred, and he thought he might have a word with Mina—and then he saw her face in his mind, eyebrows arched and lips thin. He heard the iciest of her professional voices: *I was under the impression that people should know if they're risking their lives, even if circumstances preclude giving them an exact reason.* Then she'd say something sarcastic about forgiving her presumption.

Neither Stephen's natural gifts nor the artifact allowed him to read minds or to see the future. Apparently such abilities weren't always necessary—or avoidable.

"Mrs. Hennings is still on to cook," Baldwin continued, "and I'll be handling the horses and the butler's duties. Polly and Emily and Mrs. Baldwin should be able to manage the house, and Miss Seymour has said she can lend a hand as needed. It's a bit irregular, my lord—everything is—and a bit of a pinch as well, but you haven't been entertaining much, and honestly, we've had it soft round here for a while."

"Have you?"

"Oh, aye, especially for London. At least from all I've heard."

"And Miss Seymour…volunteered?"

"Said the work would do her good, my lord, though she's not trained to it exactly."

"Well." He put aside the mental image of Mina in a maid's uniform and turned his attention to the reason that the others had left: danger, even if not the kind they were thinking of. The dark of the moon approached, and while Stephen had made a little progress, he suspected Ward would only double his efforts because of it. "As it turns out, I'll have some work for her to do myself. Tell her I'll see her in the library in a quarter of an hour."

"She's there already, my lord."

Some corner of the house or the library itself had produced a ladder, one that went high enough for a reasonably tall woman like Mina to reach the top of the bookshelf. When Stephen entered the library, that was exactly what she was doing: cradling three books in one arm, reaching for another with her free hand, and making an amused little "hmm" sound at something she saw up there.

Until he remembered to be a gentleman, Stephen noticed her ankles and the backs of her legs, and reflected on just how much of a view the angle would permit.

"What might you be doing, exactly?" he asked, once propriety reasserted itself.

Mina looked over her shoulder, keeping her place steadily on the ladder. "Cataloguing your library."

"And why?"

"Because it wants cataloguing." She collected the last book and started down the ladder. Stephen put out his hands to steady her, just in case, and told himself not to hope for an accident. "Unless you have a system you didn't tell me about. A very *original* system. One that puts Austen next to *Common Diseases of the Cow.*"

"Well—no."

Mina reached the bottom of the ladder unaided and put the armload of books down carefully on top of one of the towers. "Right, then. I'll do it the normal way: fiction by name, nonfiction by subject. You pay double if I get eaten by spiders."

"Spiders? I'd thought they'd dusted this room when I took up residence."

"The room, yes. Between the books"—Mina removed a handkerchief from her pocket and wiped gray dust from her fingers—"no. Not that I can blame them. Not like most people use the place, especially the high shelves, so no need to chance the roaring hordes of arachnids."

Stephen blinked. "Spiders don't roar."

"Ha. I suppose they don't write threatening notes in the dust, either. By the way, I found this."

A gesture toward the desk indicated a small book bound in dark blue leather with an unmarked spine. Stephen picked it up and flicked through a few pages. Handwriting covered them, not printing: a crabbed hand he didn't recognize.

"Someone's diary, I'd think," he said. "Not my father's—perhaps one of his relations'. Perhaps not. The ink's not too faded. It can't be more than a few hundred years old."

"Almost hot off the presses, then," said Mina. She looked from the book to Stephen, then asked, with a certain careful diffidence in her voice, "Do you mind if I have a look? There might be something helpful in it. You never know."

"If you'd like," Stephen said immediately. "I doubt you'll find much, but whoever wrote it is long past caring for secrets, I should think," he added, which made himself feel a little better about his first response.

Neither his father nor his uncles would have been fool enough to write down the secret vulnerabilities of the MacAlasdair blood, assuming there were any. They also would have told Stephen beforehand, and as far as he knew, the keys to his destruction were the same as for any man, only applied in greater quantities.

Certainly he hadn't much time for deciphering the hand of whoever had written the journal—and wasn't that what secretaries were for, in any case?

"If you come across anything," he said, "let me know, of course. Don't type it up just then, though."

"I'll try to restrain myself. Journals aside, what're you here for? Austen or the cows?"

"Neither, fascinating as they might be. I've actually come to request your help in something rather unusual."

"Well, that will certainly be a change."

"What I mean to say is—it's magic. Which you've not done before, unless I'm wrong."

"You're not wrong." Mina tilted her head,

frowning. "Which makes me wonder what use you think I'll be. Doesn't that sort of thing need training, or—or being a dragon?"

"It's safer if everyone's trained, aye. But I could guide you through the rite, and a spell's stronger for having more than one person in it. It gets power from…echoing, you might say."

When she was curious, Mina's face was a study in wide eyes and slightly pursed lips. "What sort of spell?"

"Protection. I've some wards up on the house already, of course, but they could be stronger. Especially now."

"All right," she said without hesitating. "What do we do?"

The first order of business was to find a corner of the library with enough bare floor. They needed a circle about five feet in diameter, which they finally achieved by moving a good many chairs and a small writing desk.

"Although you shouldn't be doing any of this," Mina said again, as Stephen lifted another chair.

"Of course I should. I'm not entirely an invalid, am I?"

"Yes you are." Mina shoved the desk to its final place against the wall. "You were coughing up blood last night and you slept until noon today. Do you get much more invalid than that?"

"A time or two," Stephen said. "And you're half my size—"

"Hardly."

"—and a woman. I shouldn't be letting you move great heavy chairs about."

"You can try and stop me if you like," said Mina, and suddenly looked down at the armchair she was pushing.

It was another of those moments where Stephen could read her mind without magic. At least, he thought it held a vague approximation of the images in his: the two of them, locked in a moment of wrestling, their bodies straining against each other. It didn't help that Mina was flushed and breathing quickly from the work, nor that tendrils of her hair were curling loosely against her neck.

She laughed, only a little bit too high, only slightly breathless. "But I warn you, I pull hair. Ask any of the girls on my street."

"I should have known," said Stephen, and applied completely unnecessary vigor to the final chair.

Then came candles, easily acquired from the kitchen, and the small silver cup that Stephen took out of a locked drawer. When he unwrapped it from its covering of green silk, Mina whistled.

"What's this, then, the Holy Grail?"

"I shouldn't think so," said Stephen. "I saw it being made, and I'm nowhere near so old as all that."

He had been very young at the time. It was one of his first memories: the glowing heat of the forge, the shine of fire from the half-made bowl, and his sister Judith's eyes reflected in it, her hands almost as steady as his uncle's. He'd known enough not to touch anything, and that had been about the limit of it.

"We have older ones," he said, "elsewhere. But even metal wears after enough time. And then there were so many of us, and we took to wandering—it was better to have more than a few such objects."

"Oh," said Mina, round-eyed again. "It's magic too, then?"

"Not so greatly as the crown, not of itself. It's a tool. But I daresay magic clings to it somewhat after enough use."

"Things start to be part of each other," Mina said, half quoting Stephen.

The quickness of her reply, and the simple fact that she'd remembered, no longer surprised Stephen. They still made him smile. "Hold on to it," he said, "while I pour the wine."

He turned toward one of the bookshelves, taking with him the sight of her: mortal hands clasped around the stem of the goblet, mortal eyes reflected in its polished surface.

Things start to be part of each other, he heard her say again.

Nineteen

WINE CAME FROM THE SAME DRAWER THAT HAD HELD the cup. The bottle was crystal, heavy-looking, and cut so that it threw off rainbows even in the dim light of the library. The wine was deep red, like the garnets in a bracelet Professor Carter kept in his study. From King Alfred's time, a thousand years ago or more, he'd said when Mina had stared at it and forgotten to be professional.

The bottle was probably newer than that, at least, and no wine could have survived so long. And Stephen had said that the goblet was younger than he was—whatever that meant.

Marveling at the bracelet and Professor Carter's other relics, reading his notes as she typed them, she'd sometimes almost felt time as a tangible thing, as if she could glimpse the past across a broad river. Now she felt that she stood on a shore and looked across the ocean, glimpsing, on some far island, the sun shining off a roof and knowing the breadth of the sea all the more intensely for that vision of the other side.

"How old was your father?" she asked.

Stephen paused, wine bottle in hand. "When he died?" His accent was thicker than normal. "Perhaps four hundred years. We stop keepin' score after a while, ye ken."

Four hundred years. Stephen was perhaps half that, if Culloden was when Mina thought it was. And she was somewhat shy of thirty.

"You're middle-aged, then?" she asked and tried to smile with it.

He shrugged, and this time, there was a more-than-human grace to the movement, a suggestion of rippling muscles even through his clothes. His smile was broader than usual too, and his teeth looked sharper.

"I suppose you could be saying something of the kind. It's no' so direct a comparison, though. We dinna' spend fifty years as spotty youths."

"Fate worse than death, I'd think," said Mina and laughed, which took the worst of the edge off. Not much more than that, though. The library was large, dark, and old. Even against the size of it, Stephen loomed above her.

She pressed her hands hard against the goblet and straightened her back, bringing herself to an almost military posture. "Right, then. What do I do?"

"Hold the cup out," said Stephen.

His voice was deep in her ears, and his eyes, meeting hers, were bright gold again. Mina's arms moved almost on their own, slowly and fluidly. She watched the wine flow from crystal to silver, bottle to chalice, and her mind went with it—flowing, rippling, then still.

Close at hand—how had he gotten so close

without her noticing? And when had he put down the bottle?—Stephen took a sudden deep breath and looked down at her with lifted eyebrows and a startled quirk of his mouth.

"Is something wrong?"

It was her voice, only it came from far away and high up.

"No. No." Stephen reached out, but stopped with his hand a few inches from Mina's hair and smiled at her instead. His teeth still looked very sharp, but the smile was warm nonetheless. "Worry not, Cerberus. This comes easier to you than I'd thought it would. That's all."

"Oh," she said. She'd have had a sharper answer if her mind had been where it normally was. Wit seemed distant now. So did worry: thank God, because she'd have been scared stiff otherwise. Runaway chariots of the sun came to mind, and hand mills that wouldn't stop making salt. "You've done this a few times, then?"

"A few," said Stephen.

For her own peace of mind, Mina decided not to press for more details. "What do I do?" she asked.

"Follow me. You'll not have to say anything. Just hold the goblet and move as I do." He did touch her cheek then. His fingers were almost hot enough to burn, but Mina turned her face toward them anyhow. The sensation was not quite painful. "Ready?"

"I'm ready."

They went slowly in a circle that felt much larger than it really could have been.

In her mind, overlaid on the image of the wine-filled chalice, Mina saw the house as if from a great height. She saw the gardens leading up to the gate; she saw the small stable behind it; she saw the tradesmen's entrance and the polished front steps. She saw the walls, sturdy and stone, and then, rising up within them, she saw another set of walls. This one was translucent and shone, patterned like stained glass with intertwining ladders of color: red and gold, brown and blue.

The first set of colors was Stephen; the second was her.

Joy followed the image, sudden and unbidden and inexplicable. What she looked on was beautiful in a way that she'd never imagined and couldn't fully understand. The light that poured through those magical barriers, or out of them—the house itself, and the people who moved in and around it—the very pace of their walking and Stephen's speech all took her breath away. Still from a great distance, Mina knew that her cheeks were wet with tears.

Later, she'd be embarrassed. Now there was no room for such emotion. There was only wonder and the need to see the ritual through.

She followed, listened, and watched as the walls came up and grew solid, watched in wonder until Stephen's hand on her shoulder brought her halfway back to herself, dizzy and blinking.

"Oh," she said again. Stephen's face was close to hers. She met his eyes, and he took another quick, startled breath. Then he brushed his fingertips under each of her eyes, wiping the tears away.

"Silly of me," she said and stepped back, her face feeling almost as hot as his fingers.

Stephen shook his head. "Furthest thing from it," he said gently. "Forgive me. I should have remembered."

"What—why—" The words for what Mina wanted to ask didn't come. Maybe it was because she didn't need to ask the first questions that came to mind. She knew why she'd been crying. It had been for beauty and joy; more than that, it had been for the certainty that there was more to the world than she'd suspected, and the knowledge of her own part in that greater whole. She'd seen a power that even she could grasp and use, as common and mortal as she was.

She settled for asking, "Remembered?"

"Magic—at least magic this complicated—has a way of overpowering you when you're new to it."

"Haven't been that in a while, have you?" Mina asked and felt some of her wonder die away even as she said the words.

"Not in some time."

There was nothing surprising in that. The knowledge settled into her chest, a hard little lump like a gemstone—and, considered sensibly, just as valuable. He was not mortal. He was not human. The more Mina had to face that, the better for everyone.

The sooner all of this was over, the better for everyone.

She smoothed her hair back and blinked the rest of the tears out of her eyes. "You should go lie down," Mina said, putting her old brisk self on again. "You've taxed yourself quite enough for your first day on the mend. And I have work to do."

Twenty

Sleep came quickly, lasted long, and because there was some benevolence to the universe, contained only darkness. When Stephen woke, it was almost sunset.

Immediately, he thought of Mina. She'd almost certainly already eaten and begun her day's tasks—Stephen wouldn't think of them as duties, since she'd taken them on herself—and the thought was a disappointing one. The one that followed was even less happy. Perhaps she preferred his absence. She'd certainly seemed eager enough for it the previous day.

It shouldn't have mattered. She was mortal. A few months ago, she'd known nothing of the world beyond the obvious physical manifestations and would have laughed off any mention of magic as a tale for children. She hadn't even been conceived when Stephen had made his trip to Bavaria. Yesterday and the day before had exposed Mina to a great deal. If she'd decided that she wanted no part of it—or of him—then the lass was showing good sense.

But he remembered the wonder in her face when she'd been casting the wards and the way her eyes had glimmered at the end.

He would have liked to see that expression on her face again.

"If wishes were horses," Stephen said darkly to the empty room, and picked up the newspaper.

He didn't read most of it. The political situation in France, the Queen's latest speech, and the theatrical reviews brushed lightly past his consciousness. Trying to keep his mind off Mina, Stephen had to send it down other paths.

His health was one. Sleep had done some minor wonders for his lungs. He could breathe without pain now; more importantly, it would be safe to transform. Injury to the human form could cause...problems...if it was bad enough, and Stephen particularly wanted to be in full control that evening. He cleared his throat experimentally, felt no pain—and then froze, suddenly focusing on a column in the paper.

East End Slaughter, the headline read.

Below it, in smaller print: *Men Butchered*, and then *Police Seek Killer*.

An unsettling set of headlines, to be sure, but not one that would ordinarily have caught Stephen's attention. London was a large city. Men had been killing each other for longer than he'd been alive.

Photographs were new.

One was of a lonely section of docks near a large warehouse. Someone had removed the bodies: no need to scare the ladies.

The other was older. One of the men had been in a police station before, brought up on charges of theft, and the officer there had been a forward-thinking man who took pictures of his charges. The picture was a few years old, and the paper didn't reproduce it that well, but Stephen recognized the man nonetheless. It was Bill, the elder of the would-be thieves.

He would have wagered everything he owned that the other corpse was Fred.

When he went to tell Mina, she was in the library again, this time frowning assiduously at one of the larger and older books. Her ledger was open before her, and she had an uncapped pen in one hand. She looked up when the door opened but didn't speak.

At first, Stephen couldn't think of anything to say, either. In all his life, there had never been a good way to break the news of a death—and a death like this, with less pain in it than guilt, was even harder in its way.

He settled on bluntness. "I'm afraid I come with bad news," he said. "I'm not completely sure, but it seems likely. You'll recall the thieves?"

"I do," said Mina. She put the cap on her pen and closed the ledger with a soft but decisive sound. "And I know. Told you I read the *Times* on my own, didn't I?" she added. "Nasty business."

"Yes," said Stephen. He looked from her eyes to her hands. The former were calm and the latter still. Her voice was a little quieter than usual, a little less brash and challenging. That was all. "I hope you're not—I hope it hasn't been upsetting you."

Mina shrugged. "Like I said, it's a grim bit of work, and I'm sure the details they don't tell us are worse. I won't deny it gave me a start—" She crossed the Turkish carpet in a few swift strides, keeping some distance between herself and Stephen but coming close enough to look into his face. "But you're taking it rough, aren't you?"

"I feel some responsibility for it, aye," he said. "After all, the feud's between Ward and myself, and the house is mine, and I'm the one who decided to question them. Had I called Scotland Yard, they'd likely—"

"They'd be just as dead," said Mina and snorted. "You think a couple of cells would stop a bloke like Ward? We already know he's got people in the underworld. My underworld, that is, as well as yours."

Stephen had been expecting to see a stricken look in her cobalt eyes, dreading the look of pain and guilt on her fine-boned face, and most of all fearing to see anger at him for dragging her into the matter, for putting blood on her hands. He would have tried to explain how the thieves' deaths were his fault, and not hers.

Faced with a creature of worldly certainty, who begged for no reassurance and demanded no explanation, Stephen could only stand and listen.

"And what were we supposed to do to keep them alive? Lie down and let Ward kill you, and then go after the Professor and whoever else got on the wrong side of him afterward?" Mina gestured in the general direction of the crown and made a revolted face. "Not hardly. You didn't make him go out and hire those poor stupid blighters, and you didn't make them take his money. You want to come over all noble and stricken, choose a cause worth your while. They're not."

She finished by glaring at him with such ferocity that Stephen had to laugh, despite everything. "Yes, miss."

"Watch it," Mina said, smiling herself. "I'm not as bad as that."

"No. Not at all," Stephen said. "Thank you."

"Nothing to it," she said. "I'm just surprised, a bit. You must've—"

"Killed men? Aye. Not so many as all that—I never went for a soldier—but it's happened a time or two." Stephen rubbed his forehead as if that would bring the right words to the front of his mind. "It's different when they're not trying to kill you. You haven't done either, have you?"

"No. I just knew men like them. Not bad sorts, really, and they didn't deserve what they got. Nobody does. But Ward's not the only man with a temper, and you're just as dead from a bullet. Even if they didn't know what they were signing on for, they knew." Mina frowned. "I can't say it any plainer than that."

"There's nobody I know who could have," said Stephen.

For some days to come, the men's deaths would weigh on him. He knew himself too well to doubt it. The worst of the burden was gone, though, freeing him to think of other things.

Ink spots, for example. Mina was a tidy woman, but fountain pens were never to be trusted, and a smudge dotted her cheek, only a finger's width from the corner of her mouth.

Then there was her mouth itself, sweetly curved and silently promising all sorts of things; the long slim line of her neck, with her hair curling against it; the swell of her breasts, not very well hidden even by her severely businesslike dress.

He could have gone on making observations for a long time, had he been more of a philosopher and less of a man. He took Mina in his arms instead.

As she'd done from the beginning, she fit there very neatly: firm and soft at the same time, tall enough that a man could kiss her thoroughly and heatedly without having to bend a great deal, and, this time, so eager for his touch that Stephen could have quite happily lost his mind then and there. After the first startled moment, after the first quick intake of breath, she wound her arms around his neck and kissed him back as if she'd been contemplating it as long as he had.

That thought did nothing for Stephen's self-control.

Neither did the way Mina wriggled against him when he cupped one of her breasts, nor the swell of her backside in his other palm. As far as the noises she made, small and desperate and half-muffled by Stephen's mouth, they went to his head faster than anything he'd ever drunk.

Under all that restraint, Mina was quite a passionate girl. Stephen had known that from the start, but never so deeply as now. After another whimper escaped her throat, he gave in to the need to find out more—and, perhaps, to satisfy both of their needs.

Fortunately, there was a desk at hand. Books thumped to the carpet as Stephen pressed Mina back into it. He was well beyond giving a damn, and though she stiffened for a moment, she didn't pull away. Nor did she flinch when he began to pull up her skirt. Instead, as Stephen's hand slid up her leg, she circled her hips, pressing her sex up against Stephen's swollen cock.

Stephen thrust back against her, finding a rhythm even with their clothes in the way, trying to retain enough concentration to remedy that. Damned skirt. Thrice-damned underthings. Women these days wore far too much under their skirts. Back when he'd been younger—he froze. Beneath him, Mina made a disappointed, questioning noise. His body simply howled.

But, he'd thought, *these days*. He remembered taking women when a skirt and a chemise was the most a man had to navigate. Generations had come and gone since then.

There was almost no distance between his body and Mina's. She lay beneath him, receptive and responsive, separated physically only by a few inches of clothing—and a great deal more in the abstract.

"Forgive me," he said and pulled away.

Twenty-one

Words didn't come easily just then. *Thought* didn't come easily just then. One minute Mina was writhing below Stephen, all her consciousness reduced to the feeling of his body against hers, his mouth on her neck, his hand—and then all of that was gone and he was halfway across the room, saying things that had no meaning at first.

Forgive him? For what? Why?

Then the air was cool against her exposed skin, and rationality began at least to come within her grasp. All the same, the answer that she first thought was: *For stopping? Never.*

Mina thought of the multiplication tables. Around five, though she still desperately wanted to pick up where she and Stephen had left off, she was able to push those impulses aside and speak almost normally.

"There's nothing to forgive," she said. "It was my doing as much as yours."

"It's kind of you to say," Stephen replied. He stood facing one of the bookshelves, his face turned away from her and his hands clasped behind his back.

Avoiding temptation, Mina thought. With his example to prompt her, she pulled her skirts back down and tugged her dress back into order. She watched her hands while she rearranged herself. Her hands were safe and familiar.

During the process, a sense of duty crept up upon her, even as she winced away. She didn't *want* to say what came next. She wanted to avoid that conversation almost as much as she'd wanted to feel Stephen's hand between her thighs or his lips on her breast.

The comparison only made the conversation more necessary.

"I don't think we can ignore this"—she waved a hand, unsure of what to call the situation and unwilling to put it into more specific words—"any longer."

"I'd not have said we were ignoring it just now," Stephen said. "But aye, you're right. Though I'm not at all sure what else is to be done about it."

"You could lock me in my room, couldn't you?" Mina couldn't help saying it, or laughing as she did—and the whole state of affairs *was* funny, really. "Or I could lock myself in, but that wouldn't be half as dramatic."

"No. If we're going to overreact, we'd best not do it by halves. I'd have to find a dungeon somewhere."

"There's always the wine cellar."

"Baldwin would never forgive me. Besides," Stephen said, and glanced back over his shoulder, "I'd not want to be hunting Ward without your help, not if I had a choice in it."

"Go on with you," said Mina. A spot of warmth started up in her chest, though, and she smiled despite herself. He'd come to tell her about the thieves, too. Another man might have kept it from her, worried about feminine nerves.

Stephen smiled. "Truly. It's a hard enough business as it is. Going it alone would be even worse."

"Could be the problem," she said. "Us being alone in this, I mean. Except for Professor Carter, and he doesn't live here, and he doesn't know what you really are. Maybe we've been…impulsive…because neither of us exactly has another, um—"

"Outlet?" She couldn't hear anything in Stephen's voice but polite contribution. He'd turned his head and was looking at the bookcase again.

"Right. Especially you. I mean, we both know I'm not exactly the sort of…of person you'd associate with normally." She would press on ruthlessly, though saying the words out loud made her hurt in a dull and foolish way, but she couldn't make herself say *woman*, or *kiss*, or anything of the sort. "Under normal circumstances. And certainly not the kind who'd know anything secret about you."

"Outside my family," Stephen said, still in that politely remote voice, "I can count on one hand those who know my other form. You're the only full human among them—the only one living, at least."

"I'm sorry," said Mina. She looked up from her hands at the straight line of his back, at his squared shoulders. "Our lives must go by pretty quickly, for you."

"Very quickly. If—" he started to say, and then shook his head. "One grows accustomed."

The air between them felt heavy with the things Mina didn't ask. She settled on a relatively safe question, one that didn't bring up the sort of people who did know Stephen well, or the identity of anyone in particular he might have lost. "You still have friends, though, don't you?"

"Friends, aye. Some."

"Oh. Well. That's what I was saying, really," she said. Stopping to think about the implications of being the only mortal to know his secret—or to wonder if he thought of her as some sort of more intelligent and more, er, *eligible* pet—would have been a disaster, so Mina pressed on, heedless of whether one sentence really led into another.

"You don't really get to see your friends right now. Or your own sort. And I'm about the place, being helpful, and I already know a few things, so—well, so it makes sense that you'd, um, turn to me."

His dark head moved, the merest suggestion of a nod. "I suppose that would be an explanation. And for you?"

Just as well that Stephen was facing the other way. Mina was blushing before she'd even begun to answer. "I'm not exactly at home myself, am I? Nobody else here knows what's going on. Until the servants got used to me, I didn't talk much with anyone but you, and even now I can't tell them everything we're doing. I'm out of my depth by half, and you're a handsome man."

"You're a lovely woman," said Stephen. "I'd rather assumed that was the main cause of what's between us."

"Polly's just as pretty as I am, and you've never kissed her. But thank you."

Stephen turned to face her, laughing and surprised. "You're far from the usual sort of woman, Cerberus. I hope you know that. And how do you know I've never kissed Polly?"

"She would've said. And you're a gentleman."

"It's nice to know how you weigh the evidence," he said wryly. "And now what? Assuming you're correct, what do you propose doing about the situation?"

Mina shrugged. "Be around other people, even if we can't tell them everything? Spend more time apart? Just knowing will help, I hope. Knowing why we feel the way we do. And that it's irrational. And that nothing would work between us," she made herself add.

It was painful, and it was true. Even if Stephen's blood had been only human, it would still have been blue. If they gave in to their passion and the worst happened, she could be his pet, if he took her as a mistress, or his obligation, if he did the gentlemanly thing. She could never be his equal. She doubted if she'd ever come as close as she was now.

All she could do was throw away the last five years of her life. All she could do was discard independence and ambition and training in exchange for physical satisfaction and a connection that would disappear as soon as the situation changed.

Stephen must have known something similar, to pull away when he did. Now, however, he didn't speak either to confirm or deny Mina's assertion. He only watched her, and the shadows from the bookcase slanted across his face, hiding his expression more than his will already did.

"They say knowledge is power," Mina added, trying to speak lightly.

"That they do," said Stephen. "They might even be right now and then."

"We'll have to hope," said Mina. "And who knows? The Yard might bring Ward in tomorrow, and I'll go home, and we can both get back into our right minds."

She didn't say *everything can be like it was before*, because it wouldn't be true for her. Dragons and demons and magic weren't the sort of thing she could *un*know. For Stephen, nothing would have really changed: he would get on with whatever lords and dragons did. Later perhaps he'd tell his family about the weeks he'd had to spend hunting a sorcerer with a stubborn mortal girl. She would be a story for some winter evening, a tale that went well with brandy.

Around the tightness in her throat, she spoke again. "You should go off and do something useful. I'll be working in here."

"I'll find you if I've need," said Stephen.

"Do that," said Mina, and turned back to the books. She didn't want to watch him leave.

Twenty-two

LORD AND TYPEWRITER GIRL, HUMAN AND DRAGON-blooded, Stephen and Mina had at least this much in common: at some point, each of them had learned that keeping busy was the best way to handle trouble. For once, that lesson had not come down to Stephen from his father, but rather from Campbell, the man who'd herded cattle and done a hundred other odd jobs when Stephen had been a boy.

He couldn't mend fences now or stack wood. He could still work. Moreover, he could work to hasten the day when Ward was no longer a threat. If that was also the day when Mina left his house, then that was also for the best.

The shard of "John Smith" would help him. He couldn't do much with it as a man since the human senses didn't attune themselves very well to magic.

As a dragon, he could see much more.

When he'd sought Mina's company, he'd taken the shard with him. It was still in his pocket when he left the library, aching in both body and spirit, and strode down the hallway to what had once been a dining room.

The chairs and table were gone these days—the idea of holding a dinner party in this house now had seemed comically insane—and the floor stretched wide and bare beneath Stephen's feet. The door was locked and chained, the walls engraved with silver sigils, and silver shutters covered a huge window on the western wall. Over the last year or so, Stephen had come to know the room well.

For the first time since he'd had the room built, Stephen turned from the locked door and opened both the shutters and the window. He placed the shard carefully in one corner of the room, then sat in the last red-gold rays of sunset and waited.

He tried not to think of Mina.

This was probably the only room in the house, aside from the servants' bedrooms, that she'd never entered. Watching the sun sink behind the roofs of London, Stephen wished for an absurd and painful second that he could have showed it to Mina, that he could have seen more amazed joy in her face or danced across the smooth floor with her.

It wouldn't be possible. She might have been more curious than afraid at the sigils on the walls, but the claw marks on the floor were another story. He would see nothing but horror in Mina's face once those caught her eye.

Before Bavaria, changing shape had never been painful. Now the curse yanked him into dragon form, twisting bones and muscles like an impatient maid wringing out clothes, and for once, Stephen welcomed the pain. It was a distraction; it was also a prelude. That night, his other form would be useful.

As dusk fell over London, Stephen's body grew and twisted. Wings unfurled from his back, filling the room; claws dug more deep gouges in the floor. He threw back his head and lashed a scaled, spined tail, feeling the room and the house and the city around him far too close for his liking. He wanted to fly. He wanted to hunt.

He turned his eye to the corner, to the shard he'd placed there. Now it shone burnt orange, and a trail of the same color rose off it, climbing into the air and out the window. Stephen looked for a long moment, drew a deep breath—there was a hint of the sharp smell of the gas, though no such thing could hurt him in this form—and sprang upward.

There were no deer in this city to chase, nor gullies to soar through, but at least tonight there would be hunting of a sort.

Stephen launched himself through the window and into the spring night. The fog hid him well. For once, he was thankful for the modern world and its coal-shrouded cities. Perhaps someone would see a mysterious shape in the sky. Most would put it down to drink or weariness or the fog itself warping the silhouette of some bird. Besides, they were only human. Stephen's other form might have worried.

When he was the dragon, those concerns were very much at the back of his mind.

He spread his wings and caught an updraft, following the trail of the shard. It led across London, occasionally crossing paths with the tracks of air sprites and other creatures, but Stephen found it easy enough to follow. He watched the lights of the city below him as they flickered and shifted, and knew pity for the people who lit them, penned in their little houses and watching the night as if it was an enemy.

He had been one of them until a few minutes ago. He knew this, but the mind of the dragon was both eternal and immediate. Now he was soaring, free and strong, with the world beneath him and the sky open above him. If he'd spent the last year as a prisoner—well, what was a year? He laughed and heard the rumble of it around him.

On the streets below, people would glance upward and mutter about coming thunderstorms.

The trail he followed led across the Serpentine, and Stephen banked sharply to stay with it, descending as far as he dared. The orange color spread out ahead of him into a nebulous cloud around a clump of tall, white buildings adorned with complicated ironwork. Stephen didn't recognize them, and he was still too high up to read signs, but his human self knew that they were the abodes of wealthy men.

Without being seen, he could go no closer, but he knew that the trail stopped here in one of these buildings. There was more, too: a presence that he'd encountered before, though he couldn't see it as clearly as he could the shard's trail. In this shape, though, he could tell that it wasn't entirely human.

Then, below Stephen, a figure emerged from one of the houses. The light around it shone very brightly to him, almost too brightly to see many physical details, and in a few moments, the figure got into a carriage and drove away, becoming quickly lost in the crowds. Stephen had a momentary glimpse, though, enough to see a thin male body and long red hair.

Stephen hadn't met the man before, but he had seen him, and he knew where to find out more.

That was as much as he could achieve in dragon form. He beat his wings again and headed upward, then reluctantly back toward his home, aware that such nights of hunting would be infrequent for quite a while longer. It was a very human thought to have in this shape; repression was obviously taking its toll.

To distract himself, Stephen flew upward, above the fog, until the stars spread themselves up above him and the wind was cool around him. From high enough, even nights over London were lovely.

He wished that Mina could have seen the view.

He could almost hear her voice, marveling, and feel her slight weight on his back, her arms around his neck. She'd be brave enough for flight, Stephen knew; she'd take to it eagerly. She'd have a hundred things to say about the stars or the city from above.

It wasn't wise to dream of her. If anything, being in dragon shape should have made the differences between them all the more apparent. Mina had stated her wishes very clearly that afternoon. She'd been very sensible about it, and perhaps her plan would even work. She was a modern woman, she had a mortal family, and she hadn't asked to be any part of Stephen's world.

All the same, he looked up at the stars and saw her face.

Twenty-three

"Not hardly," said Polly, laying teaspoon in saucer with a percussive click. "I've been to the country. *Our* whole Sunday school class went when I was twelve. A treat, they said. Not much of one, I say. It rained the whole time, and there was mud everywhere."

"Not like here, then," said Mrs. Hennings.

Polly laughed. "Oh, I suppose you've a point. Mud just seems *muddier* outside the city, though, without the paved streets and that. And I suppose the flowers are pretty, but you do get pigs. And cows," she added, with a shudder that might have mostly been exaggeration.

"You wouldn't have beef for dinner if you didn't," said Mrs. Baldwin.

"But she's right," Mrs. Hennings said. "They're unsettling beasts, alive and up close. And as for pigs, they're much better in sausage form."

Mina grinned over the top of her letter. "I might agree if I'd ever met them," she said, "but I hadn't had the chance. We always went to the seaside. I think Florrie will like a few days in the country, though, and Bert too."

"It'll do them good, anyhow," said Polly.

"Even with the mud?" Mina teased her.

"Even with. The doctors say fresh air's healthy, and I'm not one to go against their advice. I'm just glad I'm grown now and strong enough that there's no need."

"Better hope you stay that way, then," said Emily.

At midday on a Sunday, the rest of the house was quiet and clean. Stephen was out.

He'd often been out since the afternoon when they'd found out about the thieves. He and Mina still had breakfast together and still talked over the newspaper. He still kept her aware of what little progress he was making, but he made sure to stay at more than arm's length. Serious and businesslike, they talked about scrying and occult clubs; abstract and scholarly, they spoke of museums and politics, and neither of them touched on anything personal.

She didn't tease him. He didn't call her "Cerberus." In the daytime, he went out, and he stayed out until he had to come home and transform. Then, often enough, he went out again.

For Mina's part, there was the kitchen: tea and cake, as often as not, and the company of the servants. The pain that became alarmingly sharp when Mina was by herself was at least duller in company, and she was coming to enjoy the servants for their own sake, as well.

From a sensible perspective, everything was going very well. Mina wished she could have felt happier about it. That would probably take time.

"Speaking of doctors," she said into the silence,

with a quick glance back at her letter to refresh what she already knew, "Mum says they're putting in one of those charity clinics a few streets down from us. She also says—heavily underlined, I might add—that one of the doctors there is a lady."

"I've heard of those," said Mrs. Hennings, cutting herself a slice of cake. "No wonder she's practicing at a charity, though. Can you imagine anyone with a choice going to a woman?"

"Especially a gentleman," said Emily, and bit back a giggle under Mrs. Baldwin's stern expression.

"My father's of the same opinion," said Mina. She glanced back at the letter, read between the lines, and smiled. "My mother isn't going to contradict him openly, but I suspect she's mostly glad to have a doctor nearby, whatever her sex. Florrie thinks it's a wonderful idea, though. I'd imagine she's already started dissecting her old dolls."

That got a laugh.

"I think it's a splendid notion," said Polly, and tossed her champagne curls. "I've had quite enough of having to"—she glanced around to make sure Mr. Baldwin was nowhere on the premises and lowered her voice—"to undress in front of some strange bloke. *And* his assistant, like as not. I know they're not supposed to care, but they're men, aren't they? Sometimes I think I might as well go on the halls and get paid for it, instead of handing over half a week's wages."

"Polly!" said Mrs. Baldwin, switching the target of her glare, and the housemaid blushed.

"I'll have you know my sister works at the

Gaiety—taking tickets, not anything else," said Mrs. Hennings, "and it's very respectable now."

Polly sniffed. "You know what I mean. What do you think of it, Mina?"

"Music halls or lady doctors?" Mina shrugged. "The halls are a jolly good time, though I wouldn't go on them myself. I'd get stage fright something fierce, for one, and I don't think I can sing more than passably well."

"And the lady doctors?" Mrs. Baldwin asked. "What's your thinking about them?"

"I don't know," Mina said. "In principle it's sound enough. I can't think of a reason a woman can't be a doctor, and a good one. But it's new, and I'd be wary of anything new, especially where medicine's concerned." She looked down at her teacup and saw her reflection: sleek hair, crisp collar, very much the New Woman. "Now is when we say something about pots and kettles," she added.

"Well, I wasna' about to mention it myself," said Mrs. Baldwin. "We've enough nurses and midwives and that at home, of course, and half of them take charge when the doctor's too far—we've a great deal of ground to cover, of course—or too new. I recall hearing as how one young sawbones fainted the first time a birth got messy, and the midwife poured the whole kettle of water over his head. It hadn't but started to warm yet, thank God."

Women among the dragons took on different roles, Mina remembered. Stephen had talked about one of his sisters fighting in a battle, and she'd found a few older and less-well-labeled books, journals from the look of them, that suggested as much, as well as other things about dragons. In a land where they had ruled for centuries and where they'd done a great deal to keep out the rest of the world, perhaps their attitudes had spread even to those who were entirely mortal.

"Must be hard," said Mrs. Hennings, "living so far away. With so much distance between people, that is."

"Betimes it is," said Mrs. Baldwin. "But we're great walkers and fair riders, at that, and we've always been welcome into the great house if there's a storm. His lairdship's father and then his lairdship and now Lady Judith have always put up a good meal for it. Sometimes they'll have a dance or a bit of a play, and these days they'll play the gramophone. So the distance doesn't seem so far. There's been talk of putting a railway station in nearby, at that." She poured herself another cup of tea.

"Would you want that?" asked Emily. "All those people coming in?"

"No, though I suppose it wouldn't really matter. We don't have much to make them stay, so they'd just drop off a few goods and leave. And I wouldn't mind coming back to London *sometimes*," Mrs. Baldwin said, very severe on the last word, "to see the sights."

"You won't be staying here?" Polly asked.

"Not forever, most likely. I'd imagine they'll have the house kept open, of course, and come up from time to time as business demands, or for the Season."

"He'd have to come up for the Season," said Mrs. Hennings. "Oldest son and not married? They must be at him with hot irons."

The cake felt very thick in Mina's mouth. She

swallowed it, a slow and painful process, and gulped too-hot tea until she could speak again. "We don't know that he isn't married. Or hasn't been."

"He hasn't," said Mrs. Baldwin, "but he's not likely to take a wife from the London debutantes."

"Poor fragile things," said Mrs. Hennings. "They'd never survive a winter in Scotland. And he hasn't seemed terribly concerned, at that. Does his family generally choose ladies somewhere nearer home?"

Mina didn't let herself look away from the conversation. She did put her teacup down as casually as she could, while she waited to hear Mrs. Baldwin's answer.

No answer came. The bell for the study rang before Mrs. Baldwin could speak, and the housekeeper excused herself to attend the call.

"The Season," said Emily, when Mrs. Baldwin had gone. "Sounds divine, doesn't it?"

"Sounds uncomfortable," said Polly. "Not knowing if a man's dancing with you because he likes you or because he has to. I wouldn't mind one of those fancy white dresses, though. The kind with the train as long as me."

"Imagine how long it would take to sew that," said Mina, flexing her fingers and wincing. "But that's art for you, isn't it?" she added, on further consideration. "I bet Michelangelo's hands were sore too, after he finished David."

"A dress isn't the same thing," said Mrs. Hennings, mildly shocked.

"It's something beautiful," said Emily.

Mrs. Baldwin returned with her cheeks flushed and

her eyes glittering. "Leisure's over as of now, I'd say." Suiting actions to words, she began clearing away the china. "His lairdship's brother arrives on the nine o'clock train."

Twenty-four

A cab deposited Colin MacAlasdair on his brother's doorstep around quarter to ten, and Baldwin showed him into the drawing room a few minutes later. Stephen looked up from his correspondence—a particularly unctuous proposal concerning a bill in the House of Lords—and did not remark on the time. "Colin," he said, standing and holding out a hand. "It's good to see you, man."

His younger brother looked much as he'd done ten years before: taller and more slender than Stephen, ash to his oak, with silver-gray eyes and a bluish tinge to his dark hair. His clothes were in the height of fashion, and the silver pin in his cravat was an old Viking rune: fair speech, if Stephen remembered correctly.

"And yourself," said Colin, with his usual easy grin. He draped himself over a sofa. "Going over the accounts, are you? I swear I've not been spending any more than usual—and besides, I've been self-sufficient for years now."

"Have you? How did you manage that?"

"Opals. Remarkable wee stones. Went to Brazil,

dug out a fair lot when nobody was around to see me, and now I sell one off here and there whenever I need a new coat or the like. Limestone's hardly a challenge if a man has privacy enough."

"Technically, I think that's theft."

"Theft, nothing. I stayed well away from any open mines. And it's not my fault if a man can't tell where to dig, is it? Have you turned teetotal, Stephen, or might a weary fellow find a drop of wine around this place?"

Despite himself, Stephen smiled and rang for Baldwin. Wine arrived soon enough, along with a small plate of cheese and fruit. The kitchen had been anticipating Colin's visit, evidently.

"It's not that I don't welcome your company," Stephen said when they'd each had time for a few sips, "but what precisely are you doing here?"

"Thought I'd catch the Season, didn't I? It's been a few years. They must have added something new."

"I very much doubt that," said Stephen.

"The innovation or my motives?"

"Both."

"You wound me, Brother, you wound me deeply."

"We heal fast, as a rule. Who is it—father or husband?"

Colin grinned. "Uncle, actually, for a change. Very large, very unreasonable man with very large and unreasonable sons. Luckily for them, I'm a great believer in subtlety and restraint—and the family sells a fine quality of whiskey." He sat up with the sudden change that marked any of his motions and looked seriously at Stephen. "And I do get the *Times*, you know. Loch Arach, Dublin, Bath—wherever I'm keeping myself. I keep up my subscription, and I have a fair memory for names. Colonel Moore is dead and I hadn't heard from you."

"Scarce enough evidence to go on."

"Enough evidence to come down to London, surely. It hardly takes much. Am I right?"

Stephen sighed. "You are. Ward's back, probably mad, and certainly a sight more powerful than when he ran off. He's commanding demons now, not to mention more mortal forces."

"Then I'll be of use to you," Colin took another, fairly large sip of wine and stretched himself out on the sofa again, staring up at the ceiling. "Let's see. Baldwin said he'd find me a room and put my belongings there. I didn't pack much for handling the occult, but I'm sure you'll be able to supply what's needed. We'll talk about it tomorrow. Meanwhile, we've plenty to catch up on—unless the demons will come howling in any minute or you're charging out to meet the cad on the field of battle."

"No," said Stephen. "I'm waiting to see a lady who's out of town at the present. But there is one other person you should know about."

Few things seemed to have changed about Colin, and one of the eternal constants was his inability to wake up before noon. Therefore, it was at dinner that Stephen introduced his brother to Mina, and he went into the meal with his nerves on edge.

As the dining room was distinctly out of service, they ate in the drawing room where he and Mina had breakfast. By night, it took on a different air, and an odd one: formal and intimate at the same time.

When Mina came in the door, Stephen found himself acutely aware of two things. The first was that she was stunningly beautiful; the second that her life had been very different from his. She wore a violet dress printed with tiny white flowers. The color made her eyes and skin luminous, and the cut outlined the trim curves of her body, but the neckline was high and the sleeves were long. Her hair shone the color of dark honey and fell more gently about her face than usual, but it was still done simply, and she wore no jewelry.

Of course Mina didn't own a dinner gown. She wouldn't have had any need of one. Stephen was a heel for not thinking of it. Even as he stepped forward to make the introductions, he saw Mina's eyes go to his coat and tie, then drop to her own clothing. Otherwise, her face betrayed only pleasant interest.

Painfully conscious that there was nothing he could do now, Stephen helped her to the seat opposite Colin and waited as Baldwin served. He'd been nervous before; now he feared that this would be a very long hour.

"Miss Seymour," he said into the silence, "is a friend of Professor Carter."

"His secretary, actually," said Mina.

"I've heard of him. Not as much as Stephen, of course," Colin said. His accent had shifted somewhat over the last few years. Now there were shades of English in it and a bit of Irish, as well. It still conjured up memories of home for Stephen but not as strongly. "What's he been having you do, then? Lug around books on Egypt?"

"The Etruscans, mostly," said Mina, "and the Romans. The Vikings, too, lately. They're an interesting lot—a lot more complicated than you'd think, even if they didn't spin all the webs the Romans did."

"Hard for anybody to manage that, I'd think," said Colin. "Jolly strange, too. I was in Italy for a time. Gave me an absolute horror of politics."

"How fond of them were you before?" Mina asked, and both brothers laughed: Colin in admission, Stephen in triumph.

"He's got the sense to leave that to me," said Stephen, "for my sins."

"I like to put all problems into the hands of experts. Or at least into the hands of someone other than me. Luckily, being the younger son generally means I can."

"Do you have any other siblings?" Mina asked.

"One sister living," said Stephen, with a readiness that would have shocked the man he'd been six weeks ago. He'd always tried not to give specifics of his family to outsiders. "She keeps very close to home."

"These days," said Colin. "I can recall a time you wouldn't have caught Judith nearer to Loch Arach than the Channel. At least not for more than a day or two."

"Aye, but she's older than either of us, and there's only so much of the world one can see."

Mina smiled. "My mother will be glad to hear that. I've got a brother at sea—same malady that your sister used to have, from the sound of it. If he's in one place for too long, I swear he grows feverish."

Sailors' stories followed—the ones Mina's brother had told and the ones Colin had picked up over the years, or at least the less scandalous of his assortment. Mina listened avidly, talked animatedly, and laughed a good deal, with her head tilted back and her eyes gleaming.

She should wear amethysts, Stephen thought suddenly, or pearls, the large silver-gray sort. They should dangle from her ears so that they swayed when she laughed, and they should fit into the hollow of her throat, a place currently covered by far too much violet cloth. Come to that, she should have a damned dinner gown, something with silk and gauze. Mina would do more credit to such things than any woman Stephen had ever seen wearing them.

Naturally, she would never accept any such gifts from him. Men nowadays didn't give clothing or jewelry to women other than relations, wives, or mistresses. Stephen would have cursed the rule as one more modern complication, except that he didn't recall ever really *wanting* to give either to a woman before. He'd exchanged presents with relatives on the appropriate occasions; he'd given baubles to mistresses likewise, though his last such connection had been a century in the past; but he'd never really given any thought to the matter beforehand.

"…but I wouldn't say that Stephen's exactly led a settled life himself," said Colin.

Drawing Stephen out of his thoughts had doubtless not been the point of the remark, but Stephen silently blessed his brother for it anyhow. "Settled enough, in comparison. But perhaps I can travel again one day when I've untangled Father's papers and so on. I'd like to visit Russia again."

"My brother, you see, is a man of singular tastes. This one seems to be for freezing to death."

Obligingly, Mina pretended to shiver, but she also turned toward Stephen, and her gaze was far more curious than horrified. "I've seen pictures of the churches there," she said. "The ones with the domes. They'd be quite a view from up close, I'd think."

"Aye, and the icons. There's a great deal of skill there," said Stephen, "and a fair bit of history. Even if half the fake mediums today do affect a Russian accent."

"Well, if it wasn't Russian, it would be French," said Mina. "Nobody would believe that someone from Surrey could part the mystic veil."

"If they could, they wouldn't live in Surrey," said Colin, grinning.

Awkwardness was no threat. Colin and Mina got on like a house on fire. Looking at one and then the other, Stephen realized that he wasn't at all certain how he felt about that.

Twenty-five

Whatever you've heard, Mina wrote, *I promise I'm doing quite well.*

She paused and picked up her pen, examining the drying ink of her last line in the ray of morning sunlight that slanted in through the drawing-room window. Going on might prove difficult, since she didn't want to tell her family any more lies than had already been necessary. The desire for honesty dueled with the equally strong desires not to give away anything Ward could use and not to be thought mad.

Setting pen to paper again, she wrote, *Everyone has been very polite and respectful*, which was true enough, really. After the first antagonistic kiss, Mina had either initiated anything impolite with Stephen or had been a very eager participant in it. Her mother certainly didn't need to know about any of that, regardless.

> *I'm still not certain when Lord MacAlasdair will conclude his business. I do have every hope that it will be resolved soon. I look forward to seeing you again, and to—*

To what?

Resuming her old life was the obvious answer. Over the last few weeks, she'd become certain that Professor Carter *would* take her back, no matter how tarnished her reputation grew, and Mina thought she'd even been careful enough to avoid much scandal. She would go back to typing his notes, living in her boardinghouse and going home for Sunday dinners, walking in the park on fair days and visiting museums when it rained. Now she'd have at least a hundred pounds more in her pocket, and that would let her sleep very soundly indeed, shield that it was against illness or mishap.

It should have been plenty. She'd had a piece of extraordinary luck. It would give her a good foundation to go forward, and Mina *did* feel happy when she thought of it—or at least mostly happy.

The problem was that she knew more now. Through chance, she'd found out about aspects of the world that most people would never have guessed, or even believed if they'd heard. Going back to being a secretary now, having seen dragons and cast spells, would probably be as unsatisfying as staying home and marrying had seemed when she'd been fifteen and reading about expeditions to the Nile.

Perhaps Professor Carter would let her take more of a hand with his research. Or maybe she'd join one of the occult societies like the Emerald Star. Stephen could probably sponsor her, if she asked. Those were brighter prospects, but even thinking of them didn't go all the way toward lightening Mina's spirits.

When the library door opened, she looked up, glad of the interruption.

"I didn't mean to intrude," said Stephen, with an awkward smile. "I was looking for Baldwin or one of the maids."

"There are bells, aren't there?"

"It wasn't important enough to summon anyone, not with the house so short-handed. I'd wanted to find out if Colin was awake yet, is all."

Mina laughed. "I'm afraid you wouldn't like the answer. I've got no way of knowing for sure, of course," she added, "but given the last day or two, if I were a betting woman—"

"Aye, I'd thought as much myself," Stephen said. "And I've several centuries behind my guess."

"I guess he's a little old for you to have someone go in with a sponge."

"A sponge?"

"You soak it in cold water, and then you wring it out over the vic—sleeping person," Mina explained and then giggled at Stephen's grimace. "I'm surprised you hadn't heard of it. It's a handy trick when you've got brothers."

"For waking them up, do you mean, or for some sort of sisterly vengeance?"

"Well, either," Mina said as a few memories came back to her. "Though I was never much for pranks myself. That was Alice, and George, when he was younger."

"You don't seem like the sort to take that meekly," Stephen said.

"I wasn't. I had a good memory, and I was better at saving my pocket money. So I'd buy sweets and eat them in front of the other two when they made me angry. I was," Mina added, on further reflection, "a horribly smug sort of little girl. Probably deserved at least some of what I got, although I still think cutting off my braids was going too far, and so did Mum."

"I cut Judith's hair off once," Stephen admitted. "But then, she'd asked me to. It was too hot in summer, she said. That didn't save me from my mother, though." He winced.

"Strict sort of woman, was she?"

"Fierce, I'd say. But she had to be, I'd think, to live among the rest of us and have begun as a mortal."

"Begun?" Mina asked, pretending that her heart hadn't speeded up.

Stephen hesitated a moment, standing in the doorway with his hands in his pockets. Then he shrugged, stepped in, and closed the door behind him. "It changes wi' the first child," he said and looked toward the window. "It's to do with shared blood, perhaps. A mortal either gains longer life or...well, or doesna' survive, generally. The child does sometimes, even if she dies. A cousin of mine did."

"Brave women," Mina said, after swallowing past a sudden thickness in her throat. She wasn't sure what else to think. She wasn't sure it was her business to think anything about that particular subject. She dropped her gaze from Stephen's face, down to the letter she'd been writing, and when she looked up again, she couldn't meet his eyes. "Though life was more dangerous back then for everyone, I'd think."

"In many ways, aye," he said. "I think back sometimes—even to what I can remember, which isn't nearly so far—and I wonder at how we ever managed." A quick smile lightened his face. "But then, perhaps every man thinks so about his youth."

Mina laughed, taking the chance to change topics away from birth and death. "I tend to wonder how I survived, but that's mostly because of Alice and George. And me," she admitted, thinking back. "Especially when I was old enough to get into *real* trouble."

"You? I can't imagine it," said Stephen.

"Sarcasm doesn't become you, my lord," Mina said and sniffed, hiding a smile.

"It wasn't all sarcasm," he said. "I consider myself a fair man, after all, and so I'm bound to admit that I've only seen you get yourself in trouble the once. And," he added, taking one hand out of his pocket and stroking his chin slowly, "that was on someone else's behalf. Rather admirable, in fact."

Mina couldn't hide her smile, and now it no longer came from amusement. "Thank you," she said. "Professor Carter took a chance on me. It only seemed fair."

"It's not so common for women to be secretaries, not to men," Stephen said slowly, calling up facts that had never been important to his mind and had never really left Mina's.

"No. And even less common for girls from my part of London." Even now, the memory of the first few letters of inquiry she'd sent out made Mina wince, and remembering her first interview made her mouth go dry. "So I owe him a lot, you see."

Stephen nodded. "You pay your debts," he said, still in the same thoughtful voice. His eyes met hers, searching, though Mina couldn't tell for what. "And you don't go back on a bargain. You said as much, didn't you?"

"I did," she said. "And I don't." Under Stephen's gaze, she felt quite exposed. She folded her arms over her chest, putting up a barrier that was all the more necessary because she wouldn't have minded a more literal sort of exposure. "Have you found anything more? Is that why you're looking for your brother?"

"Not yet." Stephen sighed, and while that broke the uncomfortable intensity, he looked weary enough to make Mina wince inside. "I'm hoping for a message any day now, but Mrs. O'Keefe's man had little to say concerning when she'd return."

"Little to say about anything, from what you told me," said Mina, and shrugged. "Butlers are generally like that. Not that I know many of them, but that's what Alice says. I tried to be the same way with Professor Carter's visitors. You have to."

"I rather guessed as much," said Stephen, and Mina was glad to see a smile return to his face. "Perhaps you should speak with Mrs. O'Keefe's man—I'd match you against him any day."

"Now I feel like a prizefighter," said Mina. "Be off, will you, before you make the spiders angry?"

"I believe I can defend you from *those*," said Stephen, "but I'd best find Colin and perhaps wring a sponge out over him."

"I'll see who has the black eye next time we meet."

Laughing, Stephen left, and Mina stared at the closed door behind him for longer than she meant to, a fact she only noticed when she shook herself and turned her attention back to her letter.

I look forward to seeing you again, and to—

Life after dealing with Ward held bright enough prospects, if Mina went after them—and she knew she would. The real problem, the one she'd been trying to hide from herself, was how much she'd miss the life she had now.

Twenty-six

"Six weeks?" Colin leaned back in his chair and laughed. "She's a remarkably patient girl, then. I'd have been climbing the walls."

"You'd have been climbing the walls after two days," said Stephen. "Even if you'd wanted to stay inside before. Contrary-minded little devil," he added.

"Prig," Colin replied amiably. "She must be a torment to you in turn, though."

Stephen quickly stifled the reaction that went through him. Torment, yes, but not the sort he wanted to discuss with his brother. "How do you mean?"

"She doesn't seem the sort to follow orders meekly."

"You make me sound like quite the tyrant," said Stephen, because he couldn't deny Colin's statement. "I've not had any complaints. Not from most people," he added, "and Mi—Miss Seymour doesn't truly complain. She's been quite adaptable."

"Has she, now?"

"Not like that," said Stephen, glaring even as he repressed more memories. "We've strictly a business arrangement, and only for as long as Ward's a threat."

Early afternoon had found them in the drawing room again. Rather, Colin had found Stephen there reading, and now stood by the fireplace and toyed idly with the music box there while he spoke. "Pity," he said, "I'd imagine you could use a good secretary."

"Perhaps I could," said Stephen, "but she'll be employed elsewhere."

Even if he made the offer, he knew that Mina would refuse and be absolutely right in doing so. He wasn't going to make the offer, of course. Foolish idea.

"Where is the girl in question, exactly?"

"Probably the library," said Stephen, who had avoided that door. He and Mina had talked at breakfast. They would dine with Colin again, and he had no need to see her any more, even if he wanted to. Especially if he wanted to. "She's going through the books there, and it's about time someone did."

"Not surprising. Father wasn't much for cataloguing."

"Father rather lost track of this place," Stephen said, thinking of the papers he'd gone through. "Came up for a day or four at a time, since Mother passed onward, but never more, and that maybe every few years."

"I hadn't known," said Colin. "Well, I hadn't been home so very often, had I? But I might have suspected it, if I'd thought. Cities were never his glory, and this one's grown so. Did he leave things in a very bad state?"

"I wouldn't say bad. We're hardly short on funds. Only confused, and this business with Ward hasn't helped my progress any." Stephen sighed. "I'm not Father—I enjoyed London the last time I was here. I think I could again, would events let me."

"Oh, they will in time," said Colin. He put down the music box. "Even the most tangled of accounts end, and if you're really tired of Ward, you could simply go away. He'll die in a few decades."

"He might," said Stephen, "but he hasn't so far, and he has the resources to put it off, or to turn his rage on those with fewer defenses than I have. I hadn't known that he'd found more magical tutors, or I'd have hunted him down after Bavaria, whether he came for me or no."

"You're remarkably puny to try and be Atlas," said Colin. "Nobody here is in your charge, you know."

"There's a wider charge," said Stephen. "And you can't tell me you'd leave them to be set upon by demons. Not seriously."

"I tell you as little as possible seriously." Colin sighed and shifted his weight, leaning against the fireplace now. "Ah, well. If you're going to take this on, and I knew you would, I might as well help. Have you tried—"

Whatever his suggestion was going to be, it died before it reached the air, killed off by a knock at the door. Polly entered at Stephen's request, with a sealed letter in her hand.

"This came by the last post, sir," she said and handed it to Stephen.

The man you seek calls himself Mr. Green. His address follows. I've informed him of your interest. He may speak with you, if he chooses to do so.

Selina O'Keefe

"Not an invitation to a garden party, I suppose," said Colin.

"The lady I'd mentioned before. She's back in town, and it seems she doesn't want to meet with me personally." Stephen eyed the gracefully written lines, wishing they'd contained more. "She doesn't sound like she's at all easy about the whole business."

"Would you be?"

"I'm not."

"Shall I come along? I do enjoy meeting new people."

"New women, which I doubt you'll find at Green's," said Stephen, "and no. I'd rather keep you in reserve."

Colin shrugged. "Very well. I'll use the time to inspect your defenses."

"Don't inspect too closely," said Stephen. "I don't have many servants left as it is."

"Oh, now," Colin said, laughing, "I've never been the sort to make a girl give notice. You know that."

"I know if I get back and you've a palm print on your face, I'll use it for a target myself." Stephen slipped the note into his pocket and headed for the hallway. "Have Baldwin get me a carriage, will you?"

"Wounded as I am, I'll still leap to carry out your request," Colin said with a mock bow, "being the noble, gentlemanly sort that I am."

"Today would be good," said Stephen. "Preferably before nightfall."

He went to find Mina, reasoning to himself that it was prudent to let her know the situation, particularly as it involved her finding herself alone with Colin. Of course, his brother *was* a gentleman or an approximation thereof, teasing to the contrary, but she didn't know that. Consideration alone demanded that Stephen pay her a brief visit.

Stephen told himself that and also that his heart should stay absolutely still, except for the necessary blood-pumping activities, when he stood at the door to the library and watched Mina returning a book to the shelves. Even that simple action had a purposeful sort of grace to it, and when she turned, her dress shifted to outline the firm curves of her body. Stephen caught his breath.

"Oh!" She saw him and jumped a little. "I—didn't know you were there."

"I won't be. Er, I'm going out. There's a message."

"Progress?" She didn't move toward Stephen, but when she met his eyes, the distance between the two of them felt much shorter regardless.

He nodded, ignoring—or trying to ignore—the urge to reach out and draw Mina to him. "I shouldn't be gone long. If I am—" The thought of ambush had occurred to him. "If I don't return in an hour's time, assume something's happened. Get yourself to safety. And the others."

"I will," she said, and her full lips frowned. "But you take care. Do you have to go alone?"

"So the message says. Er—" He coughed. "You can trust Colin."

"If there's trouble?"

"As a general rule. He's a good enough man, whatever he pretends. I didn't want you to worry."

"I didn't," said Mina, blinking, "but thank you for telling me. How dangerous do you think this will be?"

"Not very, I should think," said Stephen, and hoped he was right. "It's only a meeting. I'd just…I'd wanted to be sure you knew the situation."

Mina smiled, puzzled but touched, and not kissing her then was one of the harder things Stephen had done lately. "Thank you," she said. "I'll…well, I'll be here."

He left her standing in a pool of lamplight, looking very small in the middle of the hallway. The image stayed with him through the slow carriage ride—it seemed that every hack in London was out that night—and onto "Mr. Green's" doorstep. A feeling of deep unease went with him too. He felt like a man watching clouds grow dark in the west and waiting to hear the first rumble of thunder.

Colin would look after everyone, Stephen reminded himself. Colin was no slouch in a fight and not half bad with magic, either, dilettante though he was. He certainly wouldn't make trouble for the staff. Baldwin and his wife knew him of old, and as for the others, Colin had always been rather engaging.

Half the dairymaids at Loch Arach had been in love with him by the time he was eighteen, in fact, and more than a few of the farmers' daughters.

That was Loch Arach, of course. London girls were more sophisticated and far more cynical. Neither Polly nor Emily seemed the type to moon about after a gentleman, no matter how charming, and Mina—well, no. Mina had a mind like a scalpel and the will of a particularly stubborn mule. Colin would stand no chance with her.

Certainly not.

The possibility wasn't even worth thinking about.

Twenty-seven

Dragons, Mina was rapidly learning, could be as boring as anyone else.

She was a quarter of the way into the journal she was reading, was reasonably sure that the author was a dragon—he made frequent mentions of "transformation" and of flying—and had spent half her time almost pinching herself to stay awake. The man had done half of his estate records in his journal, for one thing, and had also apparently had very decided opinions about his nearest neighbor.

In between sheep and hounds, Mina had found a few interesting bits: a paragraph about what seemed very coldly cordial relations with the "Great Ones of the East" (or, the way he spelled it, "ye Great Ones of the Eaft") and a mention of sending his priest to "settle" a haunted house.

Like half-buried gems, those few sentences kept her digging.

Eleanor arrived today from France,

the latest entry began,

and brought with her the children, who are growing well. She wishes to add to their number, and I have no objection, but I would wait a while before the rite, so as to ensure that our youngest may be born in the spring. Meanwhile, as I've observed before, it does no harm to practice the mortal portion of the marital act.

Mina stared.

The writing, though old, was very proper. The author hadn't yet in her reading been vulgar or even profane, which had come as a bit of a surprise to Mina in the first place. Just when she'd gotten used to a nobleman apparently fitting the image of the kindly and proper lord in children's books, he was writing about the "marital act," which apparently had extra aspects if you were a dragon and wanted to achieve the traditional result.

She knew that a number of human rituals concerned themselves with that part of life. She'd read a few books she wasn't supposed to read, and she'd typed a few pages of notes that Professor Carter had harrumphingly warned her about beforehand. From a scholarly perspective, mentions of "the rite" were quite interesting and not at all surprising.

What the journal writer meant, unless Mina was very wrong, was that if a dragon-man and a human simply had a bit of fun—as they might have said back home when they were being polite—then the lady wouldn't end up in a fix for it. At least, that seemed to be the case.

For example, if she and Stephen—

Of course, that was when the door opened.

Mina was up from her seat before she knew what she was doing, putting her back to the wall and wishing she had a better weapon than a fountain pen.

"Easy, lass," said Colin MacAlasdair, laughing and leaning against the doorway. "I promise I've not come to muck up your filing, nor yet to steal a book."

"They're your books," said Mina. She dropped the letter opener back on her desk. "I'm sorry. I'm a bundle of nerves today, it seems."

"Spending as long as you have here, I'm surprised you've *not* tried to kill anyone yet. Though I'd prefer it not be me you target when your mind does snap. You'd break the hearts of so many women."

"God forbid," said Mina. On a whim, she closed the book and handed it over to Colin. "Do you know who might've written this? Stephen didn't, but—"

A second too late to catch herself, she heard Stephen's Christian name come from her lips. Done was done; flinching or correcting herself would only call more attention to what she'd said.

"He's foisted himself on fewer of our relatives than I have," Colin said, as if he'd heard nothing out of the usual. After a few minutes flipping through the book, he laughed and shook his head.

"You don't know?"

"Oh, I do. I was just feeling sorry for you reading it," said Colin, "and a bit for my cousins, living with the man. It's my Uncle Georgie, and a man more fond of speeches you never met. Though he was a good sort, at that."

Mina glanced out past the door and saw that the hallway was empty. "A dragon named George?" she asked, keeping her voice quiet despite the immediate lack of witnesses. "Your family likes irony, doesn't it?"

"As it happens," said Colin, shutting the door, "the legend's gotten it a bit twisted. Which is just as well for us, really."

"Oh?"

Ignoring the several perfectly good chairs around the room, Colin perched on the windowsill like an overgrown schoolboy. "From time to time," he said, "one of us gets stuck, ye ken. The oldest ones didn't, from everything I can tell, but the oldest ones were free from all sorts of difficulties that we have now."

"Like, ah, continuing the line?" Mina asked. She gestured at the journal. "He mentions a, um, rite."

She looked away from Colin's face as she spoke, lest he see too much interest in hers and connect it to his brother, but his reply came easily and casually. "Aye—it's why we've not outnumbered you mortals, living as long as we do. Something about being neither truly mortal nor truly not. We're somewhere in between, like—"

"—a stuck window?"

Colin laughed. "That'll do, though it'll never make a poem. At any rate, the same thing goes for changing form. Sometimes we get trapped in one shape or another. When it's man shape, there's no worry in it, save that the man sometimes misses dragon's form. When one of us loses himself—or herself—in the dragon, though, that's a worry."

"For more than being conspicuous?"

"So I hear. It's not happened any time in my day, but…" From the windowsill, Colin eyed her for a minute, considering whether to go on. "The thing about…beings that aren't human…is that most of them aren't people."

"I'd rather assumed that," said Mina.

Colin shook his head. "No, I mean they're not just men in funny suits. They see the world differently. They see *humans* differently. You've grown into certain sentiments that I don't have, but I'm far more human than the…Elder Folk, let's call them. Not all of them see human beings as prey, mind—Stephen and I wouldn't be here otherwise—but when a dragon goes mean, it goes very mean very quickly. And a man stuck in dragon shape can slide almost as fast."

In dragon form, Stephen had been about five times Mina's size. She remembered flaming eyes and teeth like razors. "What happens then? When someone does get trapped?"

"Depends on how it happens, I'd think," said Colin. "I've heard that some of them go away to live…elsewhere…and I suppose they do well enough at it. There's more society than the human sort, after all, if you know how to find it. But if they become a danger to others, then the rest of us generally see to the matter."

"And that was Saint George," said Mina, a little faintly. Part of her was still trying to deal with *elsewhere*.

"That was Saint George," Colin agreed. "Not actually my uncle. The name's been passed down, you understand. The name of the one he killed…hasn't."

"Seems like hard luck for him."

"It might have been. Stories say he'd been an unpleasant sort even before the change. But then, we'd say that afterward, regardless. We're not completely immune to certain human tendencies, after all, and one of them is rewriting history."

Colin didn't really look anything other than human, not then. Lounging in the faint sunlight, wearing a gray tweed suit that probably had cost more than Mina earned in two years, he could have been any idle young man about town. Stephen gave off a much greater feeling of power. Certainly he was the less forthcoming of the two.

Despite those considerations—or perhaps because of them—Colin's presence was much less comfortable. Mina couldn't imagine talking to this man over breakfast, and not just because she'd never seen him there. She certainly couldn't imagine trying to reassure him when he felt guilty.

Kissing him was completely out of the question. Mina would as soon have tried to hug the tiger at the zoo.

"You said I've got certain sentiments that you don't," she said.

"It's a bit of an assumption, I admit," said Colin, "but yes. We all grow up with a set of rules, aye? And even if you break them," he went on, with an arch smile that said he had some experience with that idea, "you still know you're crossing a line and you might have to pay for it later. Your rules are different than mine. So are your consequences. When you can't just outlive your enemies—or your friends—it gives you a different perspective on the straight and narrow."

Mina took a deep breath. "And Stephen's perspective is like yours?"

"Oh, in some ways. But he's always known he was to be the next master of Loch Arach—our lands back home. That makes a difference too. An heir isn't an *entirely* separate species from his younger brother, perhaps, but then, neither are my people an *entirely* separate species from human beings."

Thinking of Florrie and Bert, and then of herself and Alice, Mina laughed. "Siblings, then? Our two… peoples, I mean?"

"As metaphors go, it'll do well enough. If you're worried over Stephen," Colin said, looking at her with sudden clarity, "don't be. He's an honorable man, and I don't mean like Brutus. Poor fool."

"Brutus or Stephen?"

"Either, I'd think. Though I've only known one of them personally."

"Good," said Mina. "I'd hate to think you'd been keeping bad company."

"Oh, I always do that. Except now, of course."

A wink turned him back from an ancient and strange creature into a feckless young man, and Mina had to giggle. "Of course," she said dryly, "and I appreciate the courtesy. Did you come in here just to compliment me?"

"Not at all. I thought I'd take a bit of a tour around the place. After all, Stephen's left me in charge of the defenses, reluctant as he might have been. I'll have to try very hard to live up to his example."

"At least in some ways," said Mina. Handsome as Colin was, she'd prefer he didn't try to follow his brother's lead in all things.

Twenty-eight

From a human perspective, "Mr. Green's" home was one towering new building in a large square of them. At noon, they cast long shadows over the street, and the door that Stephen approached was a full foot taller than he was. It was ornate as well, covered with gold leaf and fanciful designs, as well as the ironwork he'd seen when he'd flown overhead.

The whole building challenged the would-be visitor. The size and the ornamentation drew the eye but asked a question at the same time: *Are you good enough for this place? What can you offer?* Stephen, who'd seen the whole square from a vantage that made it look the size of a postage stamp, felt not a single moment of hesitation, but he recognized the demand nonetheless.

The butler who answered the door, dubious and remote, made the question more apparent. Taking in Stephen and his wardrobe with a single glance, he switched from suspicion to respect. "I'm afraid," he said, "that Mr. Green isn't at home today."

Mina had tried the same code. Mina had, even as an obstructive stranger, possessed a great deal more in the way of personal attractions, and Stephen's business had been somewhat less urgent.

"Then," said Stephen, "I'll wait until he is."

The butler coughed. "That may be some time, sir."

"As a matter of fact," Stephen said, "I rather doubt that. I'll wait in the parlor while you tell him I'm here."

Their eyes met. The butler was an old hand and doubtless *could* freeze most unwelcome visitors with a glance, but Stephen was constitutionally immune to being frozen. It rather went with the heritage.

Bowing slightly, the other man stood away from the door and showed Stephen in. "In here, sir," he said, gesturing to a doorway. "What name shall I give Mr. Green?"

"Lord Stephen MacAlasdair," said Stephen. Then, remembering what Green was—or more accurately, what he was *not*—and the urgency of his mission, he added, "Alasdair of Loch Arach's son and heir."

Stephen had always had a surname. His father had gone by "MacAlasdair" as well for the last few centuries and had laughed at it occasionally—"The youth is father to the man," he'd quoted—but he'd come of age long before a man needed more than one name. When dealing with creatures like Green, he'd always dropped the pretense.

No reaction crossed the butler's narrow face. "Very good, sir," he said without expression and retreated, leaving Stephen to make himself comfortable in the parlor.

Blues and browns predominated there, in a small room full of overstuffed chairs and strange crystalline carvings that demanded much less than the outside of

Green's home. Outside, Stephen thought as he toyed with a peacock-feather pen, the original owner had wanted to announce himself to the world. Inside, Green evidently didn't care as much.

He wondered if he would have realized any such thing before he'd known Mina. He'd always had people to deal with his lodgings and his wardrobe; he'd left the details to them. Stephen couldn't recall, now, ever thinking how the world must look to a man who was confined to one shape, or to one who didn't have money and lineage at his back.

Frowning, Stephen put the pen down and picked up a deck of playing cards. On their backs, strange creatures wandered through unearthly woodland scenes, all obviously hand-painted with some skill. He turned one over.

A blue-eyed woman looked back up at him. Her golden hair fell from beneath an equally golden crown with heart-shaped rubies marching around the band and curled on the shoulders of her rich red dress.

The Queen of Hearts.

Stephen flipped the card back over and put the deck down. Unable to sit still any longer, he rose and paced a circle around the room, glad of the challenge that avoiding footstools and end tables posed. Where the devil *was* Green? Slipping out the back, perhaps, while his man kept Stephen waiting? Stephen had half a mind to go looking.

"Mr. Green," said the butler, opening the parlor door.

At home, Green looked even less conventional than he had in Mrs. O'Keefe's club. He entered with his flaming-red hair loose around his shoulders; he wore a smoking jacket in black and gold brocade, loose silk trousers, and no shoes. His bright green eyes ran over Stephen for a long, unsettling moment. The gaze might have been lecherous or it might have been knowing; it could well have been both.

"Lord Stephen MacAlasdair," he said. "Unexpected and, I hear, insistent. How very…dramatic. You may leave us," he added, waving a hand at the butler.

Colored fire flashed in the lamplight. Green didn't wear shoes, but he did cover his hands with gemstones. Stephen wasn't surprised.

"My business is important," he said, "and a matter of some haste." Etiquette advised that he apologize for the intrusion, but etiquette didn't generally handle men who made deadly homunculi.

"So I'd inferred. Still, I'll take the liberty of assuming that it won't take us out of this house," said Green, draping himself over one of the chairs, "and ask you to make yourself comfortable. I'd offer refreshment, but I'm not entirely sure I have your sort of food." He met Stephen's eyes squarely and smiled. "Maidens are very rare these days, you know. I've seen all sorts of articles saying as much."

"And from what *I've* read," said Stephen, "I know enough to be careful of any food you'd serve me."

That was an educated guess and a general principle of dealing with the Unseen World, but it hit. Green's eyes flickered, and a hint of concession appeared in his smile. "And so the dance begins," he said. "I had wondered, you know. Reclusive as you've been, Alasdair's son, your name is not unknown in certain circles. Neither are your whereabouts."

"And you're part of those circles?"

One didn't ask for names or titles. There were rules.

"Indeed. You could think of me as an ambassador, if you wanted." For a second, Green's eyes turned from human green to the deep color of the primeval forests. "And no, I won't tell you from which court."

"I could hazard a guess or two, perhaps," said Stephen, sitting down in a chair opposite Green, "but I'm more curious about other things. Whether making homunculi falls under your diplomatic duties, for instance."

Green's mouth opened a little in surprise and, yes, dismay. "*That's* what you're here about? I had no idea you'd run into that fellow."

"No?" He didn't quite growl the word. "What *did* you know?"

"Very little," said Green. He sat up and leaned forward, his elbows on his knees. "I didn't ask, you understand. Men come to me for assistance, betimes, and their reasons for wishing it are very rarely interesting and even less often my concern. I see that I was wrong in this case," he added, watching Stephen's face, "and I *am* sorry for it. I hope this won't be a source of any trouble between us."

"Between my house and your court, you mean," said Stephen. "And you may get your wish—depending on what you tell me."

Relaxing, Green assumed some of his previous nonchalance. He turned his hand upward and studied his fingers. "I'm certain I can tell you a number of things. Shall I start anywhere in specific?"

"The man you worked for."

"I work for no man," said Green, with a scornful ring in his voice. "Say so again and I'll remind you less kindly, Alasdair's son or no."

Stephen closed his eyes and took a deep breath, stifling the urge to change. A small diplomatic advantage didn't give him all the power in the room, he reminded himself, and Green was likely to be a lord in his own manner and to serve greater lords still. The world contained mightier things than dragons.

"My apologies," he said. "I've spent too long in this world, perhaps. What can you tell me about the man you…assisted?"

"He called himself Mr. King," said Green, calming down into his prior languid speech, "and while I doubted the truth of it, I'm hardly one to question whatever name a man pleases to take on himself. He was passing tall and rather more than middle aged, as mortals go. Knowledgeable enough, in a very… scattered…sort of way. Still, he'd found out enough to know that I could make changelings and to actually assist a little in the process."

"And why did you help him?"

"A few pages of an interesting book from America. I tried to negotiate for more, but—" Green shrugged. "He had no bloodline or prospects of heirs, no secrets, no talents such as my kind value. Nothing else but money, which I didn't want, and service, which he wouldn't give. He seemed rather insulted that I suggested it."

Stephen fought back an ironic smile. "How strange. What sort of money?"

"Gold, of course. He knew better than to offer bank drafts, at least."

"Or he didn't have them," said Stephen. Ward had been not quite penniless when he'd escaped, but he'd spent some time in America learning magic. Stephen had never heard that turning lead into gold was actually possible, but spiriting money out of a bank vault or jewels out of a bedroom would certainly be within the power of most magicians. "Anything else?"

Green smiled now, his eyes dancing. "Well," he said, drawing out the word while Stephen waited and tried not to glare, "I did have him followed, of course. After he left with his new toy. He went to an office building—give me a moment." He pulled a silver rope and summoned the butler. "Bring me the book in the top right drawer of my desk."

"An office building?" Stephen asked when the butler had vanished. "He can't live there. People would talk."

"I very much doubt that he does. He came out again an hour later—but so did the sun, and my servant doesn't do well in the full light of noon. I thought I'd spent quite enough time on the man in any case. He's unbalanced, he lacks perspective, and he'll die on his own in a few years. Ah."

The butler came back and handed Green a small leather-bound ledger, then vanished.

"He has wonderful conversation," said Green, flicking through the pages, "if only you get to know him. Or so I'd imagine. Thirty-Nine Brick Lane is the building you're looking for. Consider this a gesture of goodwill on my part."

"I'll try," said Stephen.

Twenty-nine

"What are you doing?"

Colin's voice came suddenly and without prelude from the previously empty room. Up on a stepladder, her arms full of books, Mina twitched but didn't jump or scream. "Cataloguing the library," she said, rather than any of the sarcastic replies that came to mind.

She plucked a final volume from the shelves. It was bound in green leather and newer than some of the others, but the dust was equally thick. Mina held back a sneeze and climbed carefully down the ladder.

"Give over a few of those, will you?" Colin held out his hands, and Mina was glad enough to fill them. When he felt the dust, she didn't even try not to giggle at the expression on his face. "Good Lord. How long have we *had* these? And what have we been doing with them?"

"A long time and not much, from what I can tell," Mina said. She deposited the rest of her stack onto the desk with a solid *thump*.

"And Stephen still has you messing about with them? He *has* grown into a tyrant."

"He's done no such thing," said Mina, sharply enough to make Colin widen his eyes and hold up his hands in mock defense. "And he didn't give me the job. He hasn't had me do *any* work, really."

Colin eyed her as if she were some newly discovered form of life. "You mean to say you volunteered? Why on earth?"

"Because it needs doing, and I needed something to do."

"Ah." The new species was a little more comprehensible, it seemed, alien as it might be. Colin looked from Mina to the desk. "And you've been doing this all day?"

"More or less."

Less was more accurate, despite Mina's best intentions on the subject. Half her records had had blots, misspellings, or other features that had meant she'd had to cross them out and write them again. She'd written down one book twice and completely forgotten about another until she'd found it by the windowsill. Every trip up and down the ladder had taken about twice as long as normal, too.

Mina could have laid some of the blame at Colin's feet. Their earlier conversation had left her thinking about mortality and humanity, rules and consequences, and coming to no useful conclusion regarding any of it. She wasn't cut out for philosophy, she'd told herself, but her efforts to direct her thoughts elsewhere had only sent them toward that entry in not-Saint George's journal, the one about rites and children, at which point she'd inadvertently knocked a set of Johnson's works to the floor.

Work usually distracted her from troubling thoughts, not the other way around. What was *wrong* with her?

"Then I'm right in thinking it's not a very urgent matter," Colin said. "And that means you can come out with me."

Coming back from her thoughts, Mina blinked at him. "Out? Where? Why?"

"Out." He leaned against a bookshelf, counting off the points on his fingers. "Anywhere you want, within reasonable limits. Because London is quite a bit more entertaining than the inside of this library or even, if I may dare to say it, the inside of this house."

"Yes, but why me?"

"Because you're—" He looked at Mina's face, saw the skeptical expression she'd used on dozens of other young men, and grinned ruefully before switching to honesty. "You're here, and you're pleasant enough company. And I don't know many people in the city these days, or at least not many people who'd be glad to see me turn up, looking as I do."

If he felt any sorrow about the matter, he concealed it easily enough—much easier than Stephen would have, Mina thought. Still, she felt a little sympathy for him, and more so because he'd had sense enough not to try and charm her. "I can't," she said.

"Of course you can. You don't turn to dust in the sunlight. My brother would have mentioned."

"I agreed," she said, "not to go out of the house without Stephen, not until this matter with Ward is settled."

"Oh, that's the letter of the agreement, true enough." Colin waved a hand. "But the spirit of it is that you shouldn't tell anything to Ward or his men, whether you mean to or no. Stephen's presence was meant to secure as much, and so mine should do just as well. I'd hardly risk his safety or let that jumped-up fellow Ward get his hands on anything important."

"Well—"

"I'll give you my word on it."

"And what if they try something when we're not here?"

"In broad daylight? This is a respectable neighborhood, or so I hear. Besides, Stephen told me that both of you have been out of the house before this, and no harm came of it." Colin smiled at her. "So, you see, he trusts me, which means you should too."

"Does it really?" Mina asked.

"Unless you're more concerned for his welfare than he is. And if my intentions *are* evil, the farther I am from the house, the safer we all are, aren't we? Particularly if you have me out in a public place somewhere. I've not been known to do horrible things in public. Mostly."

There was a certain logic in his argument, self-serving as it was—and then, he'd never pretended that it was anything else. Like his brother, Mina sensed, Colin would never tell her that what he was doing was for her own good. As with Stephen, it was a refreshing change.

Being sought for her company was flattering, too, even if it was because she was the only remotely appropriate person around. If *Colin* thought she was a proper companion to take out into society—but no, it was best not to find that too encouraging. Colin wasn't anything like proper. He'd already said he wasn't particularly human in his outlook, and he'd *also* said that he and Stephen were very different people.

Flattery, without further implications, would still be enough. And getting out of the house would do Mina good. Given how quickly her thoughts had turned to Stephen, some distraction was certainly the best thing for her.

"Anywhere I want?" she asked.

"Within reasonable limits. I don't think it would be a terribly grand idea for us to wander over to Spain, for instance, and I'll not go to any sort of improving lecture, as my sense of chivalry only extends so far. Otherwise," he said and gave a ludicrously courtly bow, "I am at your service."

A page of the *Times* popped into Mina's head. She'd read the article over breakfast and peered as hard as she could at the few small pictures that went with it.

"There's an exhibition at the British Museum," she said. "Art from India. Some of it's thousands of years old—which might be less impressive for you, I suppose," she added, "but there are some really wonderful paintings, they say, and some statues that—"

"Art," said Colin, laughing and sighing at the same time. "*Ancient* art. I should have known."

"Should have known what?"

"It's as bad as taking Stephen out on the town."

"Well, if you don't want to—"

"No, no, I did promise. And I'll enjoy myself, too. I'm not a complete Philistine. See, you'll be having a good influence on me."

"I doubt any woman can say that," said Mina. "Give me a few minutes to change my dress, will you?"

"I wouldn't have been rude enough to suggest it, but I do think it'd be a good idea. You've most of a book cover on your collar, too," said Colin.

"Thank you." Mina plucked the scrap of desiccated leather off her blouse and headed up to her room.

Her wardrobe was such as to spare her any moment of indecision. After washing her face and hands, she put on her best dress, the violet cotton she wore when she dressed for dinner. At least it would be more appropriate for the museum. Mina brushed her hair quickly, put it up again, then pinned on her best hat and peered into the small mirror.

Allowing herself a moment of vanity, she admitted that she looked rather nice. More to the point, she looked respectable. Respectability was really what mattered on this excursion, but despite the dreams and the case of nerves she'd been carrying around all day, her eyes were bright and her cheeks were flushed. Before she pulled the self-indulgent part of her mind up sharply, she thought that it was a pity nobody would be around to notice.

At the top of the stairs, she stopped in her tracks.

As the door closed behind him, Stephen looked up at her, his hat in one hand and his coat half-undone. Despite the hat, his mahogany hair was windblown, his clothing was rumpled, and his face was tired and drawn.

Mina couldn't have imagined a more handsome man.

Thirty

Tired as he was from the trip, and struck as he was by the sight of Mina stopped on the stairs like the model for some painting, Stephen instantly grasped the meaning of her dress and hat. "You're leaving?" he asked.

"No—I mean, not for good. I wouldn't. Certainly not dressed like this." Mina laughed and collected herself. "Your brother got tired of staying in the house."

"And he wanted company, of course."

"It didn't seem like much of a risk," Mina said, shrugging, "but if you're worried, I can stay. He'll find company soon enough."

She hadn't sounded wistful. She had, for as long as Stephen had known her, controlled herself very well under most circumstances. The hat she wore shadowed her face, too.

"No, you're right," Stephen said. "It's daylight for several hours yet, and we've been out of the house before without anything particularly dire coming of it. And it'd be a shame to keep you inside when you've clearly gone to some trouble."

"Well, it's not exactly court regalia, is it? Thank you, though." She came down to the bottom step of the stairs, although no closer, and gave Stephen a closer look. "Are you all right?"

"I'll be well enough. It's been a long day, that's all."

"I'd think so. You weren't—" Mina glanced around. "Nothing happened to you while you were away, did it? Everything's been peaceful enough here."

"No, nothing happened. Not physically, at least—and no, not magically, either," said Stephen, lowering his voice. Baldwin had gone off to deal with his baggage, and the other servants were clearly about other duties, but caution would always serve him well. "I've found at least one of Ward's likely hiding places, though not where he lives."

Mina's eyes went wide. "Really?" Hope shone on her face, making it almost too bright to look at. "Then you're safe, aren't you? You can call the Yard and—"

"Best not," said Stephen. "Not without knowing more. They wouldn't know how to manage the matter. I'm not entirely sure myself, not when he's got magic at his command."

"He'd escape," Mina said, coming back down to Earth. Clearly she was disappointed, and Stephen didn't blame her. She'd almost been free of his house, free to pick her old life up again. "Or he'd kill the men who came to get him."

Stephen nodded. "Probably both. That's the sort of thing that happens when you bring outsiders into a sorcerous matter. It doesna' often end well for anyone, particularly them."

"I'll keep that in mind," said Mina, her mouth

quirking up at the corner. She folded back the end of one glove and laid her fingers against her wrist, pretending to take her pulse. "No untimely end so far, at least."

"And there won't be," said Stephen, his voice echoing in the hall. Mina looked up at him, her lips slightly parted in surprise. "That is, I take my responsibilities very seriously."

"And I'm one of them? Dutiful of you."

She didn't sound particularly happy about it. Stephen cleared his throat. "It seems the least I could do."

"Ah." Mina replaced her glove. "Well, what *are* we going to do?"

"Colin and I will have a look from above once it's darker," said Stephen, "but that's some time yet. It shouldna' be any trouble with your plans. Where were you headed off to?"

"The British Museum," said Mina, responding in kind to his attempt to lighten the mood. "Bit of a busman's holiday for me, I suppose, but they've got an exhibition—"

"The Indian artwork?" Stephen lifted his eyebrows. "I've heard the collection's very good, but I'm surprised to hear Colin's taken an interest."

"She suggested it," said Colin, coming through the door from the hallway. Naturally, he was both impeccable and fashionable; Stephen absently tried to smooth the wrinkles out of his sleeve. "Don't start thinking I'm becoming a scholar. The shock wouldn't be good for you, not after the day you've had."

"Your concern is truly moving," said Stephen, "but I think I'll bear up for a little while yet."

"Come with us," said Mina, suddenly. "If you're not too tired, I mean. It wouldn't be any more risk than we'd have been taking if you hadn't come back now."

"No, I suppose it wouldn't be—"

"And you'd be along to keep Miss Seymour safe," said Colin. "You can't really trust me to do that sort of thing, can you?"

"I'm not answering that question," Stephen said, "but I will come."

Two hours later, he stood in one of the museum's more spacious halls, eyeing a golden statue of a naga, while from behind him came the sounds of subdued conversation and the quiet click of heels against the polished stone floors. An elderly gentleman to Stephen's right was telling his grandson a story about Shiva, while somewhere behind him, three young men were earnestly debating the translation of a word that Stephen hadn't caught.

London did have its attractions. As Stephen walked along the gallery, he could feel some of the day's strain leaving him. His problems and his tasks still remained, but he could put them aside for a little while.

In the middle of everything to see, his gaze kept going back to Mina. He'd seen her looking around wide-eyed, pointing out a particularly fine landscape, examining a statue's inscription, all fascinated concentration.

Now, at his side although carefully not too close, she looked from the statue to Stephen. "The nagas turned into people when they wanted, the legends say," she said quietly. "Or at least according to the plaque."

He met the silent question in her eyes with a smile. "Aye. And it's not so far-fetched as all that. Traders along the Silk Road from India or China to Rome. Roman legionnaires crossing the water to Britain, later on. It could be—although the Russians have similar legends. Perhaps there was more than one beginning for my people."

"You don't know?"

"Not for certain, any more than I know who my more…regular…ancestors are after half a dozen generations or so. We're no better at keeping records than you are. Well," he added, looking at Mina, "most of us are much worse at it than *you* personally. I took a bit of an interest in the subject when I was younger."

"Not now? I mean," Mina added, "when you have time and leisure."

"I'm interested in the past. I've given up trying to trace back so very far, though. My family's affairs here and now started to be more important in the last few years. Or, rather, I've needed to take more of a role in them. They've always been important."

"Uneasy lies the head that wears the crown?" Colin came up to Mina's side.

"Easy enough, I suspect, compared to some men," Stephen replied. "And it's hardly a crown these days," he added, in case anyone was around to overhear.

"Calm yourself. I don't think anyone will arrest you for treason here. Looking for a resemblance?" Colin asked Mina, gesturing to the naga.

She laughed. "Speculating, maybe. It's a lovely piece of work regardless. They all are."

"Lovelier where they'd originally been, I suspect," said Colin.

A passage from one of Judith's letters came to Stephen's mind. "Still keeping company with Carpenter and his radicals?"

"Not company: they'd have a few questions about my age if I did. But correspondence, as long as such things seem reasonable. They're congenial sorts," said Colin. "I don't think I can quite manage their idealism—that sort of thing is for the young—but someone should, once in a while, and the principles behind it are sound enough for the most part."

"Says the young aristocrat."

"I said for the most part. Although we might not be as necessary as we've always thought. Or as you've always thought."

"I don't know about that. Men need a leader. Someone to organize matters and settle disputes. Although at the moment," Stephen added, "I think I'd rather enjoy being superfluous."

"No you wouldn't. Trust me, I've done it for decades—it's much more my kind of life than yours."

"You're just worried that I'll find something for you to do," Stephen said, smiling, and looked over to Mina. "And what about you, then?"

"What *about* me?" she asked with a saucy little grin. "I like to think I'm not superfluous."

"Not at all," Stephen said. "I meant what do you think—about men and leaders and so forth? Do you want to change the world, or do you like it fine the way it is?"

"I think the world will change with or without

me," said Mina. "I wouldn't mind seeing it be a little more—" She frowned, searching for a word. "Free? Open? I don't know. I think, if you want to be a—a doctor or a scholar or a poet, you should be able to, or at least to try, no matter what station you're born to."

"Or what sex?" Stephen asked, remembering their conversation over her first letter home.

Mina's grin widened. "Or that."

"Do you think it'll happen?" Colin asked, eyeing Mina with the curiosity that more than a few women had mistaken, to their sorrow, for something else.

"I think it already is." Mina showed no reaction to Colin's look, if she noticed it. She held up her hands and then made a face. "But I can't show you with the gloves on, and I haven't been typing as much lately at any rate. My fingers used to be a fair point of demonstration—the tips get callused."

"Your grandmother would disapprove?" Colin asked.

"Yours might," said Mina, and her eyes glinted in a dare-you-to-be-shocked way that Stephen was beginning to find familiar. "Mine took in laundry."

"Well," said Stephen, "one of ours kept sheep."

Mina blinked. "Really?" she asked, turning to look up at Stephen. "Your grandmother?"

Her expression might almost have been casual curiosity. Stephen wasn't entirely certain otherwise, but there was a stillness about her face as she waited for his answer that suggested she was listening very carefully.

"Oh, aye," said Colin, off beyond Mina's gaze. "Our mother's mother. They were very *good* sheep, though. And that was quite a while back. Don't let it get around."

"Even the bit about how good the sheep were?" Mina smiled, but the intensity left her expression and she looked away, flushing.

In the moment of silence that followed, the clock began to strike.

"Half an hour to dusk," Stephen said, keeping his voice mildly displeased and not swearing the way he wanted to. They were at a museum, after all. "I'd best be on my way."

"Oh," said Mina, and stepped away from the exhibit. "All right."

She sounded completely normal, even matter-of-fact, but she'd clearly been enjoying herself, and such outings were rare for her these days. That was at least partly Stephen's fault.

"The two of you should stay," Stephen said, "and take the carriage back. I'll hire a cab easily enough."

"But—" Mina began.

He had no wish to hear the offer that she'd surely make, well-meant as it would be. "No, I insist," Stephen said. "I'll make better time on my own. Colin, you'll join me when you can."

Meeting Mina's eyes only briefly, he touched his hat to both of them, then strode off toward the exit.

Thirty-one

SHE'D WRITTEN DOWN THE WRONG WORD. AGAIN.

Mina swore quietly into the silence of the library and swiped her pen through the offending line. Far more forceful than it needed to be, the motion carried her arm past the paper and into the inkwell, which tipped over. Black ink poured over the desk, the record Mina had been working on, and her skirt.

"Oh, *bugger*!"

She grabbed the inkwell and righted it, then mopped frantically at the pool of ink, first with the now-ruined page of notes and then with her handkerchief. Most of the ink came off the table, thank goodness. She didn't wish to spend her hundred pounds replacing it, and she had a feeling the entire sum wouldn't go very far.

Her skirt was a lost cause.

"Ah, hell," she said in more resigned tones and wiped the remaining traces of ink from the desk, then wiped off the inkwell itself. At least she could manage that much without disaster.

This was what came of losing her temper, Mina told herself in an inward voice that sounded remarkably like her mother's. Now her skirt was ruined. She'd have to buy another, and although this one hadn't been anywhere near her best, it hadn't come cheaply. Getting out to buy clothing wouldn't be easy in her current situation, either, and at least one of the MacAlasdairs was likely to do something stupid and chivalrous and embarrassing like offer to buy her another, which she couldn't accept, and they wouldn't understand why she couldn't accept without even more embarrassing conversation. She could have avoided all of that if she'd just taken a little more time and care with her work.

The lecture didn't help. Mostly, it gave Mina the urge to kick something, an urge to which she would have succumbed except that everything in the room would cost more money to replace than she'd had in her entire life, and hadn't she done enough property damage for one day?

Instead, she sank back into her chair and sighed.

What was wrong with her tonight? Her accounts and her typing had been full of mistakes, and she'd taken none of her usual satisfaction in sorting out a jumble of unordered books or finding a new and interesting volume.

She'd finished the rest of the diary, which hadn't been very enlightening. Toward the end, George the dragon *had* talked about his namesake a little and about the other dragon's possibly tragic end.

Some do speak of other ways to mend such cases, he wrote, such as might be witchcraft, or the sacrifice of a white deer, and others yet say that having true affection among men may yet draw a man whole from his monstrous shape, but I think, as I have been taught, that there is no change and nothing for such unfortunates but death or exile.

Cheerful stuff.

She could have chosen another book from the shelves. There were plenty that looked interesting, and even a few that might deal with magic, but Mina couldn't muster enough interest to get past the first page of anything she'd tried. She kept finding reasons to put her work aside and walk across the room or to go look out the window.

It wasn't as if there was even anything—or anybody—to see out there.

Stephen and Colin would come back to the house in dragon form, the same way that they'd left. Unless something went horribly wrong, they'd be far too high to see from the window. But nothing was going to go horribly wrong.

They were dragons, after all. And they were *flying*—what was going to attack them, a flock of angry pigeons? The image did make Mina giggle, but it didn't change her mood. She still felt aware of every second that passed.

Right, then. She wasn't getting her work done one way or the other. Maybe a walk and a bite to eat would settle her mind. Mina stood up, glared down at the ink spot on her skirt—which had helpfully taken the form of some two-headed beast—and headed out into the hallway.

With the servants away and the lamps economically turned down, the hall was very empty and very large.

Mina's footsteps echoed on the floor, steady counterpoint to the light brush of her skirt. She shivered.

She *was* in a mood, and that despite getting to see the exhibition that evening. Mum would have had a bit to say about ungrateful girls with the vapors. Mina knew she herself would have said similar things if she'd been looking on from outside.

Darkness and empty houses made a good mood hard to keep, though. So did waiting up to hear news.

From the foot of the stairs, the clock ticked steadily, like a heartbeat. Its face was pale in the gloom.

Mina swallowed, told herself that she was being silly, and opened the kitchen door.

She screamed.

She didn't mean to, and she felt completely foolish even as the sound died away, but Emily's shriek had jarred her, for a moment, out of all pretense at rationality. She leapt and yelped just as readily as the scullery maid.

"Miss Seymour!" Emily gasped, "I'm sorry! I didn't mean to scare you—"

"Likewise, I'm sure," said Mina, getting her breath back herself. She had to laugh a little, too. "Not really an evening for calm, is it? What are you doing back so early?"

"I came away before I thought I would," said Emily, looking down and biting her lip. "People I was going to visit were busy. I thought if I was just in the kitchen, it wouldn't hurt anyone."

"And it won't," said Mina, as cheerfully as she could manage. She could read enough of the girl's face. Either some youthful suitor had thrown her over, or a friend had left her out in the cold. Either way, the girl needed cheering up. "It's good to have company. Put the kettle on, will you? I'll see if there's any jam left."

Searching in the pantry helped her mood a bit, but the restlessness didn't go away entirely. It just sank down to the back of her spine.

"I was going to ask," said Emily. "You haven't seen Gussie tonight? Only I saw on my way in that he hadn't touched his milk."

"I haven't." Finding a pot of orange marmalade, Mina emerged from the pantry. "I wouldn't worry. He's probably just found another place—or a lady cat." In London, a cat's actual fate was likely far less pleasant, but there was no point bringing that up. "I bet he'll be back tomorrow."

"Hope so," said Emily. "I know it's foolish, but I like having animals around. My gran kept a dog back home. Mostly for the rats, but she was a nice little thing."

"Is this your first place?" Mina asked, but she didn't hear the answer.

As sudden and illuminating as a gas flare, the uneasy feeling she'd had before came back and swamped her, turning to real fear in the process. Mina couldn't name the threat, but she knew that there was one—and that it would likely be deadly.

"Miss Seymour? Are you all right?"

"No," Mina said, because she surely didn't look it. The blood had drained from her face, and every object in the room stood out in sharp relief. "When will the others be home?"

"Not for another hour at least," said Emily.

"Mrs.—Mrs. Baldwin said she and her husband were going to have a good dinner, and Mrs. Hennings is—"

"Good."

"What's happened? Do you need to lie down? Are you sick?"

"No. There's about to be trouble." Mina met Emily's eyes. She put every bit of force she'd ever learned into her voice, every atom of command she'd mastered dealing with younger siblings and cheeky grocers and Professor Carter's visitors. "Go to the pantry. Get into the corner."

"Why?"

"I can't explain. Please."

Mina leaned forward, taking the other girl's shoulders in her hands. "Please trust me on this. If nothing happens, you can make fun of me later or be angry, but please go now."

Now Emily's face was white and her hands shook, but she nodded. "And you?"

Mina picked up the largest knife from the butcher's block. "I'm coming too." Then, as an afterthought, she grabbed a second knife and held it out, hilt first. "At least there'll be two of us."

Thirty-two

Once again, night stretched out above Stephen, and in dragon form he soared over the rooftops of London. This time, with a destination in mind, he could watch the streets below or the stars above. This time, he also had company, as Colin flew beside him, blue scales shimmering in the moonlight.

"It's been a while," said Colin, in the wordless speech they used when flying. At such heights, the wind would have taken away all sounds. "I think we were at Loch Arach the last time we flew together."

"No, it was Italy," said Stephen, laughing at the memory. "Aunt Elizabeth's house. I remember we came in just before dawn and interrupted one of her spells, and she threatened to turn us both into frogs."

"And then said it wouldn't make much difference. Quite a blow to the pride for a young man."

"A young man as drunk as you were shouldn't have *had* much pride left."

"I'd matched Alessandro drink for drink. Considering his bloodlines, I thought my pride was well-founded, thank you. And I hadn't noticed you abstaining."

"You weren't in a state to notice much," said Stephen.

The two of them banked and curved, coming around over the Thames and then making for the east.

"She always did have a temper," said Colin absently. "And she never did understand why Mother married as she did. As though she had any grounds to talk."

"Tiberius was human enough," said Stephen, "after his fashion. And he looked human all the time, which was the important thing to her, I expect."

"I expect so," said Colin, rolling his eyes. "Knowing her."

"Be fair. Most women wouldn't want a husband like one of us," said Stephen.

"In my experience, most women want a husband who's wealthy and not around often. As long as you don't track mud on the drawing room floor, old boy, I expect the next Lady MacAlasdair won't care *what* you turn into."

"That's a nice romantic view of the matter."

Colin laughed. "Even most humans are wise enough to be cynical about marriage." He craned his head around to peer at Stephen. "And you're brooding on the topic. Thinking about the succession, are you?"

"No," said Stephen, which was true.

He peered down at the buildings below. They were rougher now, crumbling brick and stone, and the streets were smaller and darker. Had Mina grown up here? What had her life been, always in the city, always surrounded by people? Had she come to like it?

Would she ever want to leave?

"Don't worry," said Colin. "There are half-breeds to go around, and I'd imagine you can even choose yourself a tolerable one. The title alone will give you your pick."

"Thank you very much," said Stephen. "Take a look below, will you? I think we're almost there."

Finding Brick Lane required flying closer to the ground than Stephen had done for most of his previous excursions: a risk, but one that the fog again lessened. He folded his wings and came in closer. Still unable to read the street signs, he pictured the map he'd done his best to memorize on short notice and tried to match the buildings to the clusters of numbers he'd seen.

In this form, they all seemed much alike and fragile. With very little effort, Stephen could have broken through any wall he saw. Any of his bloodline could, when full grown. It was why Loch Arach had rooms lined with blessed silver and chains forged with magic. The houses and offices in front of him would crumble at one blow—at least, as far as Stephen could tell.

He could sense no significant magic. Perhaps somewhere on this street a crone told fortunes with real accuracy, or a spirit truly did linger near its loved ones, but Stephen felt nothing of the power that even his own private room, slapdash as it was, gave off. Neither did he feel the sense of inhumanity that had hung about "Mr. Green's" part of town or the chill that accompanied the manes.

There was still something wrong. Restlessness prickled beneath his scales and down the length of his spine, making Stephen lash his tail and wish, in the darkest chambers of his heart, for either enemies or prey. Below him, though, he couldn't find any trace of magic large enough to stand out.

He looked over at Colin, who'd always been better at occult matters. "Have I missed aught?"

"No," said Colin, with no trace of doubt. "Wherever your man keeps his creatures, it's not here. That means—"

Like a sudden gust from the still air, a wave of terror sent Stephen reeling sideways. Snarling, he whipped his head around to confront the new threat, his teeth bared and his body ready to lunge.

Nothing was there.

His eyes registered blank night as his mind caught up to the true situation.

"What was *that*?" Colin came up to him, keeping a careful distance.

"We have to get back," Stephen growled. "There's danger at home."

Not much light got in under the pantry door. Mina could make out the outlines of the room, but the pots and pans on the walls were only vague shapes. If Emily hadn't been wearing a light dress, Mina never would have seen her where she huddled in the corner.

Mina stood in front of the scullery maid, trying not to clutch at her knife. How did one hold a knife properly? She'd never had occasion to find out. All she knew was that it felt much heavier than any knife ever had when she'd been chopping meat for dinner at home, and that she kept having to wipe her sweating palms off on her skirt.

She and Emily had tried to move the big table in front of the door, but their combined weight had budged it all of two inches. Besides, Mina had said, they might need to get out in a hurry.

Now she wished there was something more substantial between the door and the two of them. At the same time, she was beginning to feel silly. She wasn't sure how long they'd been in the pantry, but so far, everything outside had been calm. Fear still twisted its way through her body, though. She bit her lip and tried to decide how long she wanted to heed it.

Then she took a few steps forward and bent down to peer under the door. The kitchen floor spread out smoothly in front of her. Nothing moved across her field of vision. Mina let her breath out slowly and felt her face burning.

"I think everything's fine," she murmured. "I'm sorry. I don't know what got into me."

A shadow brushed across the room outside.

Mina stumbled backwards, away from the door, bringing her knife clumsily upward. She didn't let herself breathe, but she shook her head frantically at Emily: *I was wrong, I was wrong, don't move, don't speak, don't do* anything.

She seemed to get the message across. At least, the girl froze in place. Mina snapped her gaze back toward the door.

Nothing came through, but...were those footsteps?

Yes and no, Mina decided as she listened. They were definitely steps, but she didn't know that *feet* were making them. They sounded too big and too...squishy.

She wanted to scream. She wanted to be sick. She made herself breathe quietly and slowly, and listened to the steps cross the room, then fade.

Then they paused.

Then they charged, running back toward the pantry with a sound like slopping jelly.

A huge blow hit the pantry door. The wood buckled in front of what looked like a fist the size of Mina's head. Emily whimpered behind her, and Mina glanced backward. The pantry window was too small and too high to get out.

She might have chosen very badly.

The next blow splintered a hole in the door. The hand came through, except it wasn't really a hand. Half of it was shadow, and the fingers were blurred or melted, vague around the edges and boneless. Mina's stomach hitched, and she wanted to look away.

She darted forward and slashed at the hand, putting her back into the blow. Flesh, if it *was* flesh, parted and fell to the floor with a *glop*. The rest of the hand pulled back.

Mina knew she hadn't won. The thing on the other side of the door probably had two hands, and it—she looked down at the puddle on the floor—didn't bleed. There might be more than one. She swallowed a sob, conscious of Emily behind her, and waited. She couldn't even close her eyes.

From farther off in the kitchen, she heard a snarl.

The thing at the door made more squishing sounds as it turned, and then there was a mighty crash and it hit the door again. This time, though, it was not under its own power. This time, the door held against its weight, spread out as it was, and Mina heard a boiling-water shriek. Now she heard crashing from upstairs, too, and the great roar of an angry dragon.

The cavalry, as the saying went, had arrived.

Thirty-three

"This isn't healing," Colin gasped out between his gritted teeth. "Not as quickly as it should."

He lay on the drawing room sofa, his head flung back and his eyes closed. The fingers of his good arm were clenched at his side. Stephen and Mina were splinting the other arm, which was all any of them could do until the surgeon arrived.

"It is broken," said Mina, eyes on the roll of gauze she was winding around Colin's wrist. "That's got to be more than a few minutes' work, even for you lot."

"It is," said Colin. "But I've broken bones before. I know the feel of it. This is different."

Stephen gave a moment of attention to his own wounds. None of them were particularly severe. Mostly, they were cold places where the manes had hit him, and one long cut along his chest where a tentacle had taken hold hard enough and for enough time to freeze the flesh until it cracked. None of them were healing as quickly as injuries he'd had in his past, either.

"It is," he said and looked to Colin. "Because they're not of this world?"

"It's as good a reason as any."

The thing Colin had pulled away from the pantry door at least had been physical, a hulking beast that had combined the shadowy facelessness of a manes with something like a human form, though a horribly distorted one. Dead, it had dissolved like its less substantial brethren, and the magical side had clearly been prominent enough to break Colin's arm in a way that wouldn't heal as most injuries did.

"How did they get in, anyhow?" Mina asked. "Weren't the wards supposed to keep them out?"

"They were," said Stephen. "Colin? I thought they were solid enough, but a fresh pair of eyes might help—and you've always been better at magic," he admitted, feeling that he owed his brother something.

Mina frowned at him. "Now? The man's got a broken arm."

"I've done more under worse circumstances, and it is important. Though it's kind of you to worry," Colin added, smiling up at Mina in an obvious attempt at charm.

"You'll be no good to anyone if you make yourself worse," said Mina, but she did smile back. "Go on, then."

Colin took a breath, straightened his back, and spoke the invocation. His eyes became unfocused, glowing faintly silver, and then focused again, first on Stephen and then on Mina.

"Ah," he said and shook his head. "That would be the trouble, wouldn't it?"

"*What* would be the trouble?" Stephen asked.

"The two of you."

Mina coughed. "I beg your pardon?"

"Oh, I'm not implying anything," Colin said. With an absently muttered word, he withdrew his sight back to the mortal side of the Veil. "The wards themselves are quite solid. Looking at them, it's hard to believe you were new to magic," he added to Mina, which wiped the should-I-be-offended look off her face.

She practically beamed, in fact.

"Right," said Stephen, reminding himself that his brother was injured and thus not growling about how information, not flirting, was wanted here. "Then what happened?"

"Well—"

"Doctor Banks, sir," said Baldwin.

As was almost second nature by now, Stephen left the alibi to Mina, who made up something simple about Colin falling down the stairs. Colin, Stephen was pleased to note, bridled at this clear implication that he was less than perfectly graceful, but had no chance to contradict Mina. He settled for saying that it was dark, he'd been ill, and he wasn't used to this house.

"Yes, I'm quite sure," said Dr. Banks, clearly not giving a damn. "Hold this sponge, please, miss. And don't breathe deeply."

As Mina held the sponge out with steady hands, he very carefully poured some of the contents of an unmarked bottle over it. A sickly sweet smell rose up: chloroform. Dr. Banks took the sponge back and thrust it under Colin's nose. "*You* take a deep breath, sir. Good."

The title was clearly perfunctory. Neither bloodline nor wealth carried much weight with Banks. Stephen wasn't sure even the true nature of the MacAlasdairs would make much difference to the tall, gray-haired man, not if either of them was a patient.

Obediently, Colin took a long breath in, then, on Dr. Banks's command, another, until his eyes rolled back in his head and he sagged onto the couch, boneless with unconsciousness.

Lucky Colin: the last time Stephen had broken a bone, he'd had a quart of whiskey to see him through the setting and had bitten most of the way through a leather belt despite that.

As Banks applied the cast, Stephen took Mina aside for a moment. Trusting to the doctor's presence to guarantee his self-control, he took both her hands in his. "Are you well?" He looked into her face as he asked the question, trying to see the truth beneath whatever brave mask she might put on.

"I—" Mina caught her breath when she met his eyes. "I will be. No harm done, right?"

"Right." The hands Stephen held didn't shake, but they were cold. He used that excuse to keep them in his a few moments longer. "I'm sorry," he said. "I should have known something was wrong."

"I don't see how," Mina said. "Colin said everything looked fine."

"Except for us. I should have looked."

"It might not have been obvious. We won't know what's going on until he wakes up—or until the doctor leaves and you can have a look yourself." She glanced over at the doctor, and although he was still working on Colin's cast, she blushed and let go of Stephen's hands.

Stephen let her go without protesting—without protesting aloud, at least.

As Dr. Banks patted the final remnants of the cast into place, Colin's eyelids fluttered and he muttered some sleepy words, a woman's name among them. "Ellie" or "Lilly" or something similar was Stephen's guess. He wasn't sure if Mina had heard it, and her face showed no reaction, for what little that was worth.

"Quite a constitution your brother has," said the doctor.

"You don't know the half of it. Will it do any harm for him to wake up now?" Stephen asked.

"It shouldn't. Just don't let him move around too much, and have a basin ready if he tries. I'll come back in a week. You know how to reach me if anything urgent transpires." Dr. Banks clicked his bag shut and took his leave.

"Actually," said Mina, after the good doctor was several minutes away, "it's lucky his arm *will* be slower than is usual for your lot. It'd be a bit chancy trying to explain why the bone had healed so quickly, next time the doctor comes back."

"Ah, no," said Stephen. "We'd just pack him off to France for a month or so, and say he'd healed over there. It's not a bad idea even now."

"Ha," Colin slurred. His eyes focused on Stephen, as much as they could focus on anything just then. "I know why you really want me gone. An' I'm not a—ammand—abandoning you now. I can think even if I can' fiiight."

"Can you, now?" Stephen asked, amused.

"Can once this stuff wears off. Stop grinnin' like that. Unbecomin' to a man of your years."

"I'll take that under advisement," said Stephen. "And if you think that your mind is valuable, perhaps you can continue to tell us why the wards failed. What's wrong with me and Mina?"

"Oh, that." Colin tried to wave his broken arm dismissively, swore, and shook his head. "What?"

"The wards?"

"Maybe we should wait," Mina said. "He's not thinking clearly right now."

"I'm thinkin' very clear, thankyouverymush. The wards are ver' simple, really. You two are linked to 'em. And to each other. When you're both here or you're both out, 'sallright. You're both…one thing. Coherent."

"More than I could say for you at the moment," said Stephen.

"Hush. When one of you is in the house and one's outside, the wards get confused. Stretched. Things get in through the stretched bit. Is that all? I've things to do."

"Sleep being first on the list, I'd think," said Mina, shaking her head. "We'll think about the rest of this later—and we'll need to decide what to tell everyone else," she added, looking to Stephen. "Meanwhile, I think I can take his feet if you can keep his shoulders fairly still."

"You don't have to do that," Stephen said. "I'll ring for Baldwin."

"Baldwin's got quite enough to cope with right now," said Mina. "So do the rest. I promise I won't let him drop, if that's what you're concerned about."

"It's not," said Stephen, moving to take hold of his brother's shoulders. He couldn't have said what really *was* bothering him, though—or perhaps he just didn't want to.

Thirty-four

In the ballroom, the servants stood quietly assembled, uniforms cleaned and pressed, backs straight, hands clasped in front of them. That was the way you presented yourself to your employer. It also made Mina wince with guilt, and she was relieved to see a similar expression on Stephen's face. Nobody in front of them had done anything to deserve this. Emily had done nothing to deserve that hellish half hour in the pantry, and neither she nor Stephen deserved such an expression of loyalty and professionalism.

Later, she would realize that she'd classed herself with Stephen, and neither her presumption nor her readiness to share his guilt would surprise her, though they would dismay her. For now, there was a task at hand.

"First of all," Stephen said, "is everyone still all right?"

Heads bobbed. "Yes, sir," rose in a ragged chorus, valiant and not entirely true. Polly still looked gray around the lips; Baldwin's hands twitched slightly; Emily might have been at any other reasonably solemn assembly. The resilience of youth, Mina thought. It was a wonderful thing in some respects.

"You know now," Stephen began, "that I haven't told you everything. I couldn't, for you'd not have believed me until now. There'll still be things I must conceal, for your sake and mine both, but I'll explain what's in my power."

"The monsters," said Mrs. Baldwin with an outward calm that itself spoke of inner turmoil. "Emily told us about them."

"Aye," said Stephen. "Miss Seymour told you that I'd an enemy, and that's true enough. She didn't say that the enemy had—has—some mystical powers. That he's capable of sending things other than men after me."

Nobody looked surprised, though a few people shifted and looked away, uncomfortable to hear Stephen put the situation into words so bluntly.

"I've some abilities of my own," Stephen went on. "I'd set up my own protections on this house, and I had thought they'd work well enough to keep any such things away. I was wrong, and I am most sincerely sorry for that."

The words hung in the still air. Polly swallowed hard. Mrs. Hennings closed her eyes for a second.

Stephen cleared his throat and looked over at Mina. Briefly, she wondered if he expected her to say anything—and she wondered what she would say—but he turned away again just as quickly and spoke once more. "I believe I know what went wrong. With Miss Seymour's help and with my brother's, we should be able to make the house safe from any further attacks."

Both maids turned their eyes on Mina now: Emily wondering, Polly dubious.

"However," Stephen took a long breath, "given the circumstances and the unforgivable risk I've placed you all in, I will quite understand if any of you wish to depart my service, either for the duration of this crisis or permanently. I'll provide a month's wages and a good character to anyone who wishes to leave, and I'll be glad to take you back on afterward if you'd like."

Clearly unable to help himself, he glanced for a moment at the Baldwins and then over at Mina again.

"You can speak with me privately about your decision, and you don't have to make it just now. I'll be here if you have any questions. Once again, you have my deepest apologies," said Stephen, and he actually bowed.

It wasn't a very courtly bow, particularly given the wounds he'd suffered, but the mere fact of a lord bowing to his servants drew a few gasps. After a moment of stunned silence, the servants bowed in response. They left in twos and threes, leaving Mina and Stephen alone once more.

"I'll go to the kitchens," Mina said, "and see what the mood is. They might be more likely to talk with me."

Stephen nodded, frowning, then stepped toward her with inhuman speed and put a hand under her chin. Immediately, Mina's blood began to heat, her heart to race. His lips were close, his strong body closer, and she found that she wasn't as weary as she'd thought.

His thumb brushed over her cheekbone. "I'd make the same offer to you, you know. You'd get the hundred pounds and a good character—I wouldna' bind you here, not when it's so dangerous. Not when you were nearly killed."

"I hear danger's good for the mind," Mina said, trying to breathe steadily.

Stephen's other hand clenched on her shoulder. "Mina—"

"Besides, I can't leave now, can I? Not without making a big hole in your wards."

"When Colin's well enough, we can reset them," said Stephen. He sighed and stepped back, and the air seemed very cold in his absence. "Until then—I feel the worst sort of cad, draggin' you intae this as I've done."

"You didn't drag me," said Mina. A dozen questions came to her mind, questions for which this was neither the time nor the place. In the face of Stephen's guilt, she might not have trusted the answers anyhow. She turned away. "I'd better go and talk to the others."

❧

When Mina reached the kitchen, Mrs. Baldwin was pouring out tea for herself, Polly, and Emily. "Hennings is upstairs," she said when Mina came in. "Packing."

"I don't blame her," Polly said. "Especially with her knee the way it is. If I couldn't run, I'd be out of here like a shot," she added, heedless of any contradictions in her speech.

"But, since your knees are fine…" Mina replied, with a questioning look at the housemaid.

"Oh, I wouldn't leave now for the world," said Polly, and gave Mina a daredevil grin. "I've been in service three years, and I haven't seen anything *near* this exciting anyplace else."

"You call that thing at the door exciting?" Mrs. Baldwin said, shaking her head. "I can well live without that sort of thrill, that's certain enough, and so can anyone of any sense."

Polly's eyes flashed. "People die in this city every day, you know. Typhoid's as deadly as boogeymen, and a blasted sight less interesting. Besides, I don't see you upstairs folding your petticoats."

"I've been with his lairdship for many years," said Mrs. Baldwin stiffly, "and with his family for longer, and they've always treated us very well indeed. There's such a thing as loyalty. But I don't think any of this horror is some sort of seaside attraction."

"She's right, you know," said Mina, looking at Polly and Emily. "We were lucky this time."

"And you'll have fixed the…protections…by next time, his lordship said," Polly shot back. "So it's even odds, isn't it?"

"What about you?" Mina asked Emily, giving up on convincing Polly.

The younger girl looked down and bit her lip. "I don't know," she said finally. "I'd miss it here, that's sure, and I don't know as another place would be better—um, other than the creatures, that is. But—"

"How old are you, lass?" Mrs. Baldwin asked.

"Fifteen."

"And have you family about?"

"My father, in Leyton."

"Then you'll go and see him for a month. I've no doubt he'll be glad to see you, wi' your wages and all. You'll come back after, if you'd like. One way or another, we'll know a good deal more by then."

"Oh—" Emily looked up, her face caught between delight and reluctance. "I'm not sure I should—"

"I am," said Mrs. Baldwin. "And if I go to his lairdship, he'll be too. We'll not have a child here at a time like this. I'd not sleep at nights if we did. Go and pack your things." She sent Emily on her way with a firm pat on the back, and turned to Mina and Polly. "Well, then. There's the three of us, it seems."

"Unless Miss Seymour wants to go," said Polly.

"I don't," said Mina, which was more or less accurate. She was past being dismayed by that thought now.

"No, I thought you wouldn't," said Polly. "But you're not one of them, are you? Not properly—you're from Bethnal Green. I've heard from your letters."

"And they don't breed many magicians there. At least not that I know of," Mina agreed. "I just sort of fell into things here."

"You'll have to fall into a few more," said Mrs. Baldwin. "You've been a help with the chores already, but we'll all have to take on more—"

"—and so will the gentlemen," Mina said firmly. "Or at least S—Lord MacAlasdair. I don't know if we can convince his brother, especially as Master Colin's got a broken arm. But if one of them doesn't come and work down here, they can send out for their meals and pay for it. With that and the four of us, we'll survive."

Then she remembered the manes reaching for her and the gashes in the pantry door, and wished she'd come up with another way to phrase things.

Thirty-five

Two days later, Colin was sitting up and talking. Stephen joked that it would take more than a demon to keep him silent for long. His arm was healing slowly, though, almost as slowly as a purely mortal man's would have. Stephen, as part of his share of the household work, brought trays up to his brother's room, though Colin said he would have preferred someone more attractive and less related. Because of the broken arm, Stephen let that remark pass.

He had his own tea with Colin as well, keeping his brother company and trying to figure out the next steps of the conflict with Ward.

"If he doesn't live in the Brick Lane place," said Stephen, "he'll at least have left a few traces there, perhaps. Though I'd need to find a way in, and one that wouldn't get the bastard's attention."

"The first is easy enough," Colin said around bites of muffin. "Find whoever owns the building and persuade him to let you borrow the master key. They're bound to have one. And if the building's in

Brick Lane, a tenner should do it. Maybe a bit more if the gentleman seems inclined to ask questions."

"From the sound of it, you've done this before," said Stephen.

Colin shrugged with one shoulder, which made him look even more indolent than usual. "Not under *these* circumstances. A friend had some letters he wanted back, and I volunteered, being the generous—"

"If you say 'paragon of virtue,' I'll pour the tea out into your lap."

"I thought I'd go with 'warmhearted soul,' as a matter of fact. Variety and whatnot. And if you're just going to toy with that kipper, you may as well give it to a man who appreciates good food. It must be Mrs. Baldwin's day to cook."

"Polly's, I think," said Stephen.

"Really? The girl's a wonder. You do have a talent for discovering staff."

"Makes up for my lack of choice in relations." Stephen smiled quickly, then settled down to consider Colin's suggestion. Discovering a building's owner wouldn't present any great difficulty, only wading through a bit of bureaucracy and perhaps providing enough money to grease any particularly stubborn wheels. "And if we can't," he thought aloud, "or if Ward turns out to own the place—"

"Then there are a few less legal methods we can manage. You might as well be honest first, though. You don't have the face for a scoundrel."

"You're just worried I'd be better at deception than you."

"Never."

Stephen drummed his fingers on the table. "Unless getting the key takes far longer than it should," he said, eyeing his brother's arm and the still-white look of his face, "you'll be staying here. You'll be no good at tiptoeing about and picking locks, not like this. I'll need a set of eyes here at any rate, and ideally one familiar with magic."

"Nice of you to try and make me feel useful," said Colin, "but I'm quite happy to be idle and ornamental. Still, I'll keep a lookout. What about your Miss Seymour? Are you planning to leave her here and risk the wards?"

"No," Stephen said. "She knows that part of town better than I do, and she's good with a bluff if need be. I think it'd be best if I didn't end the evening in jail or with my name in the paper. Besides, a human—and someone who knows London—might spot something neither of us would."

"You're just repeating what she told you, aren't you?" Colin smirked.

"You're a remarkably unpleasant wee churl," said Stephen, and confiscated a muffin by way of vengeance.

"You're insulting an injured man, and you haven't denied the charges."

He hadn't. He couldn't. Five minutes with Mina's ruthless logic and hard eyes, and Stephen had known a lost battle. He also hadn't wanted to stay and see where the fight would lead.

Well, he had wanted to. That was the problem.

"She says she'll keep well out of danger," he said, "and that having two people along is better in case one of us needs to go and get help."

"You'll be able to send me a message anyhow," said Colin. "At least, if you've still got the ring Judith forged."

"Aye," said Stephen. Each of the rings contained blood: his, Colin's, Judith's, and their father's. Wearing it, he could speak to Colin at some distance, though Judith and Alasdair were each, in their own manner, too far away. "But if I need more immediate assistance, it'd be good to have her there."

"If I had to choose a human to go with you," said Colin, "she's the best of the current lot by far. I never thought you'd take the opinion of one into consideration on a venture like this, though."

"She's the sort of lady who should have her say in things," Stephen said and fixed his gaze on his brother's face. "She's got a good head on her shoulders—and a good heart as well."

Colin looked up from his tea, blue-black eyebrows rising in graceful arcs. "From what I've been hearing lately, quite a few people think *all* ladies should have their say in things," he said, "but you sounded as if you were particularly warning me, Stephen."

"Well—perhaps I am." Stephen set his plate down on the nightstand and stood up. The chair he'd been sitting on, like most of the furnishings in the room, was covered with roses, an artifact of either a housekeeper's tastes or his mother's. It was rather ludicrous for the room's current tenant and particularly for the current discussion.

The whole discussion felt a bit ludicrous, at that. "I mean to say," Stephen went on, "that is, she's not like the lasses back at Loch Arach. She didna' grow up knowing how strange we were, and—and the world's different for women outside the valley."

"I'd imagine I know that better than you," Colin said, "having spent a few decades more *in* the outside world of late."

"Aye, but Mina's not like your actresses and your widows, either. She's not got very much to fall back on if anything goes amiss—and she's her family to think of—and she's not the sort to like depending on a man—"

"Exactly what *do* you think I'll do to the girl, pray tell?" Colin asked, smiling infuriatingly.

"You…I—I don't know." Stephen sat back down, defeated. "And she's a grown woman, so there's not much I can say in the matter. I just—treat her well. Honestly. Don't let her think you're in love with her."

"It was never on my mind," said Colin. "For one thing, you've given her the real sentiment already. How could I compare?"

He might have announced that he'd slipped arsenic into the teapot. Stephen went completely still for a second, then managed to make a half-choked sound of interrogation and disbelief.

"Don't swallow your tongue," said Colin, clicking *his* tongue reprovingly. "And don't pretend you don't know what I'm talking about, either. It's perfectly obvious that you're in love with Miss Seymour."

Stephen gathered himself to deny it—and found that he couldn't. Memories flooded back to him: Mina warm and frantic against him, her hair like silk in his hands and her mouth moving skillfully beneath his; Mina at the breakfast table, mouth pursed and eyebrows drawn together as she considered an article in the *Times*; Mina joking with him in the library; Mina reaching out to console him when he was worried, and prepared to face thieves with a poker, manes with a kitchen knife, and an entirely new world with the keenness of her mind and the strength of her will.

He loved her. How could he not?

The idea simply felt right, settling into his blood and his bones. When Colin had spoken it aloud, it had been the crystallization of some long-guessed-at formula.

"But it's hardly sensible of me, is it? She's mortal."

Colin shrugged. "So was Mother."

"Barely. Her whole line were magicians. And even so, she turned Father down the first time he proposed." The family story had been funny when Stephen had been young. Now he couldn't quite appreciate the humor. "Mina—she's got an entire life of her own, one that's got nothing to do with magic. She's got a family who'd never believe we exist. She loves them enough that she demanded I let her write to them when she first came here and she'd no reason to think I'd treat her very kindly. She couldn't go off and leave them without explaining."

"Plenty of women are close to their families, and there are wonderful trains these days. And I'm certain she could make up a suitable story to tell them, one that would let her keep in touch. She's good with a bluff, you said."

"*If* she wants to be," said Stephen, endeavoring to squash a small bit of hope that was sprouting inside him.

"Yes, yes," said Colin, impatiently. "*If* she wants to be. Which she will."

"Certain, are you?"

"Not as certain as I am of your feelings. But the

lady isn't my brother, for which we should all be thankful. Really, Stephen, you'll not know until you ask her. 'She's the sort of lady who should have her say in things,'" he added, in a heavily accented baritone.

"I sound nothing like that."

"You sound exactly like that, but I'm sure she'll accept you anyway. She's a forgiving sort of girl."

The prospect was too tempting; there had to be a flaw somewhere. Stephen searched and, with a sigh, found it. "I can't ask her now. Not with Ward, and her having to stay here, and me paying her. If she says no, it might be awkward enough to get in the way of magic, and if she says yes, it might be just because she feels obligated."

"Doubt it, knowing the lady," said Colin, "but wait if you'd like. Just tell her eventually, and meanwhile stop blundering about the place like a cat with its head in a sardine tin. Good Lord, Stephen, you wouldn't catch me in such a state if you offered me the Crown Jewels."

"Colin, if someone offered you the Crown Jewels, you'd say they didn't go with your complexion. Or you'd lose them at cards." Stephen got up. "I'd best go find the owner of that Brick Lane building. Otherwise, this conversation will remain academic for quite a bit longer."

"At which point I will put poison in your whiskey."

"Good luck trying with one arm." Stephen paused at the door. "Colin?"

"Hmm?"

"Thank you."

Thirty-six

A few weeks had made a night journey a much more pleasant prospect than it had been last time. The wind was gentle against Mina's face, and the night, for once, was clear. She could even see a crescent moon hanging overhead as she and Stephen got out of the carriage.

"No stars, though," Stephen said when Mina pointed it out.

"Of course there are. There's one over there—and another—" She gestured, squinting against the lights of the city.

"They don't hide so much at home," Stephen said. "A night like this would look like a spill of diamonds in Loch Arach."

"Sounds lovely," Mina said, picturing it. It wasn't the first time in the last few days that Stephen had mentioned his home. Talking with Colin must have made him miss the place, she thought, and no wonder. Everything he said made it sound halfway to Eden. "Not much like here. We're just lucky there's no fog. Though it might hide us, if there was."

"Aye," said Stephen, "but I rather enjoy breathing."

Even without the fog, Mina didn't think they'd be too obvious. People had come out to enjoy the night—walking to music halls or dances, or down along the river, trying to sell refreshments to the strollers, or just sitting on their front steps and talking. High laughter drifted through the evening air, and the need to let a group of young women pass pushed her closer to Stephen's side.

He didn't step away, even after the crowds had passed, but rather put an arm around her shoulders. "Disguise," he explained when Mina looked up at him. "May as well look as if we've a purpose in being out here, aye?"

"Might as well," said Mina, and leaned against him. After all, they were in public.

Meandering, they rounded a corner, and Stephen nudged her gently. "That one there," he said, looking toward a narrow brick building on the corner. The doors were closed, the windows shuttered, and it looked both thoroughly respectable and totally anonymous.

No light came from under the shutters, or at least none that Mina could see from outside. Either the building was abandoned or the shades were very good—or Christopher Ward was at his best in darkness these days. She felt the weight of the revolver in her pocket, a new addition to her wardrobe, and was glad of it.

"You can stay out here, if you'd like," Stephen said, "or we can find a place where you'll be more comfortable. A tea shop, perhaps—"

"No," said Mina. "We've talked about this already."

"That we have," he said. "I just wanted to know you were sure."

"Thank you," she said and smiled, both because his intentions were good and because she was glad he'd asked. Having to say her will aloud had made it stronger; she felt her feet more firm on this path, whatever it was.

"Now," said Stephen, and they started forward, both still trying to look casual, both inwardly anything but.

❧

The door led to a dark, narrow stairwell where the harsh smell of carbolic soap lay thinly over years of mold. Following Stephen up the steps, Mina kept her hands at her sides and stayed to the center, well away from the walls. She didn't look down, either. All the cleaning in the world wouldn't keep rats out of city buildings, and though she was too familiar with them to be precisely afraid, she had no desire to see one of the creatures scurry past.

Instead, she counted steps: one-two-four-six-eight-twelve and a landing. Two doors flanked them there; Stephen didn't stop at either. Twelve more steps went past and another landing, and they kept going. On the third floor, Stephen stopped, hesitated, and then turned right.

There was no light from under the door. Stephen bent and pressed his ear to it and then, after a moment, straightened up with no sign of alarm on his face. Still, Mina held her breath as he turned the key in the lock and let the door swing slowly, quietly open.

Nothing moved in the room beyond. Mina let her breath out in a not-quite-silent sigh of relief.

Inside, Stephen lit the gas lamps on the walls, which did nothing much for the room's appearance. It was a cheerless place with graying white walls. Someone had scrubbed those walls well, though. The smell of soap was much stronger here than it had been in the hall. A shining mahogany monster of a desk, all pigeonholes and drawers with brass fittings, sat near the window.

"I don't envy the woman who has to polish that." Mina eyed the pigeonholes, many stuffed with paper. "I'll take the right side, you take the left. Anything that looks odd?"

"Or that mentions a particular place. You'll know as well as I."

"Oh," she said, and turned to the desk so she could hide her smile. She'd never thought to hear those words from Stephen.

Taking a sheaf of paper from one of the pigeonholes, she shook it hard, tapping the bottom edges of the papers against the top of the desk. "Centipedes," she explained when Stephen gave her a curious look. "And similar. They like paper, and they love old buildings."

"Do they?"

"Mm-hmm. I learned typing in a place like this. We used to find them in the machines some mornings." Mina shuddered at the memory.

"But you kept going."

"It was what I could afford," she said, hearing her voice get brittle and clipped. Even the cheap, dirty school she'd attended had taken a year of saving. "I didn't have much choice, did I?"

Stephen leafed through a stack of papers. "Because you wanted to be a secretary?"

"I wanted to see more of the world, even if it was secondhand. I figured I might get a position with some old lady, type up her letters and all that." Mina smiled, remembering nights of circling advertisements in the *Times*. "Then I saw the Professor's advert, and I thought a scholar would be even better."

She put a few more papers aside. Either Ward and his correspondents were very vague, or the messages were in a code that she couldn't make out. There were many discussions of meeting "at the usual place" or "where we talked last night," but nothing more concrete. From the way that Stephen was rifling through documents and stuffing them back into the desk, he wasn't finding anything, either.

Then, pulling papers from the last cubbyhole, Mina stopped and caught her breath.

She hadn't spent a great deal of time with wealth or land, but even she knew what a property deed looked like. "Stephen," she said, and he was instantly at her shoulder, his hair brushing against her face as he leaned forward to look.

"Anywhere you recognize?" he asked. "I'm not as familiar with the city these days."

Mina frowned down at the address. "Not off the top of my head, no, but it looks like it's down by the docks. Could be a warehouse." She blinked. "Why would he need a warehouse?"

At first, Stephen didn't answer, not until Mina looked up at him and he seemed to realize she wasn't going to drop the question. "He might want room," he said quietly, "and a place where most people couldn't hear what happened inside. Creatures like he uses often have a price." He drew a sudden low breath that was half a snarl.

"What is it?" Mina asked. Stephen's teeth were very white even in the dim room, and they looked sharper than a normal man's would, but she didn't look away. She didn't even feel the urge to do so.

"The creature that came to the house last time. I think it was human once."

In a way, Mina was glad that they'd found the deed so late. It meant they could leave soon afterward. She'd known Ward could and had killed. Now she couldn't escape the thought that what she knew about might be the smallest part of the blood on his hands. The building seemed very dark as they walked down the stairs, and very empty.

"Are you going to go and"—she cleared her throat, unsure what word she should use—"find him now?"

"Tomorrow, I'd think. Midday. The manes don't have as much power then, and hopefully Ward won't, either."

"And the...other things?" Mina asked, remembering the gelid hand that had punched through the door.

"I don't know. I've not seen anything like them before."

She couldn't go, of course. She was small, human, and neither a warrior nor a witch. She couldn't reliably shoot anything more than a foot or two away from her. In a pitched battle, she'd do more harm than good.

"Will you take anyone?" she asked, her eyes on the back of Stephen's neck.

"I can't," he said, "Not unless Colin's arm heals sooner than any of us think. If I catch Ward off guard, it should go all right." He began to say something else and then stopped, so suddenly that Mina nearly ran into his back.

"What is it?" she asked, whispering again.

In answer, Stephen pointed to the window above the door, too high for Mina to see. "There are men out there. Two of them. And from the way they're talking, they're not moving for a while."

Thirty-seven

Every curse Stephen knew, in a variety of languages, went through his mind in a moment. Rather than utter any of them, he bit his tongue and motioned for Mina to go back up the stairs. He followed her. Every so often, he turned to make sure the door hadn't opened, but it stayed shut. The men outside didn't seem to have heard their footsteps.

On the second-floor landing, they stopped. Mina sat down on the first step, and Stephen sank down beside her.

"They don't know we're here," he said, once he'd started to think the situation through. "They'd have come in if they did. Or Ward would have." Ward might also have sent demons after them if he'd known, but Stephen didn't want to say that aloud just now. He glanced at his pocket watch: quarter past midnight. "He must have them guard the place regularly, this late."

"Or someone else might," said Mina. "He's not the only rich man who keeps a secret or two."

Even in the darkness, Stephen could see her grin

at him. She seemed in no danger of panic. Her voice was a little shaky, but that was all. In that respect, as in others, she was a very good companion to have in these circumstances—even if her presence did bring with it certain complications.

The stairs weren't wide. As they sat side by side, Mina's thigh pressed against Stephen's, the contact was thrilling despite their predicament, several layers of clothing, and the generally uninviting atmosphere of the staircase. He shifted his weight and fought a losing battle with his instincts.

At least it was dark.

"What now?" Mina asked.

"I'm not sure," said Stephen, fixing his mind on higher things, or at least trying to. "I don't want to kill the men outside—particularly not if Ward didn't hire them."

"No," said Mina, quiet but firm. "You said you didn't think they'd go away for a while?"

Stephen shook his head. "One of them said it was a long time until dawn. This place has no back door, either—at least not one we can get to from the staircase. We could break the lock on one of the ground floor offices and break a window from there—"

"—but that would get as much attention as going out the door."

Stephen looked down at his hands, and the silver ring caught his attention. "I could talk to Colin, at least. I'm not sure what help that would be, though. 'Excuse me, sir, but my brother and his friend snuck in there and would like to come out now.' It doesn't sound promising."

"Doesn't have to be him," said Mina, sitting up as an idea struck her. "And it doesn't have to be the truth. Have him hire someone to distract the guards. They could...I don't know, start a fire or break a window round the back and start yelling, and then run for it. You could get a couple men for half a pound each, I'd think."

"At this time of night?"

Mina laughed. "*Especially* at this time of night. It's the sort of idea that'll sound wonderful to drunk men."

Without thinking, Stephen put an arm around Mina's shoulders. "Cerberus, you're a wonder."

"A real criminal mastermind," she said and laughed again, breathless this time. "You'd better talk to your brother, hadn't you?"

She didn't move away, though, or try to shrug his arm away. Beneath his hand, her shoulders began to relax a little. Stephen rubbed his hand along her arm gently, almost absently, as he triggered the ring.

"Colin?"

"Here. And not in the wine cellar, before you ask."

Overhearing that, Mina giggled.

"I'd imagine you'd have no need to go yourself," Stephen said. "You'd just make eyes at Polly and get her to bring you half the bottles down there. We're a bit stuck here."

He explained the situation in a few words and added Mina's suggestion. Colin made a thoughtful noise. "I'd imagine that will work well enough. It'll take a while for me to get it done, though. Can you hold out for an hour or two?"

"As long as we're out before anyone else comes in," said Stephen, "that'll be good enough."

"Right, then. Try not to set the place on fire while you're waiting," said Colin, and cut the connection.

"Well," said Mina, sounding thoughtful. She leaned against Stephen's side, possibly for warmth and possibly for reassurance of a sort he didn't think she'd ask for, any more than he would. He put his other arm around her, glad for the human contact. He was also hard again, despite the clearly transient distractions of escape, and her breasts brushed against his chest when she breathed in a way that was going to drive him mad soon, but he was a MacAlasdair and several centuries old, and had at least a measure of self-control. He would be fine.

He realized she'd said something. "Hmm?"

"I said that we have some time on our hands."

Surely she hadn't meant that the way it sounded. She couldn't intend anything suggestive, even if her voice had been like warm silk when she spoke.

"Aye," he managed roughly. "It's a pity we don't have a deck of cards. And, er, a light, I suppose."

"Yes," said Mina, sounding almost annoyed. "Quite a shame."

"You've my apologies for getting you into this," Stephen said. He wished he could see her face better. Her body was tense again, though she wasn't pulling away.

"It's not your fault."

"I could have kept watch on the building beforehand," he said and tried to keep his voice even, tried not to think about the way she smelled and the way he could feel each breath as her chest rose and fell against him. "I might have seen—"

"We didn't have time. You can't know everything. Sometimes you've got to take a chance."

She fell silent. Then she took a deep breath and looked up at Stephen, her breath warm against his face. "Especially at times like these."

She leaned forward and kissed him.

As long as it had taken Mina to work up her nerve, as much as she'd hesitated at the last moment and almost backed down, that first kiss wiped away all of her remaining reservations in an instant. She clung to Stephen, every nerve in her body rejoicing at the strength of his arms around her and the heat of his mouth on hers.

If the kiss had caught him off guard, he didn't show it. He met Mina's invitation with equal parts skill and hunger. Already aroused by his nearness and by her wish to distract herself, she quickly found herself aching for more and welcoming the pressure of his body as he pulled her against him.

When Stephen's hand found her breast, she whimpered and arched up against him, not-so-silently begging him to continue. Another time, such a blatant display of need might have embarrassed her, even through her desire. Now it didn't matter. She and Stephen were alone together. They'd be alone together for a while, in the dark. Nothing counted. And the way he stroked her breast, then the harder pressure of his fingers on her nipple, felt so good she couldn't have stopped herself anyhow.

Stephen certainly didn't seem to mind. His organ

pressed against her thigh, hard and insistent, and when Mina arched upward, the friction made him groan and thrust forward. She tilted back, glad to go, eager to have their bodies line up properly for once, and—

"*Ouch!*"

The edge of the step had caught her in the spine. The pain wasn't very bad, but it was unexpected enough and in the right location to make her cry out.

Stephen pulled back instantly, though he kept his arms around her. "Are you all right?"

His touch was gentle now, with no urgency, and Mina could sense how much effort that took. "Yes," she said, "but I think we should move up to the landing."

She started to get up, but Stephen clasped her hands in his before she could rise. Despite the darkness, she felt his gaze on her face, searching and intense. "Mina," he said. "Are you sure of this?"

"Yes."

Mina spoke without thinking, but she knew that further thought would have led her to no different conclusion. She'd read George's journal and Colin had confirmed what it had said: there was nothing for her to fear in the way of consequences. And even if they defeated Ward and she could go back to her life, she knew she'd never find anyone else like Stephen.

If they didn't defeat Ward, he might well kill them both.

One way or another, this opportunity would never come again. Mina discovered that she didn't want to die—whether at twenty-seven or seventy-two—without lying with this man.

"I'm very sure," she said.

"Then I'm honored." His lips brushed hers, gentle and brief. "Wait here a bit."

"All right," she said, half laughing, and waited with her hands in her lap, feeling the yearning in her body as a sure and pleasant thing. This was good; it would take her somewhere better yet. For the moment—there was the moment.

Then Stephen touched her on the shoulder. When she rose, he took her hand and led her up to the landing. "You could lie down," he said, "if you'd like."

When Mina lowered herself to the floor, she found that the surface beneath her was soft. Exploring with her hands, she made out the outlines of a coat and a shirt, laid out in some approximation of a bed, and a waistcoat folded for a pillow.

"Kind of you," she said. "No trousers?"

Stephen's laughter washed over her. "I'd like to have some control of myself," he said and cupped her face to kiss her again.

The equilibrium she'd been holding steady spilled over again, and desire flooded through her in a second. Mina let Stephen guide her to the floor, and as he worked the buttons on her dress, she ran her hands over his bare skin. She trailed her fingers through the hair on his chest, then brushed a fingertip across his nipple and heard his quick and frustrated inhalation.

"You're not making this task of mine easy," he said, half growling.

Mina laughed. "Should I stop?"

"Nae. I've always liked a challenge," he said. With that another button came open, and Stephen slid his hand inside her dress, where the hooks of her corset proved considerably easier.

Then he slid downward, and Mina protested at first at the change in angle and the fact that so much more of him was out of reach. That didn't last long, though. Not when he took one of her nipples into his mouth and let his tongue play across it. She wasn't complaining at all then—she couldn't even remember words to complain with—and then one of his hands was beneath her skirts, sliding up her leg to her thigh, up her thigh to—

Ohhhh.

She wasn't sure if she'd made the noise or simply thought it. Stephen's hand was very light against her sex at first, but even that contact was devastating. She was melting at his touch, dissolving and yet still striving, aching, wanting more.

Slowly, very gently, he slid one finger inside her, then a second. Mina caught her breath. It was good; it was strange, though not wholly unfamiliar. Stephen's fingers were much larger than her own, and the way he stroked her was much more skilled, much more certain than she'd managed during her brief moments of self-exploration, hindered as she'd been by shared bedrooms and unfamiliarity.

However he'd learned more, she blessed his education.

"Lovely girl," he muttered against her breast, and his thumb found the spot at the top of her sex that made her cry out. He circled it slowly and then faster, and Mina's hips moved to meet his hand. "That's it—let me—"

And then desire, passion, *sensation* exploded within

her, waves of pleasure that made the darkness glow. At the last moment, she remembered that she shouldn't scream and bit down hard on her lip. If it hurt, she was miles away from noticing.

As she caught her breath, Stephen slid away from her for a moment. She heard rustling cloth in the darkness and realized what was happening. "I wish we could see each other," she said.

"Aye." He was breathless too, his voice husky. "Although it might be more than I could stand just now. If you want to stop—"

"Ask me again and I will," she threatened.

"I'll not risk that," he said, and then he was lying on top of her again, his weight on his elbows. His bare chest pressed against her stiff nipples. His legs were warm between hers, and the head of his organ was hot and rigid at the opening to her sex. Instinctively, she pushed up against it.

As before, Stephen moaned and pressed forward—this time, pushing into her with his full length. There was a flash of pain—her collision with the steps had been worse—and an odd feeling of pressure and fullness, with pleasure waiting just behind it.

He went still. Waiting, Mina realized. Without asking, he was asking, or perhaps just offering. She wouldn't have made him stop now, though, earlier threats aside. Mina wouldn't have stopped for another hundred pounds.

As an answer, she wrapped her legs around him as much as her skirts would allow, which tilted the scale very emphatically back toward pleasure. So did the sensation when Stephen began to move. He went slowly at first, with that sensation of leashed power that still excited Mina. Then, when she started to get breathless again, to writhe under him and feel desire building again, his control slipped considerably.

That was fine with Mina. That was better than fine. She thrust up against Stephen, listening to his voice come broken and ragged in her ear: *good girl* and *just like that* and *so hot, so tight*, and felt the urgency driving him. She met it with her own, surprised to find herself back on the edge but not inclined to ask questions. At the end, she bit his shoulder to stifle her scream.

Stephen reared his head back and looked into her eyes. "Mina," he said, in a voice that came from very deep in his chest. "God, *Mina*."

Then he threw his head back and arched forward, pouring himself into her. For a moment, there was nothing in the world but them and the darkness—and the darkness was fine, even welcome, because they were both in it.

Thirty-eight

Given his own way, Stephen would have lain a long time with Mina in his arms, listening to her breathing and drifting in the languid and pleasant dizziness that followed climax, particularly this time. Out of almost two centuries' experience, he could recall no interlude as intense as this one had been, nor as satisfying. He would have greatly preferred to stay where he was.

He would also have greatly preferred a light and a bed. Clearly the universe didn't pay as much attention to him as he would have liked. Perhaps that was just as well—he wouldn't have *asked* for a strange woman to come running through his house, and he certainly had no quarrel with the results.

The thought made him grin against the top of Mina's head. He'd rolled onto his back, not entirely trusting his arms to remain steady. Now she was curled against his side, and he absently stroked her tumbled hair with his free hand. The occasional disarranged pin presented a hazard to his fingers, but Stephen barely noticed.

"We'd better get dressed," Mina said, voicing what Stephen hadn't yet been able to speak. Suiting action to words, she rolled briskly away from him and stood up. He heard little clicking sounds in the darkness: corset hooks. "I don't know how long we have before Colin sends someone, but I'd guess we'll need to move quickly when he does."

"Likely enough," said Stephen.

Putting himself back together was considerably easier than the same process must be for Mina. Had there been more light, he'd have offered assistance. As it was, he'd probably only be an encumbrance. He was better at undressing women than dressing them, particularly in darkness.

He concentrated on shaking out his coat and waistcoat, on getting the buttons right and then smoothing down his hair. He kept glancing over to Mina in the process, or to where sounds revealed her to be; he could only catch glimpses of movement.

This was not how Stephen had pictured—well, anything.

Not that he would have taken it back; his entire being seemed to protest at that thought. Mina had enjoyed herself as well—he had enough experience to ensure as much and to know the signs. He had no doubts on that score, and no regrets.

He just wasn't at all certain how to proceed.

Getting out of the building would be a necessary start.

From nearby, Mina cursed, quiet and vehement. Stephen turned toward her. Uncertain what to ask or how to ask it, he ended up making a strangled interrogatory sound, neither his most dignified moment nor his most seductive.

"Oh. Nothing—I just hate buttons as much as you do. *There.*" She laughed, and then stopped and took a breath. "I should say it before we leave: thank you. I, um, I liked what we did. A great deal."

"I'm very glad to hear it."

"And you don't have to—it doesn't change anything," she said. "I'm a modern girl, after all, and I knew what I was doing. You don't have to worry that I'll want more money or that I'll hang around and make calf eyes. I wouldn't know how. I've never even seen a calf. I—wanted you to know that."

Forced lightness and real intensity twined together in her voice. For once Stephen could tell what she was really saying—and what she was avoiding. Sometimes, a man saw better without light. He laughed at his discovery.

"You're a city girl, Cerberus. I'll not hold it against you," he said. Reaching out, he took her hands in his own and drew her closer. "Trust me, worry's the last thing on my mind. Worry about the things you mention, at least."

"Well," she said, still uncertain but without that note of duty in her voice, "God knows we've got enough to fret over otherwise."

"Aye. And as far as you're concerned—*damn it.*"

The ring pulsed against his finger, and Colin spoke almost at the same time. "Ready to go, Stephen? You haven't gotten yourselves killed, have you?"

"No," he said and thought he almost sounded civil. "We're fine."

"I did say it would take a while. Get yourselves as close to the door as you can and wait. You'll have about five minutes. I'll meet you at the corner."

"We'll be there," said Stephen.

Mina, in fact, had let go of his hands already and was heading toward the stairs. She was right, and Stephen understood the impulse—the last hour or so aside, this was not a place he'd choose to spend any time—but still he cursed again. Silently, this time.

Downstairs, they waited on the last step, not talking and keeping even their breathing as quiet as they could. Stephen could see the shapes of the guards still outside and hear their voices through the door. He didn't think they could hear anything but the loudest noises from within, but it was best not to take chances.

Beside him, Mina waited. He could feel the tension in her body, the readiness to spring, but she was still except for the restless movement of her hands, clenching and unclenching on her skirt.

If not for the impending need to bolt, Stephen wouldn't have resisted the urge to kiss her again. He reached out instead and took one of her hands. Her state of mind was appropriate and useful—and so was his, for that matter, for he knew he was waiting on the edge as well. Calming down might not be a good plan, but at least he could let her know that she wasn't alone. He could reassure himself of the same thing.

Mina slid her hand into his readily enough and stroked her thumb across his knuckles, an absent gesture, but one that roused as well as comforted. Even such a short time after their earlier activities, Stephen felt himself respond to it.

Part of that was the situation, of course: hot blood,

survival instinct, and whatnot. He'd taken more than a few risks in his long life, though, and he knew that danger wasn't the only explanation.

He didn't think peace would make him grow tired of Mina.

He didn't think anything would.

"Oi, there!" One of the guards shouted from outside, jarring Stephen out of thought. "What d'ya think you're doing?"

As if in answer, a largish piece of glass went smash somewhere nearby. The guards shouted some more and then ran, their footsteps loud against the pavement at first and rapidly growing dimmer.

"Now!" Colin shouted in Stephen's ear, loud enough to make his head ring with the noise.

Later they'd have a discussion about magic and force and what volume was really necessary if one felt a proper fraternal urge to leave one's brother with intact hearing. Stephen promised himself that much.

For now, he yanked the door open and bolted outside. He would have pulled Mina with him, but there was no need. She was running right at his side. Out on the doorstep, though, she stopped to slam the door behind them, then turned. "Lock it."

There wasn't time to argue or ask questions. Stephen grabbed the key, shoved it into the lock, and nearly broke his wrist turning it. Outside, he couldn't hear the guards' footsteps any longer. Even in the relative quiet after midnight, London was too noisy to distinguish one set of sounds from a dozen others.

Grasping the key in his fingers, he took off again.

One house flew by, then another, passing in a blur

of darkness and light. The few people in his way were easy enough to dodge. Stephen could have gone on for a while, if Mina hadn't yanked on his arm again.

"What?"

He turned back, expecting her to be tired. That was no matter: she was a tall girl, but he could carry her easily enough if he needed to. She was shaking her head, though, even when he reached for her.

"Stop." She caught her breath. "We should walk now."

"Walk?"

Mina nodded. "Nobody can say where we're coming from now, and running people catch the eye. We slow down and act a bit tipsy, and we'll just be two out of many." She paused for a moment. "You might put your arm around me."

"Happy to oblige you."

They walked onward, less than steadily, leaning against each other. Mina began to hum: a loud and somewhat out-of-tune version of a song Stephen had heard in his club once or twice. Then, as the streets nearby got more respectable, she stopped, straightened up, and stepped away again.

Colin waited on the corner ahead, with the carriage nearby. He'd had to button a coat rather clumsily over his broken arm, and his hair stuck out at odd angles beneath his hat. Presenting such a flawed appearance must have been killing him, Stephen thought, and couldn't help smirking.

"Keep looking smug and I'll leave you next time," said Colin, as they caught up to him. "At least it's too dark for anyone to see me. Did you find anything?"

"Aye," said Stephen. "But I'd best save it for when we're home."

The carriage ride was quick and silent. All three of them slumped against the seats: Colin doubtless exhausted from so much exertion so soon after his injury, Stephen trying to collect his thoughts, and Mina clearly tired as well—and perhaps sore? Virgins sometimes were, he'd heard, though he'd always stayed away from them before. He should probably do the gentlemanly thing and refrain from propositioning her that evening.

He might ask her to join him in bed, though, even chastely. After the night's discoveries, he would prefer not to sleep alone.

Looking forward to a shared bed, bracing himself to explain the ring to Colin, Stephen knocked at the door. It opened to show Mrs. Baldwin, face drawn and worried. She looked past him at Mina and pressed her lips together. Not disapproval, Stephen thought, but sympathy.

"Professor Carter's here to see Miss Seymour, sir," she said. "He says it's urgent business."

Thirty-nine

Good news was never urgent business. Good news never came after midnight.

At first Mina wanted to faint, or to burst into tears and scream at the universe: *Go away and leave me alone! I'm too tired! Haven't you done enough?* But the universe rarely listened, and she couldn't do anything if she fainted.

"Should we come?" Stephen asked. "I've no notion what it's about, but if you'd rather be alone—"

"No," said Mina.

Stephen took her hand. He'd taken off his gloves, and the warm pressure of his fingers against hers took her further back from the edge of hysteria. She didn't cling to him as they made their way to the parlor, but she squeezed his hand tightly when Professor Carter stood to greet them.

"You might as well come out with it, sir," she said, before the professor could begin. "Breaking things gently never works with me."

Mina expected the news to be about her family. What else did she have? What else that would concern her and not Stephen or Colin? None of the friends from her boardinghouse would have sent a message so late or in the person of Professor Carter, no matter how severe their problems.

So Professor Carter said, "It's your sister," and it wasn't really a surprise, not a surprise at all, but still it hit Mina like a blow to the stomach. All the breath went out of her in a small cry.

"Which one?" she asked in a voice that might have been recorded. She half expected to hear the scratch and hiss of a gramophone as she went on. "What happened?"

"Your younger sister. Er." Professor Carter pulled awkwardly at his beard, searching his memory. "Flora. Florence."

"Florrie," said Mina. Florence was her name, but nobody called her that. It had always been too long and too formal for her. There was a chair nearby. Mina fumbled her way into it, and Stephen knelt at her side, taking both her hands in his. The two other men—and Mrs. Baldwin—had to notice, but Mina didn't give a damn just then. "What's wrong with her?"

"She's ill," said the professor, "and I'm afraid it looks to be quite serious, though nobody's really certain quite what's wrong. She, ah, she lost consciousness this evening, and she hadn't regained it when your brother came to find me. I'm terribly sorry."

"There's nothing to be sorry *for*," said Mina, finding and seizing a core of ferocity beneath the numbness of her shock. She sat up straighter in the chair. "Not yet. Have they had a doctor in? When did Bert find you? Where is he?"

"He came to my office about eight this evening. He said your father had gone for a doctor, but that your mother had sent him to find you at the same time, so he couldn't tell me the results. He did tell me to add that he'd already spoken to—Alice?—and that she was on her way home. And I sent him back, of course," Professor Carter added, shaking his head at the folly of the world. "A child his age on the streets after dark? I put him into a cab myself."

"That's very generous of you," said Mina, and wanted to smile and cry at the same time. Riding in a carriage would have been the thrill of Bert's life at any other time, thrill enough even to overcome his wounded pride at being thought a child or having his ease with the London streets called into question. Tonight, she thought he might hardly have noticed. "I'll pay you back, of course."

"Don't talk nonsense, girl. The price of a cab ride won't beggar me any time soon."

"Oh. Well—thank you."

She stood up, preparing to spring into action, and then had no idea where to spring *to*.

For a brief and stomach-clenching moment, she thought that maybe the harshest of the preachers from her childhood had been right, that Florrie's sickness was a judgment on her for—what? Pride? Magic? Fornication?

No. Even if what she'd done was wrong—even if plenty of people didn't do worse without consequence—no god worth the name would make a child pay for it. Besides, illness happened often enough without divine intervention. Children in the East End got sick all the time.

Children in the East End died of those illnesses all the time.

When Mina had gotten to her feet, the men had too. Now, when she turned to Stephen, she had to look up to meet his eyes. "I—"

"Colin," he said, looking past her, "order a carriage for Miss Seymour. The fastest you can get. Have Polly pack her things. Quickly, too. I want her bags by the front door in five minutes. I assume you've nothing breakable," he added to Mina.

"No," she said, dizzied for a second. "I'm sorry. I know it's not what we agreed. And I know there'll be trouble with the wards."

"Damn what we agreed. And damn the wards, too. The new moon's safely past, and there's Colin and myself to guard the place. Here." He drew out his new wallet and removed a sheaf of banknotes. "Take this. Get your sister whatever she needs—medicine, food, a private room at St. Mary's if it comes to that. If you need more, send someone here to tell me. If I can do anything, tell me. We don't know much healing, I'm afraid. We've never really had to learn."

The notes swam before Mina's eyes: a rainbow of colors, the Queen's eyes, and numbers that made no sense to her just now. It was far more than the cost of a carriage ride, though. She put the money into her coat pocket. "Thank you," she said. "I—I'll pay you back, if it's more than—"

Out of nowhere, heedless of Professor Carter's startled and disapproving *harrumph* in the background, Stephen was grasping her shoulders, his hands painfully tight. His eyes blazed like a sunset. "Anything I have is yours, Mina. *Anything*. Whenever you want it."

"The sentiment's pretty enough," said Colin from the doorway, "and I don't doubt you mean it. But perhaps further elaboration could wait for another time. Miss Seymour's bags are ready, and there'll be a cab pulling up momentarily."

"I've got to go," said Mina, stepping away reluctantly: reluctant because of both what awaited her and who she was leaving. "I'll come back, if—when—" Her throat caught. Her mind caught too, fearing to tempt fate by either too much confidence or not enough. "I'll come back when I can."

"I *could* go as well," Stephen began.

"No, you couldn't." Colin's voice was calm and cold, even if there was more than a touch of sympathy in it. "You can't do a damn thing there, and you have problems of your own here. People you're responsible for too, Lord MacAlasdair."

"He's right," said Mina, and managed a smile. "Thank you. For everything."

Stephen wrapped his arms around her and kissed her, not for very long but forcefully enough to leave her breathless, her lips tingling. "Come back to me," he said, when he finally let her go.

"Of course," said Mina, and fled into the hall.

A short time later, though it felt like years had passed, she stood in a dark room and watched her sister. Florrie slept on her side as she always had. At first glance, she looked healthy enough, at least in the dark. Only by looking closely did Mina see the way her hair was plastered to her face with sweat. Only by watching for several minutes did she see how shallow Florrie's breathing was and hear how she wheezed with each inhalation.

Mina closed her eyes. Almost immediately, she made herself open them again. She couldn't hide from Florrie's illness, and she shouldn't if she could have.

"It'll be all right," Alice whispered at her side. "We've all been sick a few times, haven't we?" But her voice lacked confidence, and the basin of water she carried shook a little. She swallowed and pitched her voice a little higher, toward the figure who sat at Florrie's side. "Mum, Mina's here."

Mrs. Seymour looked up slowly. She stood, wrung out a damp cloth for the final time, and then picked it and the bowl up before she came over to the door. Encumbered as she was, she couldn't embrace Mina, but she gave her a one-handed squeeze with what must have been the last of her strength. She looked exhausted.

She apparently wasn't the only one. "You look all in," she said to Mina. "I told your father it wasn't so bad, but—"

"Doesn't matter. I'd want to be here."

"Both of you go downstairs," said Alice. "And then to bed. I'll sit up with Florrie, and Dad's said he'll take over when I'm knackered."

"But I—" Mina began.

"Go *on*, dolt. You'll make yourself useful before long. We all will. And you'll both be more useful with sleep."

"She sounds like you," said Mina, reaching out to take the bowl from her mother as she went downstairs.

"Funny," said Mrs. Seymour. "I was going to say she sounded like your Aunt Jane."

It was good to laugh with family again, but the moment didn't last long. It couldn't.

"Professor Carter said she fainted this evening," said Mina, as they reached the kitchen. Mrs. Seymour began to fill the kettle. Falling into old patterns, Mina emptied the bowl into the sink and started getting the tea things ready.

"She did. After supper. We thought it was nothing at first. A bit of a cold, maybe, or—well, I thought it might be female troubles, though she's young for that. But we couldn't wake her, and then the fever started." Mrs. Seymour wiped at a nonexistent spot on the stove, keeping her face turned away.

Putting down the teacups, Mina hugged her mother from behind. "I'm sorry I wasn't here."

"What could you have done?" Mrs. Seymour asked sharply, but she patted Mina's hand.

"Been here," said Mina. "Has the doctor been?"

"Oh, yes. The lady doctor I wrote you about. She said to try and keep the fever down, and to give her tea and broth and similar when she wakes. She can't say what it is, though," Mrs. Seymour added.

"Just a fever, maybe. That happens," said Mina, trying not to think of stories she'd read in the *Times* or heard at Professor Carter's. Steamships came in every day from all around the world. Along with passengers and official cargo, might they bring diseases? Maybe even one that a London doctor hadn't ever seen?

Maybe she should stop borrowing trouble.

Mina let go of her mother and went to get the canister of tea.

"She'll be here again tomorrow," said Mrs. Seymour. "I'm sure—she seems very bright."

"And if she can't do anything," Mina said, glancing for the first time toward the hallway where she'd hung her coat, "we'll find someone who can."

Forty

"I'm not sure why you feel this need for urgency," Colin said.

He lounged at the library desk, occupying the seat that Mina had taken for weeks. He sat far more casually than she ever had, though, with his feet crossed on the desk and the chair tilted back, not at all worried about damaging either the wood or his spine.

He'd never needed to worry about such things. The MacAlasdair wealth was more than sufficient to replace a chair or a desk, and the backbone of a dragon scion could stand up to a kick from a horse, let alone bad posture. Stephen had never even been conscious of either for most of his life.

Of course he thought of Mina. Everything in the damn house reminded him of her.

"The arm will be better in a few weeks," Colin added in the face of Stephen's silence, glancing derisively down at his sling. "It's mending now. Ward's hated you for a lifetime, and he's been trying to kill you for months. What's another fortnight or two?"

"I didn't know what he was doing before," said

Stephen, pouring powder into the barrel of a derringer. Most of the time, he didn't bother with guns. Baldwin had owned the only revolver in the house, and Mina had taken that with her to Ward's office and then her home. This older gun, one of the relics of his father's time in London, would at least give him two shots at Ward, assuming that it didn't explode in his face. He would rather not change shape unless he had to, at least not until Ward was dead. "We killed one of his half men. I don't want to give him time to make another one."

"Maybe he already has," said Colin. "You don't send all your forces on a raid. Even I know that. Maybe he has a small army."

"Then I still don't want to give him time to make another one. He uses people for these creatures he makes, Colin."

"Yes," said Colin, "very bad form. Not worth getting killed over."

"I'm not planning to be killed."

Colin snorted. "Trust you to think people plan to get killed."

Powder, charges, cap: Stephen double-checked the gun and put it down. "Colin," he said, "he's doing this because of me."

"No, he's—" The brothers locked eyes. Colin sighed. "Fine. I'll not waste my breath. But I'm coming with you."

"You're hurt—"

"And still sturdier than Miss Seymour was last night. You're not investigating now; you're going into battle. I can cast spells one-handed, and a cast makes a fair bludgeon *in extremis*. I'm coming with you."

Argument would be futile. Stephen knew that from Colin's voice, even though his brother's posture was as casual as ever. "Then there's nothing more for me to say. At least Judith's still at home, if things go very badly."

"I thought you weren't planning to get killed."

"And I thought people don't generally plan on that."

Colin shook his head. "You're a right nuisance when you're melancholy, you know that?"

"I'm not melancholy."

"You'd think a MacAlasdair would be a better liar. At least you've slept. You have slept, haven't you?"

"Yes, Mother," said Stephen. He had, in fact. A long life had taught him how to keep his emotions from getting in the way of his body's most basic requirements. The night had been dark and peaceful. He'd only begun to worry when he woke up.

Undeterred, Colin eyed him. "She's been gone a day, you great idiot. The wards can't be causing all of this mood. Are you going to become one of those nauseating sorts who has to have his lady in sight at all times?"

"I will not, and she's not my lady yet," Stephen said, though speaking the words did lighten his mood a bit, foolishly enough. "And I wouldn't be worried if this were an ordinary sort of absence or at a better time."

"This *is* an ordinary sort of absence. Oh, it's distressing now and all that"—Colin waved a hand—"but human children get ill. They're known for it. They recover, generally, and Lord knows you gave her money enough to buy half the doctors in the East End if she feels it needful."

"And if Mina gets ill?"

"Then you'll put her in a bed upstairs and bring in half the doctors in *London*, I don't doubt. I'll even go after that bloke in Yorkshire with the familiar spirit if we need more than that, or we'll bring her up to Brigid's Well in Ireland. But things won't come to any such pass. She's a grown woman, and a healthy, strapping sort of girl at that."

"Thank you for noticing," said Stephen, only half sarcastic.

"I said I wasn't in love with the girl, not that I didn't look. She'll be back. She'll be *fine*. Now cheer up before I hit you with a bookend."

"Well," said Dr. Stevens, straightening up, "her condition hasn't gotten any worse."

"But no better?" Mrs. Seymour asked.

Dr. Stevens shook her head. The lady doctor of song and story, or at least of letter and mild dinner-table controversy, was surprisingly young, with only a touch of gray in her brown hair. She was gaunt, too—in Mina's experience, half the educated people in the world forgot to eat if left to their own devices, and the other half ate too much—and her face was sharp, softened now by a look of confusion and regret.

"It's actually rather remarkable," she said, "how little she's changed. I'd have expected—" She broke off. "I'm sorry. This isn't the time or the place to wax academic."

Mrs. Seymour didn't care, Mina knew. She probably didn't even hear most of what Dr. Stevens said because her attention was fixed on a single point. "Do you know what's wrong with her?"

"A fever," said the doctor, and spread her hands. "Some sort of influenza, perhaps. None of you have been feeling sick at all?"

"Not a one of us. Nor any of the neighbors."

"Let's hope you all stay as healthy, then." Dr. Stevens frowned down at Florrie's unconscious body. "All I can say is that you should keep going as you were. If you'd like to bring in another doctor, though, that's quite reasonable. If she doesn't regain consciousness by the time I come by this evening, I'll send for one myself."

"Thank you," said Mrs. Seymour, and turned with set face and thin lips to her youngest daughter.

Watching, Mina blinked hard to keep tears firmly behind her eyelids. She looked away, toward Dr. Stevens's retreating form. The doctor was glancing back over her shoulder, regarding the scene with puzzled worry.

Mina followed her out, stopping her on the landing. "Wax academic now," she said, too weary and scared for preambles. "I'd like to know."

"Oh?" Dr. Stevens peered up at her, surprised, but then shrugged. "It's simply odd. With most disease, there's some change from day to day, even if it's not significant. Patients get better or worse by tiny degrees. Sometimes they get a little better and then worse again, or vice versa. And I suppose that could have happened while I was gone, but—"

"But?"

"But your sister's condition, as far as I can tell, is

exactly the same as it was yesterday. It's not the oddest incident in the medical books, but it does rather stand out. And she hasn't woken up at all, which isn't common with fevers. I'd have expected at least one of you to be sick as well. It's all very strange."

"Oh," said Mina. "I see. Thank you."

She watched the doctor leave. She stood very still; there was earthquake enough in her mind without adding physical motion to it.

Nobody else was at all ill. Dr. Stevens didn't know what was wrong. Except for the fever, Florrie was asleep, sleeping like a princess who'd pricked her finger or bitten into a poisoned apple. Sleeping like the target of a wicked fairy's vengeance.

He wasn't a man to bear well with being thwarted Stephen said in her memory, and she saw again the newspaper article: *East End Slaughter.*

Servants gossiped, and Mina had read letters in the kitchen. It would be easy enough to find out where she lived and who her family was, especially for a man who could throw money around. Illness wasn't as quick or—please, God—as irreparable as the thieves' deaths had been, but it got her away from Stephen and it probably made for very satisfying revenge.

"Oh, God," said Mina, except she didn't really say it. Her lips shaped the words, but no air went past them. For one thing, she didn't want to alarm the household. For another, her lungs didn't feel like they contained any such thing as air.

She could be wrong. Asking if Florrie had touched anything or eaten anything unusual would be pointless. Children here were all on their own often enough, walking to school or running wild with friends. Even if Ward couldn't curse from a distance, there were a thousand opportunities for a poisoned apple or a stealthy pinprick when nobody was looking. Mina was no detective, and there was little time.

She stepped up to the sickroom doorway again. "Mum," she said, trying to sound calm, "I'm going out for a bit. I think I might know someone who can help. Maybe."

"This man you've been working for?" Despite her fatigue, Mrs. Seymour's eyes were sharp and knowing. "If you think there's a chance—"

"Maybe," Mina said again.

"You could send Bert."

"No." If she'd thought they'd understand, she'd have told everyone in her family to stay in the house and bar the doors. She wasn't sure if even staying inside would help—but thresholds were supposed to offer some protection, and any direct housebreaking would make the neighbors notice and raise hell. "He'll see me quicker."

Not stopping to get drawn into further conversation—even further *thought* seemed perilous just then—Mina went to her room. Alice was asleep, and that was just as well. It spared Mina questions about why she was putting her coat on, and it spared her a great deal of discussion when she took the revolver out from under her pillow and slipped it into her coat pocket.

Fog filled the street outside, thick and yellow and choking, heavy with the smell of sulfur. Such fogs were nothing new—Mina had grown up with them every few days of her life—but now, with Florrie lying ill behind her and six weeks' worth of magic and strangeness in her consciousness, everything seemed more sinister, and the fog was no exception. She thought of Hell, shuddered, and walked faster.

Then there were three figures in front of her.

She had no sense of their approach. Part of that was the fog, but not all. They moved too quickly and too fluidly to be people. She thought that they'd stepped out from the shadows under a nearby building, but there was more than one way to come out of shadows.

Mina stepped back and tried to bolt left. One of the shapes darted in front of her and grabbed her wrist with a gloved hand. As she screamed, it dragged her forward, and she could see that it *was* a shape, not a man. It wasn't entirely a manes either. She wished it had been.

It was both. Bits of human features floated in shadow: one eye, a nose, a lower lip that stretched into raw meat before the shadow cut it off, and patches of yellow teeth. The hand on her arm was boneless and cold—not as numbingly cold as the touch of the pure manes had been, but with a crushing strength that made up for that lack.

"Come with us," said the thing, its half mouth squirming around the words. "Come quietly."

Mina yanked the revolver out of her pocket with her free hand and fired at the half man's face, pulling the trigger over and over again. She realized that she was still screaming. She screamed louder when the bullets hit, when flesh and shadow tore away from the creature's head and fell to the ground, and yet it kept standing, kept pulling her toward it. Its eye was gray-white, filmy.

Someone was shouting in the background. Footsteps rushed toward them.

The things looked at each other. Then the creature holding Mina said a word she couldn't recognize, and everything went dark.

Forty-one

"THERE'S A BOY AT THE DOOR, MY LORD," SAID BALDWIN.

Events over the last few days had left the household reeling. Baldwin's face was drawn with weariness, despite Stephen telling him to rest, and the latest development had clearly both baffled and worried him.

"He says he has to speak to you."

"A boy?" Stephen turned from the last of his preparations and blinked. "I don't know any boys these days."

"No, my lord." Baldwin swallowed. "He says it's to do with Miss Seymour."

The world stopped.

"Where is he?" Stephen asked. He was already walking toward the doorway.

"The kitchen, my lord. I didn't—"

The stairs presented little obstacle; Stephen took them two at a time. He burst through the door of the kitchen and saw a boy rise hurriedly and shakily from a seat by the hearth.

Between a tall ten and an undersized fourteen, the boy straddled the gap between poverty and respectability as well. His clothes were clean, but patched and very plain. He snatched a gray cap off his head when Stephen entered, revealing a curly mass of brown hair, and looked up at the new arrival with a pair of dark blue eyes.

They were Mina's eyes. And they were terrified.

Stephen froze.

"Sir. My lord. Sir?" The boy looked confused. Men like Stephen generally didn't enter kitchens, and he was old enough to know it. "I—I need to talk to Lord MacAlasdair, sir, right away."

"That's me, lad," said Stephen, as gently as he could manage. "What's wrong?"

"I. It's Mina. My sister. Miss Seymour, she would've been to you. My lord. She said she worked for you. She went out and she's not come back, and Mum said as how she said she was coming up 'ere to talk with you." The boy's mouth worked silently for a second and then he swallowed, Adam's apple bobbing on his skinny neck. "And they say there was gunshots earlier, m'lord, and screaming."

When Stephen's heart went still, experience took over, freezing his brain and his blood, constructing an icy wall of action behind which his rage and regret became distant. When he spoke to Mina's pale-faced brother, it was with all the calm he'd ever used to lead men.

"Near you?"

"A street away, maybe. People couldn't see well for the fog."

"Is that all you know?"

The boy nodded.

Action beckoned. Stephen held back. "Why was she coming back here?"

"It was about Florrie, m'lord." Mina's brother gulped. "Um. Our other sister. She's sick."

"I know. And Mina said I could help?"

"She said you might." Now he looked hopeful as well as frightened, and Stephen felt an intense desire to put his fist through a wall.

Ward had set this up neatly.

"I'll try," said Stephen. "See here—Bert, isn't it?"

Even in his panic, the boy's eyes widened a little. "Yes, m'lord."

"Stay in here. There's jam in the pantry. I'll be back before very long, or I'll send someone else for you."

Colin met him outside. "I heard the disturbance," he said, "and the wards seem to be fine all over the house, so I take it the problem's physical?"

"Mina's gone," said Stephen. "Her brother's here. From what he's said, it sounds like Ward's taken her. And that her sister's illness wasn't natural. A trap, likely as not." He let his breath hiss out between his teeth. "I should have known."

"Yes, you really should be more omniscient one of these days," Colin said. "Now, if you could flog yourself a little later, you can get me a bowl of water and we can get to work."

"Scrying? Don't you need something of hers?"

"I've already got it." Colin grinned. "You're here, aren't you?"

A few minutes of hasty activity produced the bowl in question and sent Polly to the kitchen for supervisory and jam-distribution purposes. Then Stephen stood, his hands clenched at his sides, and stared into the bowl as clear water gave way to blue mist, which in its turn parted to reveal grimy walls and huge metal vats: a factory of some sort, obviously, though Stephen didn't know what it had made. At present, it was sheltering Ward and five of the hybrid manes, who stood in a ring around a female figure lashed to a pipe.

Mina.

Stephen growled and felt his lips draw back, baring his teeth in a threat as instinctual as it was ineffectual. His nails lengthened into claws, cutting into the still-unchanged flesh of his hands. He felt dim pain and didn't care. Rage was much closer, and much more vivid.

No. Not yet.

As Stephen watched, Mina struggled, and while the desperate energy in her movements tore at his heart, it also reassured him. She still lived. She still had enough strength left to fight.

Unless he could get to her soon, though, that strength might not do her any good. Stephen didn't know what Ward had planned, but several horrifying possibilities sprang to his mind—and he didn't know that he could get there in time to stop any of them.

He didn't know exactly where Ward's den was. In human form, it would take him at least an hour to find it. When he got there, he'd have five of the hybrids to fight, which would be no small task even with Colin—and he couldn't bring Colin.

"He doesn't have one hostage," Stephen said. "He has two."

"You think he'd kill the Seymour child?"

"I think he'd let her die. Can you break a curse like that?" Stephen swung to face Colin, prepared for another round of argument about throwing his life away for a human he'd never met.

"Does a full house beat a pair?" Colin winked. "I'll come find you once it's done. Try to whittle them down a bit, will you? Five of those things might be a bit much for me at the moment."

"I'll let you take your ease this time," said Stephen, though his voice was thick for a moment. "Bert's in the kitchen. Mina's brother. He'll take you to Florrie. And take this." He held out the derringer. "I doubt I'll be able to use it."

Colin pocketed the gun, then clapped his good hand to Stephen's shoulder. "Stay alive," he said, serious for a second.

He closed the door behind him, but there was no time for Stephen to lock it. As Colin left the room, Stephen had already begun to change shape, not caring or even really noticing as his clothing shredded around him. He did notice when he burst through the closed window, but he didn't care any more about the shattered glass than about his ruined shirt.

Launching himself into the fog, he sped toward the docks, only hoping that he'd arrive in time.

Forty-two

Touch was the first sense to return. Mina awoke to the feel of cold metal against her back and rough ropes cutting into her wrists and ankles. Her hands were behind her, and when she wiggled her fingers, she felt more metal, pitted and flaked with age. She could smell old metal too, as her head cleared, and a vague hint of rotten eggs.

Sulfur was not a good smell, considering the circumstances. At least Mina didn't see any flames when she opened her eyes.

Demons, on the other hand, were clearly in stock. Half demons. Five of the creatures from before surrounded her, human features variously afloat in shadow. Each had a different arrangement of…bits… but their eyes were all the same, gray-white and completely expressionless. Mina would almost have preferred rage or hunger—or eyeless faces like the manes had. She wasn't fond of the middle ground.

She wasn't fond of anything about this situation. She rather wanted to be sick.

It was important to keep calm. It was also important,

she realized after a breath or two, not to *look* too calm. The less Ward thought she knew, the more likely he'd be to overlook something. So she shrieked and threw herself about, imitating the heroine of every three-penny melodrama she'd ever seen, calling for help even though she knew there was nobody to hear.

Screaming and thrashing against the ropes relieved her feelings a bit, too.

At last, Mina let herself slump in her bonds, hanging her head as if exhausted. Blood was trickling from her wrists where the rope had rubbed off some of the skin. Feeling it, she thought she might have overdone the hysteria a bit.

Footsteps came toward her, echoing in the sudden silence. Mina looked up under her eyelashes. If one of the half manes was approaching her, actual hysterics became a very real possibility.

The half manes stayed where they were. The figure approaching was human, at least, although the man had very little else to recommend him in Mina's eyes. He was tall, stout, and well-dressed, his coat and hat rather absurd given their surroundings.

He stopped in front of her: not, to Mina's relief, within arm's length. "Don't bother with another show," he said. "Nobody will hear."

That wasn't just a threat. He knew what he was talking about. Mina could tell as much from his voice, and she was glad of the dim lighting. There were several dark patches on the floor that she didn't want to see clearly.

"I hope you'll be a sensible girl. I'd like to do this quickly, and I don't really *need* to hurt you. Someone *should* teach you a lesson about sticking to your place and keeping your nose out of the affairs of your betters," he added, and in the flexing of his fingers and the light in his eye, Mina saw a rage that had passed rationality long since. She shrank back as much as she could.

Whether her fear had sated him for the moment or he'd just turned his mind to more practical matters, Ward cleared his throat and went on. "But it doesn't have to be me. Not if you'll be smart."

Mina widened her eyes and raised her head. "Who are you?" she asked, letting her voice slip back into the accent she'd grown up with. "What do you want with me? I 'aven't done you any 'arm."

Ward was a big man, and past middle age, whatever spells he used to keep himself from growing any older. Mina saw his open hand lash out and had time to turn her head so that the blow missed her nose and mouth. It was still hard enough to make her cry out, and it knocked her head back into the pipe, which hurt worse than the slap.

"Don't *lie*," Ward snarled. "Don't think you can get away with it. Not gutter scum like you. I can see right through you."

He stepped back. He also rubbed his hand, which tempted Mina to smile, as stupid as that would have been. "You grew up in Bethnal Green," he said. "Then you somehow learned to speak a little bit like a lady and you worked for Professor Carter—until two months ago, when you showed up at MacAlasdair's in the middle of the night and got taken on as his personal secretary."

There was no point asking how he knew. Any of the servants or the servants' friends or their friends' friends could have told him. Mina had never tried to keep any of that information secret. Clearly it was time to revise her tactics; the old ones had earned her a bruised face and a throbbing skull.

She swallowed and managed to get words out of her throat, though it felt clamped shut. "What do you want with me, then?"

"He wouldn't have employed you for your personal charms or your skills," said Ward, and Mina wasn't sure whether he meant to insult her or Stephen, or both. "You must've found out a thing or two about 'Laird MacAlasdair.' What was it?"

The ropes were securely tied and the pipe was solid, with no sharp edges that Mina could find. The half manes stared at her blankly. Off in the distance, a rat squealed.

She cocked her head to the side. "What'll you do if I tell you?"

"Let you go," said Ward. Mina didn't believe that for a second, but she tried not to look openly skeptical. "If you don't tell me, I'll let them go to work on you." He gestured to the half manes. "They like live meat."

That, Mina believed.

Her nails scrabbled against the pipe's surface. Her hands had more hope than her mind, it seemed.

Looking down, she bit her lip. "I don't know everything," she said, very small and very frightened. She didn't have to fake that. "He didn't tell me very much."

"No," said Ward, "he wouldn't. Not even MacAlasdair would be that stupid. Start at the beginning. What did you see that made him hire you?"

Mina closed her eyes and speculated. "He—he was in a big room. There was chalk on the floor, and—and blood. I think there was a chicken in the corner. And there was something in the middle of the room."

"Something?"

Building from what she'd heard of with Stephen and Colin, she filled in the rest with imagination. "It was a bit like a man." She talked slowly, trying to sound frightened and reluctant. Every second she took was one more second that she was alive, one more second in which the situation could change. "It had arms and legs and," she swallowed, "a head. Except its hands had claws, and its head was…it looked like a big frog. With teeth. Its eyes glowed. I remember its eyes glowed."

After a moment of silence, she opened her eyes. Ward was still in front of her, but now he was scratching his head.

"What was it doing?" he asked, finally.

"Talking to Lord MacAlasdair. I, um…" Mina thought swiftly. The beast she'd constructed wasn't formed for peaceful work, and Ward would have noticed any mysterious deaths in London, just as Stephen would. "I think he was talking about affairs back in Scotland. An uncle, maybe? I didn't hear very clearly. I was scared."

"When you served him, did you have the full run of the house?"

"Not his bedroom, of course!" That got her a glare. Propriety was not a consideration here. "And there was a room in the attic." *Thank you, Florrie.* "He always kept it locked, but he went up there every night."

"Oh? Alone?"

"Mostly," said Mina, keeping her options open.

"What do you mean—"

THUD.

The sound had come from above. Mina looked up, but the ceiling itself was too high for her to see. Whatever had landed on the roof was heavy; she could tell that much.

So could Ward. He seized her by the shoulders, glaring. "What was *that*?"

"I don't know!"

Metal squealed above them.

With no place to retreat, Mina endured. Ward's hands felt like claws; his breath reeked; and the eyes that stared into hers were almost as inhuman in their rage as the half manes's. Mina shrank back and turned her face away, the best she could manage.

"What are you doing? What are *you*?"

"A girl. His secretary. I've nothing to do with this!" It was the first truth she'd spoken in five minutes, and ironically, it did nothing to convince Ward.

He hit her again, which she'd more or less been expecting. This time it was in the stomach and with a closed fist. A coldly rational part of Mina supposed that, if she *had* been casting a spell, that blow might even have been effective—physical pain to disrupt mental concentration. The rest of her knew only pain, breathlessness, and the sudden heat of blood flowing from her nose.

Much as she would have liked to blame Ward, that last wasn't his fault. He hadn't come near her face.

"It's not *me*!" she cried.

He curled his upper lip at her like an angry dog, released his grip, and stood back. "I don't feel like taking chances. Kill her," he said to the half manes.

As one, they surged forward. Terror broke over Mina, flooding her mind beyond rational thought. She shrieked and thrashed, surging against the ropes with the full weight of her body, knowing it wouldn't be enough.

Forty-three

Metal yielded easily to Stephen's claws. Brick was only a little more of a challenge. Shrouded in fog, he smashed through the factory roof and plummeted inside, roaring. One taste of destruction had merely gotten his blood up, and he was ready for more even before he heard Mina screaming.

He dove, talons out. He saw the vats and the pipe that had appeared in his vision. He didn't see Mina; the hybrids blocked his view. They were advancing toward her, unrushed but far too quickly for all that.

Stephen tore into them.

The first hybrid he reached went down in a storm of claws. A swipe of his tail knocked three others back, and Stephen clamped his jaws around the remaining creature. It squirmed in his mouth in a way no living thing had ever done, and the taste was revolting: cold and corrosive. Eating it would probably be a horrible idea, so he flicked his neck and sent the hybrid flying. It struck one of the vats and fell heavily, leaving traces of its shadowy half-flesh on the metal.

When he reached Mina, her face was white with

terror and her eyes were red with tears, but she'd stopped screaming and was holding perfectly still. Her nose was bleeding. The bastard had hit her or had commanded one of the hybrids to do it. Stephen hissed his wrath, but anger was, just then, not the wanted emotion. He stifled it, then carefully lifted one of his hands and brought a claw down through the ropes that bound Mina, slicing through them all with one blow. She stumbled forward a few steps, rubbing at her wrists.

He wanted to tell her to run, wanted to at least meet her eyes, but the hybrids were coming toward them again. Stephen roared and spun to face them.

Ward was shouting. None of it was very coherent, but all of it still sounded confident. Why not? He'd be reasonably certain, now, that he knew Stephen's secret. The hybrids were powerful and almost unkillable. One, after all, had done some significant damage to Colin, even in dragon form, and while Ward didn't know that, he'd probably gotten some idea of their capabilities in the process of creating them.

Neither he nor his creations had yet seen a MacAlasdair's full strength.

Now Mina was behind Stephen and the hybrids in front. The building that surrounded them was metal and stone, and there were no innocents to worry about.

Stephen inhaled deeply, feeling the shift and dance of magic deep in his body. This was as much a part of his heritage as his last name or the red scales that covered his skin.

He breathed out.

Fire.

Two of the hybrids melted, shrieking in horrible bubbling voices. Their bodies writhed, the shadows twisting independently of the flesh. If Stephen had had time, he would have been revolted. A third screamed and writhed as well, but didn't fall. It staggered back for a second instead, and its shape changed as the clothes it had been wearing burned away. Shadow flowed down its left arm, fusing the charred bits of its hand into something more like the tentacle its manes progenitor would have had. Shadow swallowed its left eye too, and the charred bits of muscle and bone on its side.

It swept toward Stephen, reaching out with its tentacle and overly jointed arm. Stephen snarled and lashed out, raking claws down the thing's uninjured side. He couldn't breathe fire again, not so quickly, but he'd evened the numbers somewhat. That might be enough.

He felt the impact first, high on his back, and then a rapidly spreading spot of burning pain. He didn't turn his head—couldn't, with the hybrid in front of him and the remaining one lurching toward him from where it had fallen below the vat—but he could hear his own flesh sizzling. Acid. Stephen remembered the cloud that had come from "John Smith" and realized that Ward had regained enough of his composure to cast spells.

Stephen whipped his body to the side, avoiding a bolt of chilling shadow, and took another swipe at the hybrid. This one took its legs, and the thing's torso fell to the ground, dissolving into shadow. Stephen turned to face the last and heard, from just far enough away that he couldn't do anything, Ward's voice raised in a series of blasphemous syllables, all building toward some unspeakable conclusion. Stephen didn't know exactly what the spell would do, but he knew enough to dread it.

Then a shriek and a thud cut off the chant. A series of curses came from Ward's direction, but these were the mundane sort.

Grappling with the last of the hybrids, feeling the chill of its shadowy hands against his scales, Stephen couldn't see what was happening with Ward. The sounds gave him a fair idea, though: Mina. He hadn't seen her move, but his attention had been elsewhere. So had Ward's, apparently, and he hadn't been expecting a mortal woman to do anything.

If *Get off me, you filthy bitch* was any indication, Mina had tackled him quite firmly, too.

Stephen snaked his head forward, under his opponent's outstretched arms, and opened his jaws. The hybrid's arms came down across the back of his neck, chilling it, but that was no matter now. He twisted his head sharply to the side, saw the hybrid collapse, and spat out the majority of his throat before leaping across the room to the place where Mina and Ward struggled.

She was on top for the moment. More accurately, she was on Ward's back, one arm clamped around his neck, and her legs, even in skirts, giving her purchase around his waist. She'd managed to give him several scratches across the face somewhere in the process.

The problem was that Ward's hands were starting to glow black, and the darkness was spreading up his arms. It would cover his body soon.

Mina looked up, met Stephen's eyes, and somehow read the silent message there. She let go, dropping from Ward's back with an alarming thud. She rolled out of the way quickly enough, though—out of Ward's way as he lunged for her with one shadowed hand, and out of Stephen's as he darted forward.

Instinct was almost stronger than rage just then. Stephen saw Ward and hated him. The dragon saw a small human figure, one who'd been hostile just recently. It saw prey and lunged.

Ward probably didn't even feel it when he hit the wall. His neck had snapped seconds earlier.

For reasons, silly mortal reasons, roaring in triumph was unwise. Stephen stretched himself out instead, flexing his claws and his neck. The fight had been hard, but wizards were tricky. He had done well, though the acid still burned along his side; the girl was alive and unharmed. He turned his head toward her to be sure.

"Oh," Mina said. She was brushing herself off, feeling at her arms and legs, wiping at the blood underneath her nose, but her eyes were fixed on Stephen, and huge. "Stephen?"

Stephen nodded, as much as he could in this shape, and waited for her to panic. When she looked between him and Ward's body, obviously dead, he was sure she'd start running. He closed his eyes and thought about his human shape.

"Hallo, the…er, vile lair of evil!" Colin called from behind them. Stephen's eyes snapped open. He and Mina both spun to meet the new arrival.

"I see I've arrived just in time," said Colin, strolling

inside as if the warehouse had been his club. "Nice work, well done, et cetera. Medals all round, and a tea with cream and buns, too."

Relief flooded out of Stephen with his next breath, almost as strong as the fire had been. He closed his eyes again and focused his will inward. The time for this form had passed, for now. He concentrated on being human again, on a body that was two-legged and smooth-skinned and could hold a woman without crushing her.

Nothing happened.

Forty-four

"STEPHEN?" MINA'S VOICE CAME OUT HOARSE FROM too much screaming. Her throat hurt now. Most of her body hurt—her wrists and ankles from the rope, her face from Ward's hand, and the back of her head from the pipe, as well as spots all over her body from throwing herself across the room, grabbing the sorcerer, and then dropping off him again.

Stephen had actually been fighting the half manes, though. Ward had hit him with at least one spell. Mina could see cracked patches of scales on his back and blood oozing from some of them. She wasn't sure what they'd be when he turned human again, but she was sure they wouldn't be comfortable.

"Are you all right?"

He only stared at her. In the shadowy room, his eyes shone, bright gold and the size of saucers. Mina bit down on her lip.

"Are *you* all right?" Colin asked, turning from his brother. "It looked as though you were in a bit of a tight spot there."

"Fine," said Mina, waving off the question. "But is

he?" She glanced back over her shoulder at Stephen, who had closed his eyes again. Her stomach dropped. "I need to tell him about Florrie."

"No, you don't."

"But she's—"

"Under a curse, courtesy of our late friend here. Or was. I've taken care of it. Your other sister's really quite a girl, you know," he added. His voice wasn't quite right, and his grin was too flat to be roguish.

He was trying to distract her, Mina realized, and he kept looking back to Stephen while he was talking.

"What *is* it?" Mina asked, and she couldn't keep her voice steady this time. "Ward's dead. Florrie's all right. What's wrong?"

With a scraping sound that hurt her ears, Stephen's claws tightened, digging long furrows in the cement floor. He threw his head back and roared, a world of rage and agony in that sound.

"He can't change back," said Colin when the roar died away. There was no humor in him now. His voice was flat, and his eyes were like dull coins.

All the blood ran from Mina's face as she listened. She could do nothing but listen, and Colin's words battered against the numbness in her mind even as they made too much sense.

"It was the fighting that did it, probably, the influence of the manes and the wounds he took. He's kept enough of his mind to govern his own actions—but you recall what I told you. He can't stay in London like this."

Some of them go away to live...elsewhere.

As Mina caught her breath, Stephen lowered his

head. He'd rid himself of his anger with the roar or had buried it behind a wall of self-control. The huge eyes that met hers were sad but impassive, resigned.

He crouched again, preparing to take to the air.

Mina's heart tried to beat sideways.

"No," she said and ran across the floor as quickly as she'd done to tackle Ward.

Stephen didn't move when she threw herself against his side.

"*No*," said Mina again. "Not for me. Not you. Not *this*. People need you as a man, Lord MacAlasdair. *I* need you as a man."

The diary had said that affection for a mortal might be able to reverse the change.

Stephen had never said exactly what he felt for her.

She knew only her own heart. For more than that, she just had to hope.

"If you leave," she said, and let the tears flow down her cheeks as she spoke, "I'll come with you—or I'll find you—unless you tell me you don't want me. An' you *can't* tell me without being a man, so you're bloody well stuck with me. But you don't have to leave. You don't have to stay like this."

The shape against her blurred a little, and her heart lifted—but blurring was as far as it went. Stephen bent his head and looked at her, his form still that of a dragon.

The memory of Stephen's mouth on hers, of his arms tight around her as he told her to come back to him, drove Mina on.

"I love you," she sobbed, not caring if Colin heard. "I was going to tell you that. And I'll *still* love you like this, but oh—" She caught her breath. "I want you to read the paper with me at breakfast and go to museums with me. I want to be in your arms at night. And I can't do that if you're a dragon. And you want those things too. I know you do."

Was he smaller? Standing? Or was that only her wishful thinking? Mina couldn't tell. There was no hope in his eyes, though, only frustration and despair.

There was one last thing left to try.

Mina drew back her hand and slapped Stephen as hard as she could, palm cracking against the scaled side of his face with a sound like a coachman's whip. It hurt like hell—probably far worse for her hand than his face—but the pain was just fuel. She raised her voice again and snapped, as sharply and forcefully as she'd ever spoken to anyone.

"You're not leaving me, you bastard! Change back *now*!"

Violence was the last of last resorts. If it didn't break through whatever hindered Stephen, she had lost him forever. And having started, she couldn't stop. She didn't want to watch any more, either. Mina closed her eyes, still weeping, and drew back her hand again.

Another hand caught her wrist.

Warm.

Skin, not scales.

No talons.

Human.

Mina opened her eyes.

"Cerberus," Stephen said. His voice was still too deep for a human, and a stripe of glittering red scales ran up the back of his arm, but the chest he pulled her against was a man's. Bare, too—he must have had a new shirt on when he'd changed. "Cerberus," he said again, kissing her forehead. "Mina. Lady MacAlasdair."

At first, she was too relieved to be surprised. Then she lifted her face from his shoulder—the red stripes ran down his chest, she noticed, but were nothing a shirt and gloves wouldn't remedy in public, and she'd never mind in private—and made a sound with far more surprise in it than either dignity or coherence.

"Aye," said Stephen, and then paused. "If you wish, of course."

Laughing, she leaned up to kiss him. "Someone's hand in marriage *is* the traditional reward, isn't it?" she said. "For fighting a dragon?"

Acknowledgments

There's a line about taking a village to raise a child that also seems appropriate for books. As always, I'd like to thank the wonderful people at Sourcebooks, including my editor, Leah Hultenschmidt; my publicist, Danielle Jackson; and Cat Clyne, my editorial assistant, for whipping this manuscript into shape and getting it out the door. I'd also like to thank all my friends and family for suggestions, occasional proofreading, and encouragement.

No Proper Lady

by Isabel Cooper

It's *Terminator* meets *My Fair Lady* in this fascinating debut of black magic and brilliant ball gowns, martial arts, and mysticism.

England, 1888. No one has any idea that in a few hundred years, demons will destroy it all. Joan plans to take out the dark magician responsible—before he summons the demons in the first place. But as a rough-around-the-edges assassin from the future, she'll have to learn how to fit into polite Victorian society first.

Simon Grenville has his own reasons for wanting to destroy Alex Reynell. The man used to be his best friend—until he almost killed Simon's sister. The beautiful half-naked stranger Simon meets in the woods may be the perfect instrument for his revenge. It will just take a little time to teach her the necessary etiquette and assemble a proper wardrobe. But as each day passes, Simon is less sure he wants Joan anywhere near Reynell. Because no spell in the world will save his future if she isn't in it.

"A genre-bending, fast-paced whirl with fantastic characters, a deftly drawn plot, and sizzling attraction."
—RT Book Reviews *Top Pick of the Month, 4.5 Stars*

Lessons After Dark

by Isabel Cooper

Author of *No Proper Lady*, a *Publishers Weekly* and *Library Journal* Best Book of the Year

A woman with an unspeakable past

Olivia Brightmore didn't know what to expect when she took a position to teach at Englefield School, an academy for "gifted" children. But it wasn't having to rescue a young girl who'd levitated to the ceiling. Or battling a dark mystery in the surrounding woods. And nothing could have prepared her for Dr. Gareth St. John.

A man of exceptional talent

He knew all about her history and scrutinized her every move because of it. But there was more than suspicion lurking in those luscious green eyes. Olivia could feel the heat in each haughty look. She could sense the desire in every touch, a spark that had nothing to do with the magic of his healing abilities. Even with all the strange occurrences at the school, the most unsettling of all is the attraction pulling her and Gareth together with a force that cannot be denied.

Wings of the Highland Dragon

by Isabel Cooper

Younger son of a family of shape-shifting dragons, Colin MacAlasdair has lived a long life free of both family duty and mortal cares. He takes very little seriously—including an invitation to his friend's country house. But the girl who drops onto his balcony at midnight catches his attention.

Regina Talbot-Jones didn't count on her brother's friend being so handsome, and she certainly didn't expect him to be a dragon. Reggie's empathic power has kept her distant from most people, but when she meets Colin, she wants to get closer.

Lovesick girls, interfering parents, and angry ducks: all the ingredients for a memorable house party. With an angry ghost in the mixture, though, Reggie and Colin end up thrown together even more—and discover that each has a great deal to discover about the other.

"Isabel Cooper is an author to watch!"
—All About Romance

Lord of the Hunt

by Shona Husk

Raised in the mortal world, the fairy Taryn never planned on going back to Annwyn, much less to Court. But with the power shift imminent, she is her parents' only hope of securing a pardon from exile and avoiding certain death.

Verden, Lord of the Hunt, swore to serve the King. But as the magic of Annwyn fails and the Prince makes ready to take the throne, Verden knows his days as Hunter are numbered.

When Taryn and Verden meet, their attraction is instant and devastating. Their love could bring down a queen and change the mortal world forever.

Praise for For the Love of a Goblin Warrior*:*

"Ms. Husk outdid herself in this book…
Once I got into the story, I couldn't put it down."
—*Night Owl Romance* Reviewer Top Pick

"Husk has an amazing ability to weave a
mesmerizing story with a magical dark
fairy-tale feel."—*Love Romance Passion*

"An entertaining and unique read. Shona Husk
creates a dark yet delightful world where romance
and fantasy combine."—*Romance Reviews*

For more of the Shadowlands series, visit:

www.sourcebooks.com

Prince of Shadows

by Tes Hilaire

It's forbidden for a warrior of the Light to love a creature of the Dark...

Valin has never quite fit in with the rest of the Paladin warriors. His power to manipulate shadow has always put him at odds with their purpose of using heavenly Light to eradicate evil. His warrior brothers have no idea how close he is to being lost to his dark nature.

But maybe he was never all that Light to begin with

When Valin meets the vampire Gabriella, she awakens within him something he thought long buried. But as he watches Gabriella's need for vengeance threaten to drag her down into the same dark hell that he's living, he knows his only chance at redemption is bringing her out of the dark...

Praise for the Paladin Warriors series:

"This world and series is great. If you love the warrior series books along the line of J.R. Ward or Sherrilyn Kenyon, I highly recommend that you pick these up."—*Smitten with Reading*

"Hilaire has created a unique blend of mythology and fantasy... a scorching read."—*Fresh Fiction*

For more Tes Hilaire, visit:

www.sourcebooks.com

The Magic Between Us

by Tammy Falkner

When these worlds collide

Cecelia Hewitt has lived her whole life in the land of the fae, and she dreams of a future with her childhood sweetheart, Marcus Thorne. When Marcus is called upon to dwell in the human world, it means leaving Cecelia behind and breaking both their hearts…

More than sparks may fly

Marcus was groomed for leadership in the land of the fae, but now that he has found his human parents, he will inherit his father's title and position in the British ton—and he will marry a human. As love and passion continue to burn between Cecelia and Marcus, the question remains: Can two people fated for different worlds find one to share?

"Falkner writes a good story that flows well and is full of spirit, emotions, and love…"—Long and Short Reviews

"Falkner blends the paranormal with the historical convincingly and with great passion."—Debbie's Book Bag

Enslaved

by Elisabeth Naughton

GRYPHON—Honorable, loyal, dependable…tainted. He was the ultimate warrior before imprisonment in the Underworld changed him in ways he can't ignore.

She calls to him. Come to me. You can't resist. But Gryphon will not allow himself to be ruled by the insidious whispers in his head. And there's only one way to stop them: kill Atalanta, the goddess who enslaved him. But with so much darkness inside, he can't be sure what's real anymore. Even the Eternal Guardians, those who protect the human realm and the gods, want to exile him.

Finding Malea is like a miracle. Somehow he doesn't feel the pull of the dark when she's near. And he's determined to keep her as near as possible, whether she wants him close or not. But she's a temptation that will test every bit of control he has left. One that may ultimately have the power to send him back to the Underworld…or free him from his chains for good.

About the Author

Isabel Cooper lives in Boston, in an apartment with two houseplants, an inordinate number of stairs, a silver sword, and a basket of sequined fruit. By day, she works as a theoretically mild-mannered legal editor; by night, she tries to sleep. She's only ever broken into one house, and that was in college and for very good reasons. Well, sort of good reasons. It seemed like a good idea at the time.

You can find out more at isabelcooper.org.